A GIRL'S GIRL

Emma Robertson grew up in Aldershot, Hampshire and has lived in London for the last 20 years. She and her husband like to travel as much as possible, with a particular interest in no-fly travel. Emma teaches dance and one of her specialities is wedding dance choreography, which gives her a fascinating insight into relationships as she works with couples in the lead up to their big day. She is endlessly nostalgic about the 1990s, which was a big inspiration for her debut novel, *A Girl's Girl*.

A GIRL'S GIRL

EMMA ROBERTSON

ZAFFRE

First published in the UK in 2026 by
ZAFFRE
An imprint of Bonnier Books UK
5th Floor, HYLO, 105 Bunhill Row,
London, EC1Y 8LZ

This is a work of fiction. References to real people, events,
establishments, organizations, or locales are intended only to
provide a sense of authenticity and are used fictitiously. All other
characters, and all incidents and dialogue, are drawn from the
author's imagination and are not to be construed as real.

A CIP catalogue record for this book is
available from the British Library.

ISBN: 978-1-78512-735-9

Also available as an ebook and an audiobook

1 3 5 7 9 10 8 6 4 2

Typeset by IDSUK (Data Connection) Ltd
Printed and bound by CPI Group (UK) Ltd, Croydon CR0 4YY

The authorised representative in the EEA is
Bonnier Books UK (Ireland) Limited.
Registered office address:
Block B, The Crescent Building,
Northwood, Santry,
Dublin 9, D09 C6X8,
Ireland
compliance@bonnierbooks.ie
www.bonnierbooks.co.uk

For Scott

1

2017 – Darcy

The best thing about meeting up with old friends is that you can be entirely yourself. They've admired you at your best and cried with you during the worst; there's no need for any pretence. You don't need to tie yourself up in knots in order to impress them.

Darcy knew this to be true; she'd posted an inspirational quote about it on her socials that very morning. Yet still she found herself in the Ladies at Waterloo station, faffing about with a scarf she'd panic-bought ten minutes before, trying to jazz up her jeans-and-a-nice-top combo that suddenly seemed inadequate. She knew her friends would look effortlessly chic in a way she could no longer manage, so she'd blown twenty quid she could ill afford on the sparkly scrap of silver, the twinkly fabric mocking her as she fussed with it.

She twisted and untwisted it, flipping it over one shoulder and groaning. 'I look like a knob,' she muttered, picturing her oldest, most beloved school friends who cruised through their thirties always beautifully groomed and stylish. They both had what magazines would call a 'look' that suited their personalities and lifestyles (Libby, the community outreach worker – arty, vintage, cool; Erika, HR director of a city bank – sleek, expensive, understated), while Darcy seemed stuck in same-old, same-old. Whenever Darcy tried something new, like this wretched scarf, her 'look' was self-conscious and too try-hard.

Darcy smiled at the thought of her friends; they really wouldn't care what she wore. But they had no idea how she struggled to keep up with them these days. They'd all started on the same path, through sixth form and uni and their grotty house share in Brixton, but she'd taken a different turn when she married Jon and moved back to Surrey, while Libby and Erika built their careers in London. Now, their lives always sparkled, while hers just pootled along.

Get a grip, Darcy told herself in the mirror, turning sideways to smooth her top down over her tummy and hoping the scarf drew the eye upwards. Why was she so jittery? Butterflies in her stomach threatened to fly up and out through her mouth, the urge to be snuggled up on the sofa at home almost enticing her to cry off and get back on the train.

Instead, she pulled out her phone to look at the photo she'd posted at the weekend: her lovely little family, with messy hair and muddy faces as they prepared the garden for springtime. Her heart swelled at Freya, eleven years old and displaying all the confidence that her mum seemed to have lost, while Jon looked every bit the strong provider type as he smiled into the camera. They'd earned plenty of likes and comments about what a cute family they were, mostly from other mums at the school gate and Freya's dance classes. That was Darcy's domain, where she channelled her energy into organising fundraisers and sewing costumes; generally being Supermum. Knowing that the other parents admired her always made Darcy feel better about her choices.

The phone buzzed in her hand, startling her. A WhatsApp from Erika.

She's here. I can't believe it.

Darcy's trembling hands almost dropped the phone as another message followed.

Alex Rigby is in the building!

'Oh, my God.' Darcy didn't know whether to laugh or throw up.

Alex Rigby. Just saying the name in her head propelled Darcy back to a world where mixtapes played out of tinny boomboxes while they argued about which Spice Girl they were; a world filled with the heady scent of Charlie Red and the taste of sticky alcopops. On one hand, Darcy was intrigued to find out what had become of her, but on the other . . . there was just *something*.

Darcy faced her reflection and yanked the scarf off again. For a mad moment she considered wrapping it around her hair but dismissed that with an audible snort; Libby could pull that off, but she couldn't. All around her she saw women with pashminas and other floaty things she didn't know the proper names for and they just seemed to throw them on and go about their lives without another thought. Why was this being stylish business so difficult?

An image of Alex flashed into her mind, a skinny teenager in a dress that was far too old for her, standing in front of a mirror just like Darcy was now. Darcy remembered Alex scrunching handfuls of tissue to shove into the bra that she so desperately wanted to fill. Alex was always doing stuff like that, dressing outrageously and mooning around after boys.

One boy in particular.

Darcy blinked away the teenage memory and turned back to her thirty-six-year-old reflection with a sigh. She fluffed her low-maintenance dark brown bob and wondered if Alex remembered her with long hair, back when Darcy was the one turning heads rather than showing up as the frumpy friend. In those days she'd have worn the scarf as a belt, slung around her hips to draw attention to her enviable midriff, rather than trying to hide her stomach under forgiving layers.

Sod it, she thought, shoving the scarf in her handbag. She'd put it in her Ottoman of Unwanted Gifts and

Other Impulse Purchases until she had an opportunity to wrap it up and gift it to someone else.

She fired off a quick wow face emoji to Erika before pocketing her phone and heading towards the tube. No wonder she was nervous. Alex Rigby had almost legendary status in their memories now, so long had it been since anyone had seen or heard from her. Even with social media and the fact that they all came from the same hometown, Alex and her family had somehow dropped off the radar since moving to Spain in the late nineties.

Libby had been devastated – Alex was her best friend, like Erika was Darcy's. Two pairs of two in a gang of four through school and sixth form, and then in the summer of 1999, Alex had left a message on Libby's answerphone: she wasn't going to university after all; she was leaving with her parents when they retired to Spain. She'd promised to call with the address once she got there, but never did.

There was an older cousin, Darcy remembered as she squeezed onto the Waterloo and City line. Susie? She'd worked in the print shop in town and laminated their fake college IDs for them with a knowing grin, stating repeatedly that she didn't want to know anything more about them. Libby had contacted her when, months later, she still hadn't heard from Alex. Susie said she'd try, but time passed with no word and eventually Susie moved away with her husband, and that was that. Alex was gone for good.

As the train squeaked and juddered towards Bank, Darcy tried to calm the growing knot in her stomach and acknowledged that part of her earlier antsiness was because Libby had told her Alex might make an appearance. At their last meet-up, Libby had been fizzing with excitement to tell them, before they'd even ordered drinks, that Alex Rigby had not only appeared on Facebook at last but had also *friended* her.

'Alex *fucking* Rigby! Let me see.' Erika had lunged for Libby's phone.

'I wonder why she didn't come up as people we might know?' Darcy had mused as Libby showed Erika the profile.

'It's on ultra-private settings,' said Libby. 'Maybe because of her daughter? She's divorced from the father, I think.'

'She's got a daughter?' Erika squealed. 'In my head she's still eighteen. I just can't imagine her as a *mum*.' Darcy bristled at the way Erika said the word *mum*, always aware that child-free Erika and Libby had very different lifestyles from hers. Before she could reply, Erika continued, 'Oh Jesus, have you seen her? Is that really her?'

Erika turned the phone towards Darcy, mouth agape in a very unlike-Erika fashion. Darcy could immediately see why. The profile picture looked a little like Cameron Diaz. Darcy actually laughed. 'No!'

'Yeah, that's really her,' said Libby, nodding. 'I know!' she added when they both made exclamations of disbelief.

'Come on, remember she used to lie about stuff all the time?' said Erika. 'The affair with the married man? The time she "won" the lottery, but her mum threw the ticket away?'

Libby, who'd always been Alex's defender back in the day, shook her head. 'She was just insecure. She wasn't *that* bad.'

'Come on, Libs,' said Darcy. 'Remember that time she was supposed to be on the radio?'

'And how Hunter from *Gladiators* was hitting on her at the summer fete!'

Even Libby laughed at that as she took her phone back. 'It's definitely her; there are other pictures.' She scrolled through Alex's short, newly created profile and showed them a picture of her with her teenage daughter and another one with her parents, who were now completely white-haired in stark contrast to their somewhat leathery skin, deeply tanned after so many years in the Spanish sun. In each one, Alex looked stunning. Tall and slender but with enviable curves. Her hair was a richer golden colour than they remembered, complementing her sun-kissed skin.

'They stayed in Spain then?' said Erika, as Darcy struggled to reframe Alex Rigby as a beautiful woman rather than the plain teenager she remembered.

'The parents did, but Alex has been in the States for a while,' said Libby, putting her phone away and reaching for the cocktail menu. 'When she messaged me, she'd just moved back here from New York.'

Darcy had felt sick when she heard that. It hit her again then, as she shuffled in a sea of suits towards the train doors to exit. She'd always wanted to see New York but so far hadn't even been there on holiday, yet this shiny new Alex Rigby had been living there all this time. That wasn't how it was supposed to go. Alex had been nothing special at school; she'd been way down the pecking order of popularity compared to Darcy. Darcy had been the one destined for greatness, not Alex sodding Rigby. If any of them should have been living it up in New York, it should have been *her*.

And now she had to go and be reunited with this glamazon and hear tales of her fabulous life. Darcy's phone buzzed again. Erika. *Come on! Where r u?*

Darcy replied as she left the platform. *Be there in a few mins.*

She took the wrong exit, as she almost always did at Bank, with its myriad options designed to confuse day-trippers, and had to check her phone to track down the bar where they were meeting. Multiple people walked smack into her with exaggerated, pass-agg sighs and she eventually arrived red-faced and irritable. She took a deep breath and swallowed her nerves as Libby waved at her through the window.

It was a typical city bar, dark and crowded, with groups of braying corporate types spilling out onto the street into the spring evening, clutching pints. A boom of macho laughter made Darcy jump as she picked her way through the wooden barrels being used as outdoor tables, the smell of beer and expensive perfume tickling her nose.

It had been a sunny day for March and with the evenings growing lighter, some of the more low-key punters were making the most of it by drinking Aperol spritzes and sharing a dish of olives as if they were sitting in an Italian piazza rather than standing outside a pub on a back street off Bishopsgate. Inside, she headed towards Libby's table, seeing Erika sitting beside her, and the back of a blonde head across the table beside the empty chair.

'Hey!' Libby stood up to hug Darcy as she approached, followed by Erika, who always greeted with two air kisses and a squeeze of the hand. 'Look who's here!'

Darcy turned to the remaining woman at the table, who was still sitting and watching her impassively. She was just as striking as she had appeared in her Facebook photos, with her hair loose to her shoulders and wearing a simple white shift dress that drew attention to her tanned, toned arms. Darcy swallowed hard. 'Alex. I can't believe it.'

Alex paused, appraising her for the merest of moments, Darcy thought (or was she imagining it?), before standing and enveloping her in a hug too. Darcy couldn't help but flinch. They were never huggers before. They'd been at the opposite ends of their friendship group, with Libby and Erika to buffer the sharp words and constant competitiveness between them. But Alex's embrace felt warm and affectionate, holding her so close that Darcy could feel her hard and unyielding chest. *A boob job?* Darcy wondered, before tucking her tummy in a little in case Alex was similarly assessing *her* contours.

Eventually, Alex released her and stood back, holding her at arm's length. 'Darcy.' She smiled, almost indulgently. 'Darcy Starr. I've thought about you a lot over the years.'

'It's Brooks now,' Darcy corrected, taking a moment to really look at Alex. Now she could see echoes of the girl she remembered, highlighted and enhanced by expertly applied makeup, plus Botox and fillers, she'd wager. 'I married Jon Brooks.'

Alex smiled again. 'Of course. Jonny. How is he?'

'He's great, fantastic, thank you,' Darcy replied, putting her coat and bag on the empty chair so that she could break eye contact. She rarely confessed to anything less than marital bliss, even when it was just the three of them, feeling on the back foot as she so often did these days. The one thing she had in her corner was a perfect home life. 'Can I get anyone a drink?'

'It's table service in this bit, honey.' Alex sat down and patted the seat of Darcy's chair. 'I reserved us a table as I knew it would be rammed.' Darcy's eyes met Erika's briefly at *honey*. She knew that would come up in the debrief later. Was it an affectation she'd picked up in New York? 'I took the liberty of ordering a round of negronis before you arrived, Darcy. I hope you like them?'

Darcy was loathe to admit that she'd never tried one. Usually she stuck to prosecco to start with and would then move on to white wine with dinner. Libby liked cocktails but only if they were 2-for-1 because she was saving for her wedding. Erika was the adventurous one who had tried every drink on the block.

'You'll like it, Darce,' said Erika, as the waiter arrived with four dark orange cocktails.

'Oh, you've never tried one?' Alex smiled again. 'Well, you'll love it. I can't imagine you're still drinking Malibu and Coke!'

They all laughed, including Darcy, despite the fact she did still sometimes have a Malibu and Coke at home on a Saturday night and didn't see what was so funny about that. She took a sip of the cocktail and stifled her reaction to its bitterness. 'Thanks, Alex.' She lifted her glass and they all clinked. 'It's definitely unusual.'

Erika snorted. 'Sorry. But you know what is unusual?' She waited a beat. 'Having *Alex fucking Rigby* sitting at our table once again! I'm sorry,' she added more quietly, when a couple at the next table turned to look, 'but this is so weird, after all these years. Libby has told us almost nothing about where you've been and why no one has heard from you.'

Darcy realised that Libby had hardly said a word since she arrived. On every night out in the past few months, she'd been giddy with excitement for her wedding and the hen trip to Croatia. Now, she looked tense, picking at the trendy blood orange crisp that sat atop her glass. 'That's because I know almost nothing,' she murmured.

Alex laughed. 'Well, the short version is that I decided to follow my folks into the sun because, once they'd sold the house, I guess I just didn't feel ready to take care of myself.'

'But we were all going off to uni anyway,' said Erika.

'I know, but I realised there'd be no base to come home to in the holidays and they'd be so far away if I needed them. And I wasn't excited about my course; I only applied because everyone else did.'

So far none of this surprised Darcy because she'd always thought Alex was immature and more reliant on her parents than the rest of them were by then. Alex was a late-in-life surprise and her parents had tended to indulge her, even baby her, in Darcy's opinion. 'But why didn't you keep in contact?' she asked now.

There was an awkward pause as Alex looked at Libby, who had moved on to tearing narrow strips in her napkin. 'I do feel bad about that. I do, Libs,' she added, forcing her into eye contact. 'I guess it took me a while to find my feet and, although it was my choice, I felt like you'd have all left me behind with your exciting new uni lives. I never intended to leave it this long but, you know, life gets in the way.'

Libby nodded and took a slurp of her drink. Darcy didn't know what to say until Erika broke the silence. 'I suppose the big question is this. Why did it take you so long . . .' she paused, and they all looked at her, waiting, '. . . to get on bloody Facebook?'

Everyone laughed and Darcy was grateful to her for breaking the tension. She couldn't relax with this new, grown-up Alex; the woman was a total stranger. No one could have ever mistaken Darcy for being her biggest fan, but at least teenage Alex had some spirit and character. This woman beside her didn't feel quite right, and as of yet she couldn't put her finger on why.

'Good question,' said Alex, sipping her drink as Darcy watched her curiously. 'I have Instagram, mostly for my business, but Kyle – my ex – wasn't a fan of us sharing our private lives on social media.' Alex smiled directly at Darcy, making her wonder if Alex had already seen *her* rose-tinted profile. 'I guess I changed my mind because I was coming home and wanted to look up old friends.'

Old friends, Darcy mused as Alex wrapped her perfectly manicured fingers around her half-finished negroni. *Is that what they were?*

2

2017 – Darcy

'No, absolutely not,' said Darcy, almost falling onto the sofa in her hurry to sit down. 'She can't be serious?'

Darcy's head was throbbing and she'd almost thrown up when Jon's morning alarm had startled her awake and into the horrors. She couldn't believe she'd been talked into drinking so much on a school night. Now that Jon was at work and Freya was off to school (thank goodness Freya walked with her friends now and didn't need her to drive), she'd been trying to get her act together for her shift at the hotel, but was seriously considering phoning in sick for the first time ever.

'She is. Alex railroaded her after you left last night.' Erika's voice down the line was supplemented with the click-click-click of a keyboard and a hum of distant conversation, which indicated she was already at work. Darcy looked at the clock; it was almost nine. She had a nine-thirty start, negotiated when she still had to take Freya to school each morning, but she would be cutting it fine now, especially as she'd have to walk.

'Can I call you back? I've got to phone work; I'm not going in.'

'Oh no, are you that bad?' Erika didn't get hangovers; she simply wouldn't stand for them. 'You never take a sick day.'

'Yeah, it's that bad. Call you back in ten?'

'Better make it half an hour, I've a quick meeting at nine.'

Darcy agreed and hung up before phoning work and pleading food poisoning. She felt it was half true; it was definitely something she'd consumed last night that made her feel so rough. Her boss was lovely about it, which just made her feel guilty on top of everything. 'Don't you worry about anything. We'll manage,' she soothed down the phone. 'It must be bad if you're not coming in. You never take a sick day.'

Darcy closed her eyes and imagined her gravestone. *Darcy Brooks, née Starr: 1980–2017. She never took a sick day.*

Darcy worked on reception at a boutique spa hotel on the edge of town, and she'd taken pride in being ultra-reliable and professional since she'd started there five years before. After Freya came along, Jon had encouraged her to find something closer to home that she could fit around school hours; her office job in the city with all the commuting and socialising expected of her wasn't working for them as a family, they'd both agreed.

The hotel had been a perfect solution and Darcy became popular with the mums at Freya's dance school thanks to the discount rates she could offer them on massages and treatments. But she was right to stay home this once, she justified to herself. Just the thought of having to be front of house and acting effortlessly professional when she was feeling this dog-rough made her want to throw up again.

The previous night had been so bizarre. The new and improved Alex Rigby had totally dominated the evening as if the three friends were guests at her party, rather than it being *her* who was the outsider after all these years. She insisted on treating them to dinner at some Michelin-starred Indian restaurant, even though she had never liked Indian food and barely touched her plate, and Darcy found herself swept up in the strangeness of having her there.

She drank quickly at first, to take the edge off the tension, and then ate everything that was put in front of her with a vague idea of soaking up the booze, but nothing could shift the unease in the pit of her stomach. It felt like foreboding, although she didn't feel quite ready to examine why that might be.

And now, according to Erika, Alex wanted to come on the holiday that was supposed to double as Libby's hen do. The thought of spending a week away with her, feeling totally unable to be herself and relax around her oldest friends, felt almost as bad to Darcy as the dreadful intensity of her hangover.

Reaching for the sugar she had sworn off in an attempt to shift a few pounds – this was an emergency – Darcy plunged the coffee and poured it to the brim of her 'Wine o'clock' mug, the jaunty text mocking her. A Secret Santa gift from Erika the previous year, Darcy suspected it was meant entirely as a joke; she knew Erika wouldn't be seen dead using something so unstylish. However, it was the largest mug Darcy owned, which was what she needed today.

Shuffling in her fluffy slippers to the living room until it was time to call Erika back, Darcy clutched her coffee mug in one hand and phone in the other before easing herself back onto the sofa. She opened Facebook and went straight to Alex's profile. Last night before she'd left, Alex had insisted they *friend* one another.

There was a new post. *Great catch-up with old mates last night*, it said. *And we haven't changed a bit since school!* Signed off with a winky face emoji and followed by three photos. The first one was a bathroom selfie that Alex must have taken at the start of the evening, look-ing gorgeous, hair and makeup immaculate. The second was of all four of them at the dinner table, taken by the waiter. Alex still looked fresh and perky while the other three looked rather worse for wear. Darcy grimaced at how red-faced and bloated she looked.

The third one was another selfie, this time of Alex with her arm around Libby and with Erika holding the phone out in front of her, all three of them grinning happily. Darcy swallowed. This must have been taken after she had gone home. Having the farthest to travel, Darcy had dashed off back to Waterloo for the last direct train to Weybridge, whereas the others all lived in London so weren't in a rush.

Alex was apparently staying rent-free in a Belsize Park townhouse belonging to her ex-husband's family. Darcy wasn't sure of the exact arrangement; some details from the previous night were foggy the morning after. And just as when she'd heard that Alex had been living in New York, Darcy had been forced to fight her feelings of envy once again. Partly because Alex waltzed straight into London life with a massive house in a chichi, affluent part of town, and partly because of that photo of the three of them grinning. They looked like they were having so much more fun than in the earlier photo when Darcy was there too.

She scrolled through Alex's profile, scanty as it was. It seemed she'd only joined at the start of the year and there was little more to see other than the photos she'd seen before. Alex's privacy settings were so stringent that Darcy couldn't even see who her other friends were. Darcy thought it strange; Alex hadn't said anything to suggest her ex was a dangerous man or that they were on bad terms. She'd spoken of him quite fondly and they were obviously still friendly enough for her to stay in his family's property. Why did she need to be so secretive? The point of social media was to see and be seen, surely?

Unless Alex only wanted to see?

The phone in Darcy's hand started ringing, startling her so much she sloshed coffee over the side of the mug and onto her dressing gown. 'Fuck's sake,' she muttered, putting the mug on the table in front of her and dabbing at the mess with her sleeve.

'I thought I was calling you back?' Darcy greeted Erika.

'You were, but it turns out I have, like, ten minutes before I have to sit in on a disciplinary panel. Don't ask,' Erika added, not that Darcy had been about to. She always told Erika she was happy not to have such a stressful job anymore and that was particularly true today.

'Anyway, short version is: Alex wants to come to Dubrovnik and she's bringing her daughter,' Erika continued when Darcy didn't answer. 'To be honest, she wasn't exactly asking. She just basically invited herself.'

'But why? How did it even come up?' Darcy said eventually, massaging her forehead. She'd been pleased when Libby was uncharacteristically quiet about her wedding and hen plans the night before, hoping that meant Alex was still NFI. The trip to Croatia was planned for less than a month away and the wedding itself was in August;

the invitations went out in January. Alex couldn't possibly be offended about having not been invited, seeing as Libby hadn't heard from her since the last millennium.

'Alex already knew Libby was getting married; I guess she told her when they first started messaging. And after you left last night, we went for a nightcap,' Erika said as Darcy quietly seethed. 'Somehow the conversation came around to the hen, I don't really remember how, and Libby told her about Dubrovnik and that it wasn't really a hen, it was a holiday, and that you were bringing Jon and Freya.'

Darcy winced; she was still a bit embarrassed about how that came about. She simply couldn't justify a holiday abroad just for her; it was too much to ask. Luckily, Libby hadn't minded at all, claiming she didn't want a traditional hen do, and as far as she was concerned, it was the more the merrier.

'The next thing I know, she says she should bring Tatyana – that's her daughter, by the way – and how it would be great to get your girls together.'

Darcy sighed. How typical of Alex to choose such a show-off name for her offspring. 'And Libby said yes?'

'Not exactly, but you know Libby, she can't simply say no,' said Erika with a snort. 'She ummed and ahhed and said it was probably too late, but Alex got her phone out and made her give her the details right there.' Darcy groaned quietly to herself as Erika went on. 'Like I said, she railroaded her. Got the resort name and the dates and found it herself. She's on a different flight but staying at the same hotel as us.'

'So it's a done deal?' Darcy couldn't believe it. 'She's actually booked it?'

'Yeah, I think so. We were all so wasted, it seemed quite funny at the time.' Erika paused and Darcy heard her say something in the background. 'I've gotta go, Darce.' Erika was back. 'I'll message you later.'

'Hang on a sec,' said Darcy quickly, as something occurred to her. 'Who was looking after Alex's daughter last night? I've only just wondered because I keep forgetting she's a mum now.'

'Oh – get this.' Erika laughed. 'There's a *housekeeper* at the Belsize Park pile.' Of course there was. 'Honestly, I think we are going to get some comedy mileage out of all this if nothing else!'

Erika rang off, leaving Darcy staring into space. Comedy was not the word she would use.

She felt a wave of frustration at the thought of Alex taking over every social event from now on. Last night had been bad enough with all the talk of her interior design business and the stories about how she'd met her then-husband in Spain.

'I was working as a waitress in a cocktail bar.' Alex's opener had Libby and Erika falling about laughing; they were several drinks in by this point.

'Come on!' Erika shook her head.

'He asked for a sidecar, but our place didn't do them; our clientele were more into Sex on the Beach and buckets of bright blue crap. He came and stood by the bar and talked me through how to make one for him.'

On and on, to a chorus of encouragement from the others, Alex had waxed lyrical about how Kyle was handsome, rich, classy . . . it had taken all of Darcy's self-control not to ask her why they had split up if he was so bloody perfect. She'd thought Libby had implied that Kyle had ended the marriage, so why was Alex so intent on painting him as Mr Wonderful? But Libby and even Erika seemed to be enjoying themselves so she'd kept quiet.

Darcy opened her phone again and searched for Alex's Instagram. As with Facebook, the profile was fairly new and didn't reveal much, mostly artfully arranged photos to show off her interior design skills. Maybe she reinvented herself after her divorce, Darcy thought. It would be very on-brand for Alex simply to start again as if her old life belonged to an entirely different person.

There was one photo from the previous night: a black-and-white close-up of an espresso martini. *Late night conversations with old friends*, the caption read, and was signed off with a heart emoji.

Had they been talking about her? Darcy reached for her now-cold coffee. She was used to the fact that Erika and Libby had a closeness that had excluded her to a certain extent since she left London. That had been her choice; her family were her priority now. Even though Libby had Pete, their relationship was so laid back, Libby had more in common with steadfastly single Erika. Hell, Darcy thought, the only reason they were getting married was because Libby had told Pete time was running out for having children and she wasn't trying for a baby without a ring on her finger; her own upbringing made her stand firm on that.

Darcy massaged her pounding head, feeling excluded once again. Alex had always wanted what was Darcy's. Now they were all going to be stuck together for a week, not just the women but their daughters too.

And, of course, Jon.

3

1997 – Alex

As we headed out that evening, I could smell anticipation in the air, and I for one was ready for an adventure. Libby was clutching my arm, the two of us practically skipping with excitement (as much as I could skip in my dress) to get to the club at opening time, while Darcy and Erika dragged their feet behind us, too cool for school and not impressed with turning up at 6 p.m. to somewhere called the Manhattan Showlounge.

'The place should be done for false advertising,' Libby's Auntie Karen said while we were getting ready in the caravan. Not really Libby's auntie, Karen was her mum's friend, and always came on holiday with them to the same caravan park in Dorset. This year, we were all there too; Libby was allowed to bring me, Erika and Darcy as a treat for finishing our GCSEs.

I chose my new favourite dress, a red sheath that was so tight I could barely walk in it. I'd bought it from a car boot sale without my mum knowing. 'Isn't that a bit OTT?' Erika had squinted at me as I shuffled across the caravan floor like a geisha. She was wearing jeans and a lumberjack shirt. I looked around and saw they all looked decidedly more casual than me; Libby in a denim skirt and Pulp Fiction T-shirt (which was bound to get a rise out of Darcy at some point as she insisted the rest of us didn't *get* that film), and Darcy herself sporting the trendy ladette look in loose combat pants and a tight vest top.

'I just want to look, you know,' I lowered my voice, 'eighteen.'

Libby's mum Pam had laughed. 'You don't need to hide your intentions on my behalf, love. I've seen those fake IDs, I don't think I've much to be worried about.'

'Anyway, Mum did much worse things when she was our age, didn't you?' Libby batted her eyelashes at her mum with a fake-angelic smile and Pam flicked her with a tea towel. We all knew the story of how Libby's mum fell pregnant with her at a Northern Soul all-nighter in Wigan. High on life and God knows what else, Pam didn't realise she was pregnant until three months later, by which time she had no recollection of who she'd spent the night with. As a result, Libby had never known her father, and as Pam was a fair-skinned redhead, could only assume that her tightly curled hair, brown eyes and tan skin came from him. She joked about it but, privately, she'd told me many times she felt she was missing out on a big chunk of her family history, and she would never, ever have children unless she was married to the man first.

Manhattan's was dark and half empty, the smell of stale beer, cigarette smoke and vinegary chips hitting me full in the face as Libby insisted, 'That's the smell of holiday right there!'

The others pulled faces but poor Libby looked so excited, I smiled and pretended to agree, folding myself onto a chair as best as I could in my dress.

'Boob.' Erika pointed at me. I'd asked them to be on boob-watch, as the only place my dress had any give was around the cleavage area where it gaped rather sadly.

Darcy announced she was going to the payphone in the entrance to call Bradley, her boyfriend at home, and while she was gone, Libby strove to reassure us the evening would improve. 'It will get busy later, I promise.'

'Then why did you make us come down so early?' Erika shook her head. 'I wanted to see if we could get channel five on the telly in the caravan.'

'Why? What's on channel five?'

'I've no idea, I've never been able to bloody get it!' Erika laughed.

'Whereas I'm getting it all the time,' announced Darcy, who'd returned without us noticing. 'Except this week, when I'm having to go without.'

'We're not talking about channel five anymore, are we?' I leaned over and whispered to Libby.

Darcy stuck her tongue out at me before nodding towards my chest. 'Boob.'

'Oh shit.' I sat back again.

'At least I think it was a boob, it's pretty hard to tell with you.' Darcy smiled, smoothing her black vest top down over her own ample chest. Libby always insisted that Darcy didn't mean anything by it when she spoke to me like that, but in any case her smile was enough to wind me up. She somehow looked more mature these days; I wondered if it was because she wasn't a virgin anymore. Was that why she seemed more sophisticated than the rest of us?

'So, who's going to the bar?' Libby changed the subject, tapping the table impatiently before the conversation about boobs led me and Darcy into another argument. We debated our strategy to get served for some time, as I was keen to ensure we played this just right, until Erika pointed out that me repeatedly mentioning the word *underage* was possibly not helping matters.

'OK, OK!' Libby put her hand up. 'Two of us will go and buy drinks for all of us.'

Darcy stood up and felt for her purse and fake ID in the many pockets of her combats. 'Well, I think we're all agreed that *she* shouldn't go up,' she said as she pointed at me, dismissive as ever. 'Erika and I should go because we're the oldest.'

Erika's birthday was precisely three days before Libby's, but I let it go because I was happy to let them have the first attempt, so off they went to the bar, Erika looking shifty and Darcy strutting overconfidently.

Libby and I turned our attention to Silly Billy, the children's entertainer who was getting started on the dance floor.

'Good evening, boys and girls!' he bellowed.

'Good evening, Silly Billy!' we chorused along, giggling like mad.

'Grow up, children!' said Erika, reappearing with Darcy, both with hands full of glasses and bottles.

'Oh yay!' Libby exclaimed. 'You got served!'

'Be. Cool.' Darcy set down Libby's Bud and her Malibu, while Erika handed me a pineapple Bacardi Breezer and swigged from her own glass of Archers and lemonade.

'Nice lads behind the bar. Don't think they cared to be honest.'

'Very nice lads!' Darcy grinned, as she sat down.

'Oh?' Libby looked interested.

Darcy winked and nodded, but said nothing.

'You've got a boyfriend,' I reminded her, and she looked at me like *duh*.

'What's this shite?' Erika nodded at the children singing and jumping around on the dance floor.

'Don't be such a killjoy!' Libby said to her. 'Get that drink down you and lighten up.'

'Libby fancies Silly Billy,' I joked. 'From now on we have to call her Sibby Libby.'

Libby and Erika laughed. Darcy shook her head and muttered, 'Children,' but she did at least crack a smile.

Emboldened by our first drinks, Libby and I took our turn to go up to the bar next. I felt my pulse quicken a little as we waited to be served and rearranged the neckline of my dress as Libby fidgeted. 'Do I look OK?' I asked her, meaning, *do I pass for eighteen?*

She nodded. 'And me?'

'You look *gawjus*,' I replied, making her laugh as I knew it would.

'Yes, ladies?' The barman came over to us, blowing his floppy Hugh Grant-style fringe out of his face.

I opened my mouth but nothing came out; suddenly, it was parchment dry. He was the most gorgeous boy – man – I'd ever seen in real life, like he'd just stepped out of a *Just Seventeen* poster.

He raised an eyebrow as he waited, but Libby jumped in to rescue me. 'Archers and lemonade, Malibu and Coke, a Bud and . . .'

'And a pineapple Bacardi Breezer?' he finished, with a grin.

My body flooded with heat and I laughed, too loudly. 'Yes! How did you know?'

'I did this round for your friends about half an hour ago.'

Libby and I looked at each other, my attraction stalling for just a moment as I remembered where we were and wondered if we were in trouble.

'Don't worry, girls. Jonny never forgets an order, do you, mate?' A second barman with a Scottish accent and a freckly face had appeared. When he said girls, it sounded like *gerrils*; I was enchanted by the pair of them. I felt like I was dreaming, so far removed was this interaction from my normal life.

Beside me I was aware of Libby reaching for her fake ID when I noticed that the second guy had moved on and Jonny – I assumed that was his name – was off pouring our drinks. 'What just happened?' I whispered to Libby.

'I think . . . were they flirting with us?' she whispered back, eyes wide.

'Oh, my God!' I prayed that she was right. 'I really like him. The one with the fringe.'

'Yeah?' Libby grinned.

'Oh God, yeah.' I took a deep breath. 'I'm going to say something to him.'

I fiddled again with my neckline as Jonny returned. I opened my mouth but before I could say anything, he'd turned away to get the bottles out of the fridge.

'Go on,' Libby encouraged me.

I cleared my throat. 'So.' The volume of my voice took me aback and I realised I was shouting. 'Your name is Jonny.'

He stopped and looked at me in surprise and amusement. 'Yes, your honour.'

I laughed again, way too loudly, and Libby covered her face with her hand.

'What's yours?' Jonny smiled at me.

'Thanks, mate, I'll have a pint of lager!' The Scottish one reappeared with a grin and Jonny gave him a good-natured shove before turning back to me.

'He never misses a trick,' said Jonny. 'Any sign of a free drink or a fit girl, and there he is. I meant,' Jonny leaned forward on the Boddingtons pump and looked directly into my eyes, 'what's *your* name?'

I flushed crimson. 'Alexandra. Alex.'

'Nice to meet you, Alexandra-Alex.' Jonny reached over the bar and gently shook my hand. My breath caught in my throat as he continued. 'This is my mate Rob,' he indicated his freckled friend, who gave a little bow, 'and you are?' He turned to Libby, who seemed charmed by their double act.

'Libby. Just Libby.'

'Alexandra-Alex and Libby-Just-Libby, got it!' Rob saluted, before moving along the bar to serve the next person. We handed over our money to Jonny and made 'Eek!' faces at each other behind his back as he went to the till.

'See you soon, I hope, ladies,' Jonny said with a teasing smile as we walked away with our drinks, trying to stay cool until we were out of sight of the bar.

'Ohmygodohmygodohmygod!' I finally let it pour out, as we arrived back at the table.

'Did you get IDed?' Erika looked at me in concern.

'No! The barmen flirted with us!' I wanted to squeal with excitement.

'And? They flirted with us too, I told you.' Darcy reached for her drink.

I refused to let her take the wind out of my sails. 'They asked for our names and one of them, Jonny, shook my hand,' I said, with a hint of triumph.

'Oh big whoop, he told *me* he liked my top.' Darcy straightened it, sticking her chest out a little more in the process.

I felt my face fall. 'Jonny did?'

'The Hugh Grant lookalike? Yeah.'

'He did,' Erika confirmed. 'And the Scottish one said he liked my accent.'

'But you don't have an accent?' I was confused; Erika's family was German but she didn't have a German accent.

'My English accent.' Erika laughed.

'Ah well, it's cool to have some friends behind the bar.' Libby smiled, sensing, as she always did, that Darcy had got to me.

'But I liked that Jonny, I mean I *liked* him,' I whispered to her. 'And it's not fair – Darcy already has a boyfriend.' I let my dislike of Darcy shine openly in my eyes as I watched her sip her drink. 'It's not fair!'

Libby squeezed my arm, but I knew she didn't get it, not really. This wasn't some teenage crush. I knew that this was the start of something big and I wasn't about to let Darcy ruin it for me.

4

2017 – Darcy

Darcy threw another dress on the floor and resisted the urge to kick it. Nothing in her wardrobe was suitable; anything she liked didn't fit her anymore, or *at the moment*, as she preferred to rephrase it. It didn't fit her *at the moment*, but it would again soon, she vowed, as soon as she got her shit together.

She sat on the edge of the bed and surveyed the pile of abandoned outfits. With the Dubrovnik trip less than a week away, there wasn't enough time to begin yet another health and fitness regime, and the cute summer dresses from holidays long past were destined to spend another season languishing at the back of her wardrobe.

'How's it going?' Jon appeared in the doorway, holding two steaming mugs. 'Aren't the clothes meant to go *in* the suitcase?'

'Haha.' Darcy reached for one of the mugs as Jon picked his way across the mess and found space on the bed beside her. He looked tired, she noticed. When he sat down beside her, he gave a groan as if he were pushing eighty rather than forty.

Darcy blew on her coffee, letting the sweet-smelling steam tickle her nose. 'Is there sugar in this?'

'It's one of those mocha sachet things; it was near its date.'

Darcy pulled a face and tried not to think about empty calories.

'What's up?' Jon sat back, bumping his back on an open suitcase. 'You've not been yourself for a while.'

She'd not been herself, Darcy Starr, for some years now, but she knew he didn't mean that. He meant the last few weeks, since Alex had exploded back into her life.

'It's this trip,' Darcy began. She'd still not told him Alex was coming. Technically, Jon knew Alex was back in the country as there'd been the photos from their night out, so Darcy had dropped her name as nonchalantly as she could get away with. He'd nodded then, with little interest; Darcy wasn't even sure he remembered who she was talking about, and if he'd seen the photos – Jon rarely used Facebook – he'd not made any comment.

'Is it the money?' Jon took a sip of his mocha and grimaced. 'Wow, this really is crap, no wonder we left them in the cupboard for so long.'

'Yes!' Darcy seized on that. 'Yes, I'm worried about how much this is all going to cost. Buying drinks and eating out, you know.'

It was true; they did have to be careful. Jon worked hard to provide for them, but his middle management job at a plant hire company in Woking just about paid their mortgage and bills. Darcy's job helped towards little treats, but they didn't have cash to flash, hence combining Libby's hen do with their main holiday of the year.

Jon put his mug down on the bedside table and reached for her free hand. 'It'll be OK; it's not like they'll expect us to go to posh restaurants every night. I know Erika can afford it, but Libby doesn't have loads of money, does she?'

Darcy shook her head; Libby was budgeting for the wedding. Yet even though she and Pete didn't make a fortune either, they always seemed to have enough. Was it the classic formula of double-income-no-kids? Or was it just because Libby could throw on an outfit made entirely from charity shop bargains, travel by bus and trim her own hair, and still look like she was living her shiniest, most sparkling life?

But Darcy didn't begrudge Libby, or even Erika. Something, or more accurately someone, else was on her mind.

The previous week, still feeling unsettled about their reunion, Darcy had decided to take the bull by the horns and meet Alex for coffee — something else she hadn't mentioned to Jon. They'd met in London so that Darcy could combine it with a bit of holiday shopping, but it had been a mistake. More than a mistake; a total disaster. Darcy had seethed her way around the shops of Oxford Street, running on fumes of envy and loathing, knowing Alex was going to arrive in Dubrovnik with cases full of designer gear like an A-lister on vacation, making Darcy feel even more invisible.

Alex had breezed into the coffee shop, turning heads and shooing away compliments. 'Please! I look like shit!' she'd trilled when Darcy grudgingly told her she looked good. She'd been full of how her design business was coming along and how well Tatyana was settling in at school. Darcy knew her own news of having an afternoon in lieu to use up, allowing her to come up to London for a treat, sounded utterly banal. Alex had openly laughed when Darcy told her what she did for a living.

'Bloody hell, I never pictured Darcy Starr working at a hotel reception! You were so confident at school I fully expected you to become a TV presenter or Prime Minister or something!' Darcy had pasted on a brittle smile as Alex appraised her, Alex's eyes resting on Darcy's middle for slightly longer than was polite. 'But I guess we've all changed a bit since then.'

Returning with a few new pairs of leggings and a flowery top she'd seen in the sale, Darcy wished she'd saved herself the train fare and simply shopped at a

Primark closer to home. Darcy knew she hadn't imagined the looks and the digs designed to undermine her, particularly Alex's parting shot about Erika having a fling with someone at work.

'I think you've got that wrong.' Darcy shook her head. 'Erika isn't seeing anyone. She loves being single.'

Alex wrinkled her nose, at least she wrinkled it as much as she could with all the shit she'd had pumped into her face. 'You know, the younger guy? She's really going to have to be careful there as she's further up the chain than him and it's so not a good look for someone in human resources!' Alex laughed, then tilted her head in a condescending manner when it was clear that Darcy had no idea what she was talking about. 'She told us the other night. Oh no – of course, you'd gone home by then.'

Darcy's face flamed with humiliation as once again she pictured them having a better time without her there, the three of them laughing behind her back. 'Can't wait to hang out with you all again – this is going to be so much fun!' Alex tinkled, with an infuriating little wave, as Darcy fled the coffee shop, feeling far worse than before, a feeling that had stayed with her ever since.

Yes, a total disaster.

Darcy realised Jon was still waiting for her to say something and she took a deep breath. She needed to take control of the situation.

'Jon, I forgot to say, there's a few more people coming on this holiday now. Libby's friend Alex has invited herself along and she's bringing her daughter.'

Yes, *Libby's friend*, Darcy told herself after she blurted it out. No one important.

'Oh right. Someone else for Freya to hang out with then?'

Darcy could tell that Jon hadn't processed who Alex was. 'You remember, from years ago? The one who . . . had a bit of a crush on you?'

Darcy watched Jon closely as recognition dawned in his eyes. 'The skinny blonde?'

'That's her,' she said through gritted teeth. She couldn't read his expression. 'Remember I said she was back? She came out with the girls a few weeks ago.'

He shook his head. 'I don't think I knew you meant her.'

Probably wasn't even listening, Darcy thought. 'Well, I did. And I'm not keen on her to be honest, so I'm hoping we'll be able to give her a wide berth on the trip.'

Jon shrugged. 'Suits me. I barely remember her.'

'Really?' That came out more sharply than Darcy intended.

'Yes, really!'

Darcy was silent, wishing with an urgency she'd never felt before that she'd been single when they first met so they could have been together from the start.

'You're not worried about her being there, are you?' Jon persisted, forcing her to make eye contact with him. 'Because that was a lifetime ago and I wasn't even interested in her. I only ever wanted you.' He took her mug and placed it beside his on the dresser. 'It was always you, you know that.'

'Even now?'

He drew her into his embrace. 'Of course even now, you daft bint. Always.'

Darcy buried her head into Jon's shoulder and breathed him in deeply. Jon wasn't perfect but he was hers. That bitch couldn't touch them; nothing she had could hold a candle to this, their little family. Nothing any of them had, in fact – Libby's effortless style, Erika's successful career, not even Alex with her hard new tits and wads of cash could compare with what she and Jon had together.

Darcy called Freya into the room and took a grinning selfie of the three of them with the open suitcases in the background. *Getting ready for holibobs! #family #friends #blessed,* she posted.

As the likes rolled in and the three of them abandoned the packing to have a proper cuppa in front of the telly, Darcy felt lighter, unburdened. She'd never admitted it to anyone, but she'd felt lost like this before. At uni, where her personality had been dwarfed by the big characters around her, and it dawned on her that she was nothing special: she'd just been a big fish in the small pond of their school. Then after graduation, when everyone she knew seemed to overtake her in the career stakes. Most recently, when they'd failed to have a second child, as all her NCT peers were growing their families and she was left behind as they went through motherhood a second or even a third time. It was as if she was failing at life, and everyone else was doing better than her in every way.

But she looked again at the photo of the three of them and smiled. This was what she was good at. The comments rolled in, *beautiful family*, *well jel*, *you look fab hun*, mostly from the dance mums who spent their whole lives on social media.

As she snuggled next to Jon on the sofa, Darcy had a notification that Alex had commented on her photo. Steeling herself, she opened it and saw one word: *Gorgeous*.

Darcy's breath caught in her throat. Who was gorgeous? All of them? Or just one person in particular? She zoomed in on Jon, tilting her phone away from him so he couldn't see what she was doing. He looked good in the photo, but then she'd deliberately picked one where they all did. She'd taken the shot nine times from different angles until Freya threatened to walk away if she didn't stop.

Then, while she was still looking at the photo, another notification told her Alex had also reacted to her post. The laughing emoji.

Darcy pictured Alex's own laughing face and threw her phone down on the sofa.

5

2017 – Darcy

Freya was staring at Tatyana in adoration. Ever since they'd met in the hotel bar earlier that evening, Freya had been smitten.

Darcy watched Freya in amusement as she copied Tatyana – or Tatty, as Alex called her – who was teaching the younger girl how to peel a prawn. Freya would never touch seafood at home, let alone pick up a whole prawn and shell it with her bare hands, but it seemed that anything Tatty did, Freya was willing to try.

She couldn't blame her daughter for being enchanted; Tatty was a beauty and had a sweet nature to go with her looks. Darcy also knew Tatty's American accent would have added to her allure in Freya's eyes, her daughter being a huge Disney Channel fan.

It amused Darcy that Alex had a daughter so unlike her, at least unlike the Alex who she remembered from school. In fact, she found it hard to believe that Alex was a mother at all, let alone to this clear-skinned, white-toothed, all-American princess.

She'd asked Libby earlier if she knew how old Tatty was and she'd said, 'Thirteen I think, maybe fourteen,' which would make her only two or three years older than Freya, who'd turned eleven in January. Yet, Darcy thought, Tatty might be a little older than that as she was a clear foot taller than Freya. It wasn't just her physical appearance either; there was a definite maturity in her manner and the indulgent – but not condescending – way she spoke to Freya, that made Darcy think she might be closer to fifteen or more.

'I like your bracelet,' Freya said shyly, having noticed it as Tatty reached for a napkin.

'Thanks.' The older girl smiled at her, admiring it herself as she wiped her hands. It was silver and adorned with little dolphins in Swarovski crystal that sparkled in the evening sunshine. 'My daddy gave it to me for my birthday.'

Darcy tuned in, hoping Freya might ask Tatty how old she was, but instead her daughter asked, 'Where is your dad – daddy?' Darcy noticed her falter; she'd grown out of calling Jon *Daddy* some years ago now but clearly wanted to fit in with Tatty's Americanisms. 'Isn't he coming on holiday with us?'

There was a pause as Tatty looked to her mother for direction and Darcy sensed that everyone was holding their breath.

Eventually Alex smiled and reached for the wine bottle, pouring an inch into her own glass before passing the bottle to Libby. 'Tatty's daddy and I don't live together anymore, sweetie,' she said brightly. 'He stayed in New York when Tatty and I came to England for a while. But it's OK,' she continued, seeing Freya's frown, 'because he loves Tatty very much, and he's going to come over and visit her in the summer when he can get away from work.'

'And we're having Christmas in New York, right, Mom?' added Tatty.

'I said maybe, not definitely.'

Tatty shrugged and turned her attention back to Freya as the adults resumed eating. It was a tense atmosphere, Darcy thought, and had been all evening. No one was comfortable, despite everyone trying their best to be good company. Perhaps they were trying too hard, she thought, as Libby said for possibly the third time that evening how beautiful the view was from their table on the waterfront and the others obligingly chorused their agreement.

Jon was quiet, she noticed. He'd hardly said a word all evening and only then when he was spoken to. Darcy was still stung by his reaction when Alex walked in. To say that his jaw had dropped would be a cliché, yet there was no other way to describe it. She'd been tempted to reach over and close his mouth with her hand.

It was earlier that evening as they waited in the hotel bar as arranged. Erika and Libby were already sitting at the bar with a pitcher of the local lager when Darcy, Jon and Freya found them. Darcy had been struck by how carefree they looked when the rest of the party weren't around. Libby was laughing loudly at something Erika had said, holding onto the bar with both hands so that she didn't fall off as she leaned back on her stool.

Libby looked vibrant and fit (in both senses of the word) in a denim skirt and sparkly gold vest top that enhanced her skin tone. Knowing Libby, it would have cost about fifty pence from a market stall but somehow looked fun and summery rather than cheap and tarty, which Darcy knew it would look on her. Libby's natural curls were liberated for once from their standard pony-tail and bounced loose around her shoulders, restrained only slightly by the Jackie O sunglasses perched on her head.

Erika looked groomed and understated as usual with her sleek, dark bob and an expensive-looking black maxi dress set off by simple silver jewellery. Completely different to Libby, but somehow the two complemented each other and were attracting admiring glances from a group of young men, probably almost half their age, sitting on the other side of the bar.

Darcy looked down at herself in her lemon yellow tunic top over black leggings. Even though Freya had told her she looked 'pretty, like a buttercup', and Jon, when pressed for an opinion, had said she looked *nice*, Darcy felt matronly and past it.

She was almost thirty-seven years old, she reminded herself angrily; she'd been married for twelve years and had a pre-teen daughter. Why shouldn't she look and feel comfortable and appropriate for her age? Just because Libby and Erika were living some sort of arrested-development, child-free London lifestyle, did that mean she should feel pressured into dressing like she was twenty-one again? Wait until they joined the real world and had children, she thought, then they would understand that there was more to life than looking hot.

Erika noticed their arrival and waved them over with a grin. Darcy's gut twisted with shame at her private snippiness as she watched Erika pour her and Jon a glass of beer each, while Libby pulled up a stool for Freya and ordered her a Coke. She hadn't meant it, not really.

Jon seemed glad of other adults to talk to, Darcy noticed, as he fell into a conversation with Erika about the flight. 'I say this with all respect and love to my German family members, but I am not down with people clapping when the plane lands,' she heard Erika tell him. 'It's like, well done for doing your job, Mr Pilot, and managing not to kill us all! It's cringey as fu—' She remembered Freya just in time. 'Fudge!'

The adults all smiled as Freya sipped her Coke and pretended not to be listening. Ice broken, Darcy could see that Jon was relaxing, looking around the bar and out to the view beyond.

'You picked a great hotel, Libby,' he enthused. 'Thank you for letting us tag along.'

Darcy had felt a little disappointed when they'd first arrived, taking in the boxy exterior they were faced with when they walked up from the bus stop. The road entrance led straight into the upper level of the hotel, with the floors underneath built into the hillside descending to the water's edge below. Once inside, however, she'd noticed that one wall of the reception area had floor-to-ceiling windows and the view made her stop and catch her breath; cerulean blue sea edged with the lush greenery of the coastal path was laid out before her, and from then on every time she turned a corner or looked out of a window she was treated to more of the same. It was just perfect.

'It's my pleasure. And it's gorgeous, isn't it?' Libby looked so happy that Darcy felt happy too, relishing being with her family and her oldest friends, all enjoying one another's company in such beautiful surroundings.

Then Alex's arrival at the bar took them all by surprise, and not necessarily in a good way. Darcy, aware this would be the first time Jon had seen Alex since they were teenagers, noticed that he didn't recognise her when she first approached the group. Even Erika did a double take.

'Hey, ladies!' She grinned, pulling Libby in for a hug and air-kissing Erika and Darcy before solemnly shaking hands with Freya and introducing Tatty. Resplendent in a white halterneck top that showed off her enviable shoulders and arms, worn with black skinny jeans and wedge sandals that made her legs look longer than ever, Alex was instantly holding court among the little group.

Eventually, after it didn't seem like she was going to acknowledge Jon, Darcy interjected, 'Alex, you remember Jon? My husband.'

Alex turned to him with a vague smile, as if she couldn't quite place him and Darcy saw then the way he looked at her – a mixture of confusion and admiration – and her stomach turned over with an unnamed fear.

'Jonny, of course!' she murmured, leaning in for a hug and planting a kiss near his left ear. Darcy noticed him tense, then she caught his eye over Alex's bare shoulder as he coughed and released her.

'Don't you all look lovely tonight?' Alex smiled as they took their drinks over to a table where they could all sit down, prompting Libby and Jon and even

– grudgingly – Erika to retort that she also looked very lovely.

'Oh no, I just threw this on as it was near the top of my case. I'll unpack properly later – I couldn't wait to get the fun started!' she said, flourishing in the limelight.

Darcy sighed, realising that Alex was likely to dominate the whole evening if permitted, but after noticing Jon (or *Jonny*, as she mimicked in her head) being so in thrall to her, she found she couldn't think of anything to say.

'But no, truly, everyone looks wonderful. Don't these two look cute together?' she chirped, and everyone chorused their agreement as Alex gestured towards Freya and Tatty who were sitting together at one end of the table, Freya totally absorbed in what the older girl was telling her about going to school in New York.

'Erika, that dress looks amazing on you,' Alex continued. 'And, Libs, I love that top. Jonny,' she added. 'You haven't changed a bit!'

'Hardly!' He laughed, running his hand over his head, where Darcy knew he was self-conscious about starting to recede. Darcy also noticed him tuck his tummy in and sit up a bit straighter. Pathetic, she thought. Were all men so susceptible to flattery from a beautiful woman?

'Honestly, you haven't aged a day. Neither have you, Darcy,' Alex added as an afterthought, somehow making it sound as if it weren't so. Alex was smiling warmly at her, but again Darcy felt she was being slighted. What was Alex's problem? Was it just that Alex wanted to be top dog when the group were all together – or *was* it to do with Jon?

Don't be ridiculous, she chided herself immediately, as Alex engaged Libby in a discussion about the wedding plans. Look at her, Darcy thought, she could have any man she desired, and has just spent the last however many years living the high life with a wealthy American. Why on earth would she still be interested in Jon?

Yet the feeling remained niggling at Darcy as the evening went on, amplified by having Jon sat beside her. After the meal was cleared away and everyone accepted another glass of wine, except Freya and Tatty who ate their pudding happily, the conversation was still rather stilted. Darcy, emboldened by the wine, was fed up with feeling invisible and determined to take control of the conversation.

'So, what's Pete up to this week, Libby? It's a shame he couldn't have come along, be someone for Jon to talk to,' she said with a smile.

Libby looked embarrassed. 'Well, as it's my sort of hen do, I didn't invite him. He didn't mind, he's not into beach holidays; he's more of a camping guy. Oh – and he totally understood why Jon was invited,' she quickly added. 'I've left him chasing RSVPs, if he can be bothered, and tomorrow his brother's coming to stay for a few days. They'll probably be at the pub most nights, or sat in front of the PlayStation.'

'Has he been much help with the wedding planning?' Darcy knew full well that he hadn't. 'Or is he like Jon, who left everything to me?'

'Hey, I did stuff!' Jon protested. 'I sorted out all the transport and I drove to Calais to get the wine.'

'Yeah, that's right, you did cars and booze, all the difficult jobs,' said Darcy, smiling through her sarcasm.

'Pete has done a few bits.' Libby looked awkwardly between Darcy and Jon. 'To be fair, he said from the start that if we were doing this, then he expected me to organise things – after all it was me who wanted it!'

Libby gave a little laugh that sounded unconvincing to Darcy, who remembered the many conversations they'd had about how Libby was keen to get married and Pete wasn't.

'So, what was your wedding like?' Alex grinned at Jon. 'If I remember the Darcy of old,' she continued teasingly, and Darcy wondered if she had imagined a slight emphasis on the word *old*, 'then I'll bet it was beautiful, lavish and just a trifle high maintenance!'

Alex gave her a playful squeeze on the arm, and once again Darcy was left wondering how to take her words. High maintenance? Could that be taken in any other way?

'It was beautiful,' confirmed Libby, coming to her rescue.

'But not lavish. We didn't have the money for lavish, especially not in those days,' Jon added.

Darcy worked hard to keep her voice neutral. 'It was laid back and relaxed, just a really fun, happy day.'

And it had been, Darcy remembered. They'd had a ceremony in the local church and the reception in the pub across the road which had a marquee in the garden for functions. Erika and Libby had decorated the venue with paper garlands and fairy lights as their present to her and for the wedding breakfast they'd had a hog roast, followed by dancing to rock 'n' roll records played on Jon's dad's beloved old Wurlitzer jukebox.

She'd worn her mum's dress, a simple seventies floor-length gown in cream, and carried a posy of wildflowers tied with a ribbon. Her hair had still been long then and, despite everyone telling her to get a hairdresser to create an elaborate up-do, she'd worn it loose and flowing around her shoulders with just a short veil held in place with a pearl comb. When Jon had seen her walking down the aisle, he'd had tears in his eyes and the biggest grin on his face she'd ever seen. Remembering that look made Darcy flush with warmth; they'd been so hopelessly romantic back then.

Smiling, she turned to him. 'Remember when you took that—' she began, stopping abruptly when she saw his attention was focused on Alex, who had taken her phone out and was showing them all a photo from her own wedding.

The photo was one of her on her own in a white lace dress, which looked very intricate and expensive, as far as Darcy could make out. Her hair was in a chignon with a gleaming tiara sat atop it and her makeup was expertly applied.

Darcy thought that Alex must have been mid-transformation at this point. Gone was the gangly awkwardness, disastrous perm and teenage acne, but she wasn't yet the groomed goddess who sat before them. A surreptitious glance between the photo and the real-life Alex in front of her confirmed what Darcy had suspected – she'd definitely had a boob job since then and possibly some work on her face too. The girl in this wedding photo was the missing link between the annoying old friend that Darcy used to tease and the beauty who was now – somewhat unexpectedly on holiday with them.

Darcy wondered if the photo reminded Jon of how Alex used to be. She saw him now, grinning inanely at something Alex was saying about her wedding dress, something that would have been of no interest to him whatsoever, if it wasn't being said by someone he found attractive.

Jon always had been an incorrigible flirt, Darcy thought. His cheeky confidence and the fact that other women were often so readily charmed by him were all part of the attraction for Darcy in the early days. He might give other women attention, but they meant nothing to him; *she* was the one he was coming home to.

Darcy recognised the soppy grin on his face as the same expression he wore when the well-proportioned blonde in their local takeaway gave him an extra shovel of chips on the house. It never bothered her because she knew it was as harmless as when she exchanged double entendres with the guy at the butcher's with the big arms.

But this was different, and this did bother her, because Alex was newly divorced and had once fancied Jon, enough to make a play for him. More importantly, Darcy couldn't remember the last time *she* had made his face light up like that.

Alex finished her story and everyone laughed loudly, even Jon. Even *Freya*, which Darcy took particularly personally.

As Alex began another anecdote, Darcy reached for the wine and poured herself another glass.

6

1997 – Alex

The morning after we met Jonny, I told Libby I was serious about my feelings for him as we whispered, heads together, in the back of Libby's mum's car. It was the first time I'd been able to talk to Libby alone; even though we shared a room in the caravan, the walls were so paper-thin that when I'd tried to talk the night before, Erika had sing-songed, 'We can heeear yooou!' from the other room, shutting me up immediately.

I knew I had to stake my claim before anyone else (let's face it, I meant Darcy) declared an interest. Even though she had Bradley, she still flirted with other guys wherever we went. It was like she couldn't help it; she fed off their interest and desire. She had to be the centre of attention, even if she didn't really want the guy. I couldn't have her doing that with Jonny. He was already too special to me; I'd never had a man flirt with me like that before. It had to mean something.

Pam grumbled that she felt like our chauffeur with no one in the passenger seat but she was soon singing along to Sunday Love Songs on the radio. Darcy and Erika were with Karen in her car, all of us on our way to a café in Dorchester, for what Karen called brunch. I'd never heard the term 'brunch', but it seemed trendy and sophisticated. I was a young woman, on holiday with her friends, who flirted with fit blokes in bars and was now going out for *brunch*. Life was good.

'I had a connection with Jonny. You saw it!'

'Those boys might just talk like that to all the girls.' Libby generally tried to walk a fine line between us all; she hated conflict. And although I knew she would always be on my side, she still insisted on seeing the good in Darcy too.

'Well, I'm just saying now that I like Jonny. I mean I *like* him. So if Darcy goes after him now I've said that then she's a bad friend.' The fact he would only be in our lives for a week made no difference to my analysis.

Libby didn't say anything, which I took as her agreement on the subject, and I turned to look out of the window, the rain beating down in typical British summertime fashion. I imagined how my next conversation with Jonny would go; I just knew he would be kind and interesting and considerate – and I already knew he was funny, not to mention gorgeous. It would be perfect, I just knew it.

Upon arrival, the six of us commandeered a booth, ordering all-day breakfasts and sticky buns along with strong coffee served in cafetières, which I also thought were classy as anything.

'Hey, Erika – I wonder if they'll have any German bread?' said Darcy with a wink.

'German bread!' Libby and I cried in unison, rubbing our tummies and laughing as Pam and Karen looked at us, bemused.

Erika shook her head. 'Are you never going to let that drop?'

I remembered the school trip to the Lake District two years before, where we'd experienced our first proper continental breakfast buffet. Erika was extremely excited to show us how delicious German bread could be, and the catchphrase had stuck, with us all shouting, 'German bread!' and rubbing our tummies whenever the opportunity came up.

'Never!' Libby laughed. 'We'll still remind you of that even when we're properly old, like in our thirties.'

We spent a relaxed morning eating and chatting, the only flashpoint being when Darcy spotted me smiling into my coffee and asked if I had wind, but Libby defused the tension by pointing out the computer in the corner.

'That wasn't here last year.' Libby, Pam and Karen visited the same haunts every summer. 'Three quid for a go on that internet thing.'

'I'll have a go!' Darcy jumped up. 'Bradley and I got Hotmail accounts, so I can send him some *hot mail*.' She pouted as she headed off to the computer and I noticed even Erika rolling her eyes.

Getting ready to go out in the evening, I spent even longer on my hair and makeup than the night before while Erika played her summer mixtape on the battery-operated boombox Libby had brought from home, and we had a little boogie in the caravan to get us in the mood.

Of course, that was the point at which Darcy walked in from yet another trip to the phone box, and she fell about laughing at the sight of me.

'Kiss my arse, Darcy.' I glared at her.

'I would if I could find it.' Darcy smirked at Erika, who sniggered. That annoyed me more than anything, as I'd been having a nice time with Erika before Darcy returned.

'Better than having a fat one.'

'Are you saying I've got a fat arse?'

I was silent. Obviously Darcy didn't have a fat arse; we all knew she had the best figure out of all of us.

'Well, are you?' she persisted.

I shrugged and went back to my makeup; I was determined not to let her ruin my evening.

'Because I promise you this,' Darcy continued. 'If a guy had to choose between your bones and my curves, it would be curves all the way. Any bloke you can think of,' she added with a smile, and I wondered if she meant

Jonny. I knew Libby did too because I met her gaze in the mirror.

That night, remembering our conversation in the car, Libby engineered it so that I went to the bar with Erika while she kept Darcy busy. I was sure that if I appealed to Darcy to stay away from Jonny, she would be even more likely to seek him out just to annoy me and prove that she could have him if she wanted him.

It was Rob who came over as we approached the bar, so I let Erika chat to him while I waited to catch Jonny's eye.

'Hello again.' He smiled his lopsided smile and I took a direct hit to all of my vital organs. 'Is my mate here taking care of your needs?'

For a moment, I couldn't speak. Was he flirting with me?

I smiled back and found my voice. 'He's doing a grand job, but I'm sure I could think of something for you to do, as well.'

I couldn't believe my boldness. I was totally out of my depth; for me, this was about as daring as it got. As soon as the words came out of my mouth, I blushed hard, right from my chest up to my forehead. I knew he could see it happening and he looked amused. Curious. He narrowed his eyes and hesitated before saying anything else. *Oh my word.* The pause was electrifying, charged with tension and sex and anticipation and lots of other feelings I couldn't even begin to name.

I waited to hear what his reply would be – would he flirt back? (Did he realise *I* was flirting?) Would he ask me out? But the spell was broken as Rob totalled up our order and Erika elbowed me back to reality.

I couldn't leave it there. 'I was thinking perhaps we should get two rounds now so that we don't have to come up again during the show?'

Some inane 'family fun' game show was about to start and Erika squinted at me in confusion, knowing we didn't care about watching it. 'Well, maybe you look after that lot and I'll get some more in, yeah?' I nodded at her as she side-eyed me but didn't argue. Rob started to assemble another round of what he'd just served us, with a small smile playing on his lips, as I turned back to Jonny.

'So, what is it that I can help you with? It looks like Rob has got the drinks taken care of.' Jonny leaned onto the bar and his hair flopped into his eyes. I had to clench my hands into fists so as not to reach forward and brush it out.

I shrugged, bravado gone now he was giving me his full attention. I couldn't think of a single thing to say, let along something clever, funny or teasing.

'You're really pretty, you know?' He smiled at me again, tilting his head as if appraising me. 'I bet you get guys telling you that all the time.'

Breathless, I opened my mouth to reply, but was distracted by a grinning Rob placing the drinks in front of me. 'Erm, haha, no, well, no. Not really.' Distracted, I pulled a tenner from my purse and handed it to Rob without looking at him.

'Well, you are. Isn't she, Rob?'

'Aye, she's a picture,' Rob agreed, handing me my change. 'Pretty as.'

'You are . . . You should take a compliment . . . er?'

'Alex.' I swallowed hard. I thought I'd told him my name the night before but I didn't mind; I knew he must meet a lot of people in his job.

'Alex. Of course. Do you have a boyfriend, Alex?'

Rob, still grinning, excused himself to serve another punter and I found myself alone with Jonny's gaze again. It was so intimate. I'd never had a man's attention like this before. He was so worldly, so mature. So mesmerising.

'No.' My voice came out as a hoarse whisper and surprised me. I cleared my throat. 'Not at the moment.'

'Well, that's just a tragedy. Isn't it, Rob?' Jonny called over his shoulder to Rob who was behind him at the optics.

'What's that?'

'The lovely Alex here doesn't have a boyfriend.'

'What? That's pure crazy!' Rob clutched his chest like a Victorian maiden at the sight of a nude ankle and I couldn't help but laugh.

'Would you like one?' Jonny was all serious again, sweeping his heavy fringe back and resting his head on one hand as he looked at me.

'I . . . don't know.' I was thrown again, from the change between playful to intense. Was he asking me out? Obviously, I wanted to say yes, YES, of course – this was going even better than the fantasy conversations I'd been having with him in my head for the past twenty-four hours.

'Ah, well then, maybe I should ask your friend here instead?' Jonny stood up straight and smiled, but not at Erika, who was back silently standing on my right, but at Darcy, who had appeared on my other side.

'What are you doing here?' I blurted, more angrily than I meant to. I glanced over to our table where Libby was mouthing 'Sorry!' and shrugging theatrically.

'Charming!' Darcy smiled at me and then turned her gaze full beam towards Jonny. 'I just fancied some nuts.' She put her foot on the bar rail and pushed herself up and forward, making a show of looking over the bar as Jonny watched her in a mix of pleasure and amusement. 'Do you have any nuts?'

Both the boys laughed. 'Yes, we have nuts, don't we, Rob?'

'Yes indeedy.'

Darcy winked. 'Glad to hear it.'

Filled with impotent rage as all their attention turned like lasers to her, I looked to Erika for her reaction, but she had her head down, piling our fresh round of drinks onto a tray. Was I the only one who could see what Darcy was like? I wanted to slap her smug face as she accepted her packet of peanuts and glanced at the label.

'Big Ds,' she commented, mock-innocently.

'Aye, we have those as well,' Rob quick-fired back, and the three of them laughed.

I was invisible by that point, as was Erika, not that she seemed to care. I couldn't think of a single thing to say to bring myself back into the conversation, let alone into the glow of Jonny's approving gaze. I watched helplessly as Darcy tore the bag open with her teeth and shook some into her hand, which she then offered to Jonny. 'Want some?' Her words were a challenge.

Jonny gave her a slow, knowing smile. 'I'd love some, but not when I'm working.'

'Another time then.'

'Definitely.'

Rob slammed the till drawer shut and, suddenly, I realised it was over. The guys had moved on to serving other people and Erika was picking up the tray to take back to the table. Darcy, with her damn peanuts, strutting behind her. Jonny hadn't even acknowledged me again before turning away and I was left wondering if I'd imagined my moment with him before *she* turned up. I followed the other two, my spine prickling with a creeping, unmistakable feeling of dread.

7

2017 – Darcy

Darcy woke to the sound of the balcony door sliding open and then closed. It took a moment to remember that she was in Lapad, Dubrovnik, rather than at home and it didn't help that her head was fuzzy from a poor night's sleep and too much wine. She really needed to stop drinking so much, she thought as she wriggled up to a sitting position, but with Alex always around these days that was a challenging prospect.

She could hear Freya gently snoring in her sleeping area and registered that it must have been Jon who had stepped out onto the balcony. What Darcy really wanted to do was pull the duvet over her head and go back to sleep, but she resolved to make an effort and, with a stretch, reached for her robe. She wasn't going to spend the whole holiday on the sidelines watching Alex being the fun, lively one while she faded to a resentful nothingness.

Thoughts of a little alfresco snuggle were banished to the back of Darcy's mind as she realised she could hear Jon talking to someone out there.

'Yeah, why not? I'll look after you,' Darcy heard him say as she pulled back the sliding door, finding him pulling an exaggerated muscle-man pose.

'What the hell are you doing?' Darcy's voice came out louder and more sharply than intended.

Jon jumped and dropped the pose, leaning nonchalantly against the balcony rail. 'Stretching.'

'Were you talking to someone?'

'I . . .' Jon looked around with a shrug as Darcy stepped out and peered over the rail to the pool below. 'Not really,' he said eventually.

'Not really?' Darcy turned back towards the hotel and looked at the balconies either side of theirs. 'I heard you say something.'

Suddenly Alex appeared on one of the previously empty balconies nearby. 'Hey, Darcy!' she called, leaning over the rail and tilting her head back with a smile.

Darcy froze. 'Hey.' She took in the sight of Alex in skimpy pink pyjamas and slowly turned back to Jon again. Had she been there the whole time?

'Oh, hey – hey, Alex,' Jon added, averting his eyes. 'How are you this morning?'

'Hot!' Alex called back. 'But I don't think I will join you for that swim just now, thanks.'

Darcy's cheeks flamed. Why was he out here talking to *her*? And why did he just lie about it?

'Going for a shower now. See you at breakfast, guys!' Alex trilled, before either Darcy or Jon could say anything else. Jon gave a little laugh as if to say, *that was weird*, before heading back into the room, Darcy wordlessly following.

Jon whistled softly as he pottered around in the room in the half-light, picking things up and putting them down again. His sunglasses, his phone, the Factor 50 sun cream that Darcy had brought for Freya. Darcy watched him, unable to work out if it was fake nonchalance on his part – an attempt to breeze past her annoyance – or if he was genuinely cheery.

'You're not usually so perky in the mornings,' she muttered.

'What?' he whispered back, glancing in the direction of where Freya was still asleep. The room had a pullout sofabed separated from the rest of the room by a voile curtain, so there was an element of privacy, but she was still only a few feet away.

Darcy sat on the edge of their bed and enunciated through gritted teeth. 'I said: You're not usually so *perky* in the mornings.' When he looked blankly back at her she continued, 'Don't give me the innocent face. I find you out there chatting with Alex *in her underwear* and now you're all zippity-fucking-doo-dah—'

'Will you watch the language?' Jon cut in. 'Do you want our daughter to hear you effing and jeffing?'

Darcy balled her hands into fists and took a sharp intake of breath. 'Don't tell me how to behave. Do. Not. Tell me how to behave.'

'I don't know where this has come from.' Jon ran his palms over his head and leaned back against the wall. 'I went out on the balcony to see the view and there she was.'

Darcy snorted. 'See the view! Well, you got a nice eyeful of the view when she draped herself over the balcony for you.'

'You're being ridiculous, you know that? I saw her there and called hello. There was nothing more to it than that.'

'So what were you doing when I came out? You were – I don't know – *gyrating* or something.' Jon scoffed at that, and Darcy glared at him before carrying on. 'I don't know what you were doing. But you said you were stretching, and she hid round the corner when I came out.'

'I wasn't bloody gyrating.'

'You watch *your* language.'

Jon shook his head. 'Babe, you are losing it. Would you be like this if it were Libby or Erika I was chatting to?'

'Of course not. But she's . . .' Darcy stopped, about to say *she's always fancied you*, but reluctant to remind him of that awkward fact. Instead, she said, 'Why did you ask her to go swimming with you?'

'Oh, for God's sake.' Jon walked in the direction of the bathroom. 'It was just banter. I wasn't really inviting her.' He went in and closed the door.

'Banter!' Darcy stared at the door. Jon tended to retreat when he'd had enough of discussing anything or if the conversation became too difficult. Sometimes Darcy could see that it was a useful technique, to stop things getting out of hand when tempers were frayed, but other times she wished he would stay with her and help her get to the bottom of what was bothering her.

Was she being unreasonable? she wondered. Was having Alex around making her paranoid? She wished she could confide in Libby or Erika, but she couldn't, especially with them all about to spend the week together. And this was meant to be Libby's hen do. She couldn't trash that. Nor could she let them know that she doubted Jon, not even a tiny bit. And, it pained her to admit, she wasn't sure whether they'd be sympathetic, now good old Alex was back and taking charge of everything. Could she trust them to take her side if anything happened between her and Alex? She wasn't sure.

Darcy's phone vibrated with a Facebook notification, making her jump. *Alex Rigby added a photo with you.*

Frowning, Darcy opened it and saw that the photo was of Alex alone, but she'd tagged everyone who was on the trip.

I guess there are worse places to wake up #humble-brag #bedhead

The photo was of her on the balcony just now, a head-and-shoulders selfie with the dazzling blue of the sea over her shoulder setting off her golden skin and white teeth. Her hair was naturally tousled (the hashtag bedhead, Darcy noticed, drawing attention to it and inviting people to wonder who had tousled it), and her head was dipped down demurely so that she could look up through her lashes, Princess Diana-style, with a cheeky smile that instantly filled Darcy with jealous spite and white-hot rage.

Throwing her phone back down, she paced the room, walking off her anger. 'Smug bitch,' she muttered, remembering how Alex had always been an exhibition-ist, even when she'd had very little to show. Her constant attention-seeking drove Darcy mad – then and now.

But am I just angry because she looks so good? Darcy wondered. She stopped in front of the mirror and appraised herself. She was only a few months older than Alex, but comparing her reflection to the photo Alex had just shared, it looked like there could be ten years between them. If a woman like Alex was after her husband – as unlikely as that idea might seem – then what power did Darcy have to stop her? Or him.

She heard Freya stirring and vowed to pull herself together. The Brooks family were the envy of their local parents' circle. They were a strong unit in their own way. Jon was only human and bound to enjoy a gentle flirtation with a beautiful woman, but he wouldn't throw away almost twenty years together for that.

The bathroom door opened and Jon stepped out with a towel around his waist. He was in pretty good shape, Darcy noticed; in fact, she preferred his body now to when they first got together. The Dad Bod was all the rage and Jon wore it well. When did she last tell him that she still found him attractive? She couldn't remember.

'You OK?' Jon noticed her watching him.

Time to stop the rot, Darcy thought, walking over to him and placing a kiss on his cheek. He looked at her quizzically, as well he might, given how they had left the conversation before his shower, but after a pause he reached for her and drew her in for a proper kiss.

Darcy wrapped her arms around him and increased the intensity of the kiss, leaning in and drawing him closer to her. He slipped his hands under her pyjama top and she felt him stir underneath his towel. 'Uh-uh,' she said into his neck, pushing him away. 'Freya.'

He groaned quietly as she released him, then noticed the open bathroom door. 'Would you mind helping me with something in there for a minute?' Jon raised his eyebrows and Darcy couldn't help but laugh at his hopeful face.

Darcy glanced towards Freya's sleeping area. 'Maybe later,' she said, pulling a face. They hadn't had sex in ages, but a quickie against the bathroom wall while their daughter lay a few feet away was not what she had in mind for their romantic reconnection. She kissed him again; a long, lingering kiss like the ones they'd indulged in as teenagers. 'Definitely later,' she murmured.

'Oh, what are you doing to me, woman?' Jon laughed, drawing away from her reluctantly and shuffling back into the bathroom, no doubt to sort himself out.

'Still got it!' Darcy whispered to herself with a smile as she turned to pull out her clothes for the day. There was no way she would be swimming; the idea of donning swimwear was never her idea of fun these days but the thought of standing half naked beside Alex Rigby and inviting the inevitable comparisons, even just those in her own head, was an absolute non-starter. Instead, she selected a pale blue summer dress with a white kimono-style top to dress the bingo wings, and a pair of strappy white sandals. She laid them out on the bed and waited for Jon to come out of the bathroom so that she could shower.

Picking up her phone, she noticed that the likes were coming in for Alex's post and took a moment to look at it again. *Sad really, that she's so desperate for attention,* Darcy thought.

Erika and Libby had both liked the post and a few other names she didn't know were commenting inane things like *Fire!* and *U look gorgeous hun!* as was the way of social media.

Then, as she had the phone in her hand, a notification popped up: *Jon Brooks likes a photo you are tagged in.* Darcy's eyes flew to the closed bathroom door. This meant he had his phone in there with him and was looking at the same teasing image of Alex that she was.

He must have known she would see this, she reasoned, as her stomach churned once again, thinking of him looking at suggestive pictures of *her* while he was naked and half aroused already. If he was doing it publicly, surely that meant it was all above board – just a friendly *like*; absolutely nothing to see here. Otherwise, he wouldn't have been so brazen about it.

Yet . . . Jon hardly ever used Facebook. Why would he have chosen this morning, this particular moment, to log on?

Darcy clicked onto the post again and looked at who was tagged. Alex, Darcy, Libby and Erika of course, but also Tatty, who had her own Facebook account (Darcy filed that information away for future snooping), but not Freya, who wasn't allowed one. Then, finally, Jon.

Jon was tagged in the photo which, with Alex's stringent privacy settings, meant that she must have sought him out and added him as a friend at some point. And he'd gone into Facebook and accepted it, even though Darcy could count on one hand the number of times he'd been active on there in the past year. Now that Alex was in the picture, he was on there at least twice in just a few days.

'Fucking bitch,' Darcy whispered to herself.

'Mum?' Freya's voice startled her. Darcy spun around and saw Freya drawing back the voile between their sleeping areas. 'Did you say *eff*?'

Darcy knew there was no point pretending she hadn't; her daughter had a knack for catching her out.

'Yes, sorry, babe. I stubbed my toe.' Darcy pointed to her bare foot. 'I couldn't help it.'

'Ouchy,' said Freya, rubbing her eyes. 'Where's Dad?'

'In the bathroom.' *Probably wanking over a picture of that slut from school.*

Freya climbed onto their bed, rumpling the dress that Darcy had carefully laid out for herself. 'Freya!' Darcy cried. 'Can't I have anything nice, just for once?'

Freya looked at her, wide-eyed. 'Overreact much?'

'And don't get bloody cheeky with me, miss,' Darcy snapped. 'I've already had about as much as I can take from your father this morning.'

'Hey, hey!' Jon came out of the bathroom to find Darcy on the verge of tears and Freya totally bemused. 'What's happened?'

Darcy glared at him. 'You tell me.'

Jon looked at her and then to Freya, who was still watching intently. 'Freya, go and have your shower.'

'But, I—'

'Now please,' he cut her off. 'Let me and Mum sort this out while you get ready and then we can all go for breakfast.'

Freya hesitated. 'Go, Freya,' said Darcy. 'I'm fine. I'm just cranky because my toe is sore. Remember to put your swimming cossie on under your clothes,' she added, forcing a smile.

Freya looked at Jon, who nodded, and she returned the smile then slid down off the bed, careful to avoid her mum's clothes this time, and went into the bathroom.

Once the door had closed, Jon looked at Darcy. 'Now, what's this really all about? What's wrong with your toe?'

Darcy almost laughed, despite herself. 'There's nothing wrong with my toe. Freya heard me swear so I told her I'd stubbed it.'

'And why did you swear?'

Darcy looked at Jon. He was so familiar to her that she rarely stopped and really looked at his face. He was looking back at her curiously, as if searching her face for the same familiarity that she was seeking in his. This was the man she had loved for twenty years, the man who'd promised to be hers forever. The man who held her hand and soothed her while she brought their daughter into the world, not minding at all when she'd screamed that she hated him and he was never to touch her again. He had looked at her then with amazement, admiration, like she was an impossibly beautiful warrior.

She tried to reconcile this man who was so much a part of her, with a stranger who might flirt on balconies and make friends with women on social media without mentioning it. He looked like Jon – he had his same crinkly-eyed smile and gentle touch – but he felt like someone new. Someone she couldn't entirely trust.

'Darcy? What happened?'

She sighed. 'Nothing, it's . . . Freya jumped on the bed and messed up my clothes. I'm . . . cranky this morning; I think I might be a bit hungover.' She turned away from his gaze and smoothed out the dress.

'And that's all it is?' He moved to stand behind her and rested his chin on her shoulder; his signature move for cheering her up when she was down. 'You're sure?'

'I'm sure.' She faltered for a moment but then tilted her head towards his, allowing him to nuzzle her neck the way she always did. 'It's all good.'

8

1997 – Alex

All through the holiday, I knew that, despite claiming to be deliriously happy with Bradley, Darcy was enjoying her moments with Jonny, but there was no way I was giving up on him. Whenever she went to the bar I was there too, even if it meant standing in near silence as they teased one another. Any little smile or word that Jonny threw my way still felt like a win. I held on to how lovely he was to me at the start and I knew that, if only I could get Darcy out of the picture, he would be again.

I sensed I was losing support from the other two, even Libby, as they accepted the inevitability of Darcy having things her own way *again*. Usually, even *I* would roll over if I could see the way the wind was blowing. Hanging on until the last minute and fighting her for things was not my way, because I knew she would win, she always did, and I couldn't let her see me feel bad about it. At least then I didn't hand her quite such a smug victory.

Not this time, though. I was hanging around to the bitter end because I wanted Jonny far more than I'd wanted anything we'd fought over before. And I just knew, if she weren't around complicating matters, he would want me too.

'Are you sure he wasn't just being chatty?' Libby gently tried to talk me round. 'You know what guys can be like. He might talk to all the girls like that.'

'What she's trying to say is, it might have meant more to you than it did to him.' Erika was blunter, pulling me aside for some tough love before Darcy returned from yet another trip to the phone box.

During the final few days, it seemed like Libby and Erika had come to a tacit agreement to keep me and Darcy apart as much as possible. A week in a small caravan stuffed with hormones and old, unsettled scores hadn't helped heal our friendship, unsurprisingly, and I resented it when the others stuck up for Darcy, trying to tell me she wasn't as bad as I made out. They just couldn't see through her like I could.

On our final full day, we'd all gone to Poole where the adults took a boat trip around the harbour while we looked around the shops. Erika steered Darcy to look at makeup while Libby tried to talk me out of blowing my remaining holiday money on a Wonderbra.

'Ignore what Darcy said about curves.' Libby wrestled the padded, satiny thing from my hands. 'Different boys – men – like different types of girls. Don't waste your money on this contraption.'

'It's not about *her*. I'd just like to know how it feels to have boobs for once.'

'So this is nothing to do with impressing Jonny?'

I shrugged, allowing her to put the bra back onto the rack. 'I just . . . I don't know how to get him to notice me again. Especially when *she's* there giving it all,' I thrust out my tiny chest, 'hey, Jonny, check my curves!'

We both started laughing and I realised how silly I sounded. I didn't know how to explain about the connection I'd felt, but I knew in my heart that I was right.

Of course Darcy insisted that she didn't even fancy him. 'I'm with Bradley, I'm not going to give that up for a holiday romance!' Yet I'd seen the spring in Darcy's step when she returned from their chats at the bar.

The party on the final night was my last shot to make an impression. Jonny and Rob had invited us to a blowout at one of the staff caravans after Manhattan's closed. I was out of my mind with excitement at the thought of spending time with him when he wasn't working, not to mention the thrill of doing something so grown-up.

Libby's mum had been surprisingly easy to convince. 'OK, but be back at the caravan by one thirty please, we've got to pack up and be out early tomorrow morning.'

I blocked out the reference to going home in the morning, as I couldn't bear to think about that yet. The rest of the evening passed in a blur; I'd spent all week fantasising about being alone with Jonny and knew exactly how it would go, the sweet words he would murmur to me in a quiet corner, allowing myself to fall even harder for the idea of this man who was going to bring me all the love and romance I'd been aching for.

By the time we arrived at the party, I was vibrating with excitement. We stood in the doorway, holding the cheap booze we'd stashed earlier, taking in the scene and trying to look cool. It was my first proper grown-up party with people all around us chatting, drinking, smoking. Then Jonny appeared, pushing his hair out of his eyes, and making a beeline for us.

'Darcy, hey.' He leaned in and kissed her on the cheek, as I stood, stung, my jaw on the floor. Even Darcy looked surprised, as if she didn't expect such an effusive welcome, especially when he only nodded at the rest of us. I saw Libby and Erika raise their eyebrows at one another but I was rooted to the spot, unable to move.

'Girls, help yourselves to drinks, make yourselves at home,' Jonny said, waving us in the direction of the kitchen area. 'Darcy, can I get you something?'

Darcy hesitated, looking uncertain for once. I stared at her helplessly – pleadingly – and it seemed to make up her mind, as she turned her back on us and told Jonny she'd love a drink. Jonny grinned, grabbing two cans and showing her through to one of the bedrooms so that they could 'have a chat somewhere away from the music', and she followed him without a word.

I must have stood there for a full five minutes or more, while Libby and even Erika tried to talk me round.

'They might just be talking.'

'I'm sure there's nothing in it.'

'Darcy wouldn't cheat on Bradley, would she?'

'No! I don't think so. Do you?'

'No!'

'No, you're probably right.'

I wished they would shut up but knew that if I said anything, my voice would break and tears would come. We'd all seen those girls crying over boys at parties, but I refused to let it out in front of these strangers, all older and more sophisticated than we were.

'Let's get you a drink,' Erika said eventually, heading into the throng around the kitchen area as Libby led me to the bench seating. I recognised Rob cuddling up to two tanned, laughing girls and he nodded at me. He must have noticed my expression as he broke off from his flirtatious threesome long enough to say, 'Dinnae bother about Jonny-boy, Blondie. Plenty more fish in the sea.'

I nodded back at him, still not trusting myself to speak, and Erika returned with three egg cups. 'I couldn't find any glasses left,' she explained, setting them on the table in front of us as Libby retrieved the bottle of strawberry-flavoured MD20/20 from the carrier bag we'd brought with us.

After pouring a slug of the sweet red liquid into the eggcups, Libby proposed a toast. 'To us, and to never letting boys come between us!'

'To us!' Erika repeated, throwing the shot down her throat and wincing.

I swallowed mine without toasting – or tasting – and held my eggcup out for a refill. I saw Erika and Libby make eye contact, but they didn't refuse. After my second shot, I felt ready to say, with all the dignity I could scratch up, 'It should be me in there with him. She's got a boyfriend and she doesn't even like him like I do.'

Libby poured a third round of eggcup shots, the little bottle almost empty, and as we lifted them to our lips, the door that Jonny and Darcy had disappeared behind opened and she walked out, looking around with a frown. Spotting us, she came straight over. 'I'm not feeling too good, I'm going back to the caravan.'

Still holding the eggcups aloft, we paused in confusion. Jonny was standing in the doorway, showing no sign of following her.

'What happened?' Erika said as she looked between the two of them. 'Is everything all right?'

Darcy folded her arms. 'It's fine. I told him I'm with Bradley.' Libby and I shared a glance and I felt a flicker of hope. Maybe they *were* just chatting. 'But I think I'll go now.'

Erika and Libby chorused variations of *no, don't, stay*, etc., while I just stared at her, hatred filling me from my very core. It occurred to me then that through all the comforting platitudes the other two had given me just now, not once had they suggested Darcy might not go for it with Jonny out of loyalty to me.

'Sorry, guys, I don't mean to spoil the night but I'd really rather leave.' Darcy stood there, looking at us expectantly, waiting for us to come with her. Well, she could whistle.

'I'm not going,' I announced, before anyone else could reply. 'I'm having a good time and I'm staying until our curfew.' Defiantly, I threw back the sticky eggcup shot and looked Darcy in the eye. 'Take care walking back now, won't you?'

Libby and Erika looked at each other. 'I don't think Mum would like it if any of us went off on our own.' Libby turned to me and I shook my head. 'I'll stay with Alex,' she said eventually.

Erika looked at the full eggcup in front of her and frowned. 'I guess I'd better go with Darcy then.'

'Thanks.' Darcy turned on her heel and went without another word, clearly pissed off that we didn't all run after her. Erika sighed and followed on, giving us a sad little wave as she went. I shrugged at Libby and picked up Erika's abandoned drink, downing that as well.

'Steady.' Libby looked concerned.

'Honestly, it's fine. Let's dance!'

The change in my mood was partly down to the shots but mostly I was elated Darcy was gone and Jonny was still here. It was like restarting the evening with a clean slate. I decided to forget that he'd approached her first because I accepted that guys always went to her like flies around shit; an analogy that made me smile. But with her gone, hopefully Jonny would come to his senses.

Some women who must have been thirty *at least* were doing the Macarena along with Silly Billy the children's entertainer. The living space of the caravan could hardly accommodate us, so I took the opportunity to edge closer to the doorway where Jonny was still standing, swigging beer and looking morose.

I tried to catch his eye but he stared steadfastly ahead, as if seeing something unmissable in the distance. I refused to waste the opportunity so I persisted, moving closer until I was almost touching him as I danced. 'Hi,' I ventured when he still didn't acknowledge me.

He took a swig of his beer, swallowed, sighed heavily and finally replied without turning his head. 'Hi.'

'Great party.'

'Is it?'

I considered the crowd squashed together clutching cans and cigarettes, jumping up and down, shouting along to Blur's 'Parklife' and thought that for me, yes, this was pretty cool. Especially now I was standing next to him. 'Don't you think so?' I asked instead.

Finally he looked at me. He opened his mouth as if he were about to launch into a rant but hesitated and closed it again. He took another swig of his beer and then regarded me thoughtfully. 'What's your name again?'

'Alex.' I was gutted that he still hadn't remembered, when Darcy's name had tripped off his tongue the moment we arrived, but I chose not to focus on it. Flies around shit, I reminded myself. He couldn't help it.

'Alex, are you sixteen?' He looked me right in the eyes this time and the intensity threw me. That, and the fact that I'd pretended to be eighteen all week.

'I . . . I'm eighteen?' I said eventually, the rising inflection of my voice making it sound like a nervous question. 'I'm eighteen,' I repeated, more convincingly the second time.

He swigged his beer and gave me the side-eye. 'Come on. I know you girls are underage.' For a minute I couldn't breathe, but then he smiled his gorgeous smile and I felt relief wash over me. 'Be honest, are you sixteen?'

'Yes, OK. I'm sixteen.' I nodded, giving him an *OK, you got me* face. After all, if we were to have any sort of relationship, he would find out.

He didn't say anything and I wondered if Darcy had told him, but I didn't want to put her back in his mind now I'd finally captured his attention. 'And you're nineteen?'

He laughed. 'Yes. I have no reason to lie.'

'When do you go back to uni?' He'd already told us that he was going into the second year at Southampton, not a million miles away, and his family home was in Guildford, which was even closer to home. I *so* wanted to bring the conversation around to potentially meeting up once we got home. When he didn't immediately answer, I added, 'Will you be going back home for a bit first?'

He shook his head. 'No. I don't know. Listen . . .' He hesitated.

'Alex,' I supplied, with an indulgent smile.

'Right, yeah.' He finished his beer and put the can down by his feet, the room too over-populated for him to be able to reach any available surface without fighting through a mass of bodies, who were now singing, 'Let's all meet up in the year two thousand!' at the tops of their voices and bouncing up and down, the thumping of their feet on the caravan floor reverberating through the walls and making the whole flimsy structure vibrate.

'Listen, Alex.' He fixed me with an intense stare that caught the breath in my throat again. 'I'm not really up for small talk. What I'd really like to do is—' He stopped and leaned in—'this.'

He kissed me, just one soft touch from his lips to mine, and I was so stunned I couldn't move. I'd been wishing so hard for this to happen that I couldn't believe it was truly real. I stumbled slightly as my knees buckled and Jonny drew back to look at me. 'Was that all right?'

I nodded; there was no way I could speak. He smiled and put one hand around the back of my head, drawing me towards him and kissing me again, harder this time, his beery tongue probing my mouth. I found it strangely horrifying, but electrifying at the same time.

I had never been kissed like that before; truthfully, I'd never been properly kissed at all before that night. A few pecks from boys during spin the bottle was all I had to offer in the way of experience, but those sad, immature encounters could not compare with what was happening there with Jonny. He was a man. A gorgeous, sexy man who knew what he was doing, and what he wanted to do was to kiss me.

Hesitantly, I wrapped my arms around him, unsure if that was the right thing to do, and tried to respond enthusiastically with my tongue. He drew me closer to him, his other hand on my back, pressing my body hard against his. I felt his heat and urgency and my own body responded, sparking up eager nerve endings that were hungry for his touch.

He pulled me through the doorway that he'd been leaning on, drawing me into the room where he'd earlier disappeared with Darcy. I banished that thought; I was the one in his arms, nothing else mattered. As the door closed behind us, he guided me down onto one of the twin beds, still kissing me, and it occurred to me for the first time that he might want to do more than just kiss. The thought terrified and excited me at the same time. It hadn't even crossed my mind that we might get this far. I wanted to have him in my arms so much, but was this too soon?

His kisses became more urgent and he slipped the hand that had been on my back around to my hip and then inched it slowly upwards. When it found my breast, I flinched, and he drew back. 'No?' he panted, looking at me with an intensity that made me shiver.

I didn't know what to say. I didn't want to disappoint him, but this all felt too fast. He must have read something in my face, however, because he pulled away from me and sat up.

'Don't stop,' I whispered, but it was too late. The spell was broken.

I saw him close his eyes, his face full of regret. When he opened them again, I searched his face, trying to regain the intimacy, but the shutters had come down; the passion of a few minutes earlier had disappeared.

'I'm sorry,' I said eventually, my voice still hoarse from a throat clogged with emotion. 'Please don't be angry with me.'

He shook his head but still didn't look at me. 'I'm not angry with you, sweetheart. I'm angry with myself. This was a mistake.'

I reached out to touch his hand, but he stood up as if my touch burned. 'Jonny?' Surely he wouldn't have kissed me so passionately if he didn't feel at least something for me.

'Ah . . . look, it's getting late. We should probably call it a night.' He reached for the door without looking at me. The intimacy we'd shared was replaced by a cold, distant politeness, like it had never happened. I could have kicked myself for hesitating when he touched me. I would have given anything to be back in his arms again.

I stood up, feeling foolish as I followed him back to the party. Most people were out on the decking, bouncing around in a conga line led by Silly Billy. Rob was kissing one of his two girlfriends while the other one sat with her arms folded, expression thunderous.

I decided to try one more time. 'Jonny.' I took his hand. I felt him stiffen but he didn't pull away. 'Jonny?'

Finally he met my eyes and I searched for any sign of the tender connection we'd had in that tiny, cramped room, but his expression was unreadable. I took a deep breath, knowing this might be my last shot, and asked him if he'd like to meet up again sometime. I tried to keep the hope out of my voice. I wanted to appear cool and breezy; I knew that guys didn't like it when girls acted all desperate.

He flicked his floppy hair out of his eyes. 'Ah, maybe, sweetheart. But I'll be pretty busy once I'm back at uni.

This is a mad year for me so I'm not sure I want to get into anything heavy.'

'Maybe just a phone call then, when you've time?' I strived for nonchalance but feared that my true feelings were creeping through.

'Maybe, yeah.'

'So, can I have your number?'

'Ah, I don't really have one. I mean, we have to use the phone boxes here and I don't know the number of where I'll be living at uni yet.'

My heart sank; I didn't want to believe he was giving me the brush off, but it was starting to feel that way. I was just wondering if I were brave enough to ask for his number at his parents' house when he sighed and said, 'Why don't you give me yours?'

My heart lifted with relief and love, and I gave him a huge smile. 'Yes, of course.'

He found me a scrap of paper and I used the kohl pencil in my handbag to scribble my name and number on it. I handed it to him and he looked at it before putting it in his pocket. 'Alex. Thank you.'

'Bye, Jonny. Call me whenever you like.'

He leaned in for a brief kiss, his lips warm on my cheek, before withdrawing quickly. 'Safe journey home, sweetheart.'

I felt tears pricking my eyes, so I turned and left before he could see. On the decking outside, Libby was slow dancing with Silly Billy but she pulled away from him as soon as she saw me. 'You OK, Al?'

Was I? I wondered, as we linked arms and made our way back to the caravan. I felt utterly changed from the girl I'd been when I sat next to her less than an hour before. Somewhere between the heaven of having been in Jonny's arms and the hell of having to leave him behind, I was existing in a state of dizzy pleasure-pain. Was this what real love felt like? It must be.

'He kissed me!' I told Libby, as soon as we were out of sight of the party.

'Oh, my God!' She swung around and grabbed both of my hands, jumping up and down. Even in the darkness I could see the light in her eyes and I could feel the manic excitement coming from her as she pumped my arms up and down. 'That's so cool!'

We picked up our pace as a light came on in one of the nearby caravans. 'Did you get off with Silly Billy?'

'No!'

The curtain twitched at the window of our caravan and I pulled up short, thinking that it might be Libby's mum, but it was Erika. She eased the window open a crack. 'Get inside, will you?' she whispered, before pulling the window shut again. Inside, she hovered by the converted sofa where 'Auntie' Karen was fast asleep and gestured that we should go to our room rather than hers.

'Darcy's had a bit of a crisis,' said Erika, in a serious voice, without her trademark sarcasm, once the three of us were squeezed into our little bedroom. 'She's asleep now but she was really upset.'

'What's happened?' Libby looked concerned as I tried to keep my eye-rolling to myself.

'She kissed Jonny,' Erika blurted out. 'And now she doesn't know what to do about Bradley.'

'No!' I heard Libby exclaim, as I felt myself drowning. It sounded as if they were talking in the distance; I couldn't hear them through the roar of the sea in my ears. I was hot and cold simultaneously. This couldn't be happening.

'Yes,' Erika insisted, too full of the drama to notice my despair.

'But Jonny just kissed me.' I shook my head, wanting them to understand. 'She . . . Darcy turned him down. How could he have kissed her first?'

I wasn't really asking; I knew the answer. The reality dawned on all of us as we looked at each other, appalled.

'Ew,' said Erika eventually, breaking the silence. 'Ewww.'

I wanted to scream. I wanted to rail against the injustice of her getting there first every single time *and* being better and more beautiful and more popular. But I couldn't do it; I was just too sad.

'Look, it was a party. These things happen.' Libby patted my arm in a way that was meant to be comforting. 'Let's chalk it up to experience, eh? I'll say the same to Darcy.'

'No, don't tell her!' I looked between Libby and Erika in alarm. 'Promise me?' I could already imagine her crowing about sloppy seconds and how she was the one he really wanted. I couldn't bear it.

Erika frowned. 'I don't know . . .'

'Why upset her more?' I knew that she'd be more likely to keep quiet for Darcy's benefit than for mine.

Erika looked at Libby, who nodded. 'OK.'

'Great.' I finally exhaled. 'No big deal.'

9

2017 – Darcy

The morning so far had gone better than Darcy dared hope, with them all hanging out together at the hotel. They'd already decided the previous night that, as it was a Sunday, they would leave exploring the Old Town until the Monday in case some of the shops were shut.

'Also,' Alex said, 'there's a cruise ship docked here on Sunday so the town will be heaving with slow-moving tourists. I can't see anything on the port schedule for Monday so it should be quieter.'

Smart arse, Darcy thought at the time, internally pulling a face, but now had to admit that she was grateful not to be plodding around in large crowds as the sun was already baking hot by 11 a.m. and she was very happy to be lounging under a parasol by the pool, with the breeze from the shore taking the edge off the humidity.

Breakfast was a little awkward at first as they'd mumbled polite good mornings like delegates on an away day rather than old friends. Alex and Tatty, Libby and Erika arrived first and spread themselves out over two tables of four so they could hold seats for the rest of the party. On arrival, Darcy immediately sat herself at Libby and Erika's table and sent Freya to sit with Tatty, leaving Jon with a choice of seats – beside Alex or opposite Darcy – and it seemed to Darcy that everyone was holding their breath waiting for him to choose.

Of course, that was absurd, she said to herself, when he naturally sat across from her. The others were paying him no attention whatsoever. Tatty and Freya were chatting happily about some yogurt Tatty had tried last time she'd been to Croatia, Alex was flagging down a waiter to order more coffee for them all and Erika and Libby were raring to go to the buffet now they no longer needed to hold the table.

'I'm starving!' Libby patted her tummy, smooth and brown between her cropped T-shirt and denim shorts, as she squeezed through the gap in the tables. 'Hey, Erika – I wonder if they'll have any German bread?'

'German bread!' Darcy joined in, the two of them rubbing their tummies as Erika gave a theatrical sigh.

'Oh my God, you guys!' Alex laughed. 'You still do that?'

The good vibes continued as everyone tucked in, making small talk about the sunny weather and stunning scenery, and Darcy was able to relax a bit. Alex didn't so much as look at Jon, she was joining in with

Tatty and Freya, who were now onto something about different shades of blue. Alex was describing the sea that was shimmering invitingly at them through the open windows of the breakfast room as being *Pantone Lapis*, presumably something to do with interior design, while Tatty was nodding in agreement. Freya clearly didn't know what they were talking about but was lapping it up, looking between the two of them in wonder, eyes shining with open admiration.

Darcy tried not to let that bother her and tuned out, switching her attention to Erika, who was talking about a colleague who had recommended taking the cable car while they were there, and idly wondered if there was any truth in what Alex had said about Erika being in a relationship with someone at work.

Erika was intensely private about her personal life. Darcy knew that she dated, but she didn't know how often or with whom. No one ever seemed to stick around for long and she sensed that was Erika's choice, as she treasured her independence. She was also more than a little intimidating; her innate self-confidence and direct way of speaking meant that those who didn't know her well found her a tough nut to crack.

Jon had said something funny when she hadn't been paying attention and everyone had laughed, so she joined in, glad that he was relaxing and her friends were enjoying his company. She just hoped that no one was enjoying it more than they should have been, as she noticed Alex laughing, perhaps a little *too* hard.

But apart from that, Darcy thought, it was not a bad morning. They were now comfortably ensconced on daybeds under huge parasols beside the pool and the companiable atmosphere had been restored. She'd been concerned for a moment, when Jon had suggested that Erika, with her German heritage, should have come down first thing and put towels on all the sunbeds for them, but luckily Erika had just laughed rather than taking offence.

As it happened, finding space had not been a problem. They established a corner of the pool terrace and were stretched out happily. The girls were in the water and the adults amused themselves by reading or snoozing. Darcy was enjoying the view and indulging in her favourite guilty pleasure, people watching.

The young couple holding hands across the gap between their sunbeds, holding their phones aloft with their free hands, squinting at the screens. The man sitting at a table in the shade with a coffee and a laptop, tap-tap-tapping away and ignoring his elegant surroundings. The large, older woman with a cane who landed heavily on a lounger with her legs spread wide, only the stripy fabric of her summer dress saving her modesty. Darcy liked to watch them all, wondering what their backstory was; what brought them to this place. What they hoped for out of life.

'I'm going for a dip.' Alex's voice caught her attention. 'Anyone else?'

Darcy immediately declined, as did Erika. Libby readily agreed and jumped up, tossing her paperback onto the lounger behind her. Darcy sensed Jon shift as if he were going to get up too but then thought better of it. 'Maybe later.'

Darcy tensed as first Libby whipped off her shorts and T-shirt and bounded towards the pool in a sporty black two-piece, her lean, athletic limbs gleaming in the sunlight, before Alex slowly rose to undress. Whereas Libby's approach had been a no-nonsense, quick strip-off-and-get-straight-in affair, Darcy was horribly sure that Alex was going to put on a bit of a show for them all.

She was almost disappointed when Alex simply slipped out of her dress and padded barefoot after Libby in a fairly chaste white one-piece, casually pulling a hairband from around her wrist and tying her hair into a messy knot atop her head. She looked great, Darcy had to admit, staring covetously at her perky bottom as it walked away from them, but there was none of the pouting, preening and hair tossing that Darcy had been expecting her to perform in front of them. Maybe this idea that she was flirting with Jon was all in her head?

'I can't get over how different she looks now,' Erika said, turning her sunbed slightly so they could chat.

Darcy spotted the opportunity to have a little gossip about Alex and wondered what she could get away with saying in front of Jon.

'I know,' she began neutrally. 'I mean, she was always slim—'

'She was scary skinny, Darce,' Erika cut her off. 'She looked unhealthy. Now she's like some goddess. I wish my arse looked that peachy.'

Darcy forced a laugh and looked surreptitiously at Jon. She didn't need him hearing chat about Alex's peachy arse. He had his sunglasses on so she couldn't read his expression.

Erika took Darcy's lack of reply as encouragement. 'I wonder how much of what she told us about New York is true,' she mused.

'What do you mean?' Darcy whipped her head back towards Erika. 'Don't you believe her?'

'Oh, clearly much of it *is* true, Tatty is testament to that. I don't know.' Erika paused. 'I guess it just seems a bit far-fetched, this idea of the wealthy American swooping in and taking her back to his millionaire New York lifestyle. It's totally the sort of thing she used to make up when we were younger. Remember the married man?'

Darcy did remember. Alex used to insist she was having an affair with a married man when they were at sixth form, known to them only as G. They'd never seen any tangible evidence of him existing at all and it had never quite rung true to Darcy.

'Do you know what happened between them?' Darcy leaned forward towards Erika. 'Why they broke up?'

'No, and that's another thing.' Erika dropped her voice a notch. 'Don't you think that's weird when she's just come out of a divorce? She only ever talks about how wonderful it all was at the start. And she's living in one of his houses and spending his money yet she shut Tatty down straightaway last night at dinner when she said about seeing him at Christmas, which is ages away.'

Darcy looked over at Jon, lying back, watching the water. It didn't look like he was going anywhere anytime soon and she was itching to talk freely with Erika. 'Shall we go and get a cool drink? The bar's open.'

Erika grinned. 'I thought you'd never ask. Jon, will you watch our stuff?'

'And our daughter,' Darcy added drily. She could see Freya playing happily in the water and tried to ignore the gut punch she felt when she saw Alex teaching the girls how to do a handstand and high fiving Freya after her plucky attempt. Injecting false lightness into her voice, Darcy turned to Jon, saying, 'We'll bring you back a beer?'

'Sure, thanks.' Jon waved them away without even turning his head.

Darcy followed Erika to the bar, admiring her flowing cobalt blue (or was it *Pantone Lapis*?) ankle-length skirt and white strappy vest top. Erika often wore brands that Darcy had never heard of but her clothes always looked well cut and chic. She suspected that the white vest top was not a two-quid Primark job like some of hers were.

'What can I get you, ladies?' The server and her musically accented English saved Darcy from saying anything else.

Erika was ready, having already memorised the menu. 'I'll have a Hugo, please and . . . what kind of beer would Jon like?'

'Oh, the local lager, please. I'm sorry I don't know how to pronounce it.' Darcy smiled apologetically at the young woman who inclined her head benevolently, clearly accustomed to English tourists and their typically poor language skills. 'And a diet Coke for me, please.'

'What? Come on, Darce, don't let the side down,' Erika interjected, putting a hand up to stop the server from walking away. 'Cancel the Coke and make it two Hugos, please.' She looked at Darcy and raised her eyebrows. 'OK?'

'OK.'

Erika handed her card over and took her phone out for a quick scroll as they waited for the drinks. Darcy tapped her fingers on the bar; she needed to find a way back to talking about Alex without it seeming like she was too bothered, but as she worked herself up to a casual opener, Erika suddenly swung her stool around to face her.

'Oh! Wait, I've found him!' Erika looked at her expectantly and Darcy tilted her head at her to continue. 'I googled Kyle Kaplan.'

Darcy was nonplussed. 'Who?'

'Alex's ex-husband. *Kyle.*'

'Oh, that Kyle! I don't think I knew his surname.' Darcy was immediately intrigued. 'And?'

Erika turned the phone screen to face Darcy. 'Well, he's real, so that's a start.'

Darcy took in the photo that Erika had found on LinkedIn. With his neat salt-and-pepper hair and strong jawline, he looked entirely the all-American, rich-older-man stereotype that she'd imagined. 'What else is there?'

'It's all business stuff I think. This was the only thing I could find with a photo.'

'Alex did say he hated social media.'

'I've just searched Kyle Kaplan Alex Rigby and there's nothing useful.'

'Maybe try Kyle Kaplan wife?'

'Hmm.' Erika scrolled for a bit. 'There's quite a few Kyle Kaplans in the world. I got lucky with the LinkedIn one because it said about his businesses in New York.'

Darcy's eyes widened as two large wine glasses filled with a pale yellow liquid and lots of greenery were set in front of them, along with Jon's lager. Darcy had never had a Hugo before and hoped it wasn't going to be another negroni-type affair. She thanked the woman, who smiled and said, 'You are welcome!' in that melodic accent of hers before retreating to the other side of the bar.

'None of them seem to be Alex,' Erika said, putting her phone down and reaching for her drink. 'Cheers! *Prost*! And whatever they say in Croatia!'

Darcy clinked her glass to Erika's, wondering what was in it.

'Look me in the eye!' Erika demanded. 'Or it will be seven years' bad sex!'

Darcy snorted. She'd have to have sex for that to be true. Erika was probably having more sex than she was and she was single. Or was she?

Darcy took a sip of her Hugo, which was sweeter than it looked and not bad at all really, and wondered how much she could say to Erika. Erika, who might be having some hot affair with a younger man, even risking her career for it, but hadn't yet confided in her. Erika, who thought that Darcy and Jon's marriage was picture-perfect. It was a lonely feeling, sitting beside one of your oldest friends and not being able to talk to them honestly about anything real, she reflected.

'We should take Jon's beer back to him.' Erika made to slide off her stool.

'Hang on.' Darcy stopped her. 'He can wait a minute. I want to ask you something.' She took a deep breath.

'Oh?' Erika looked intrigued and wriggled back onto her stool. 'Go on,' she prompted, when Darcy hesitated.

'Do you remember when I first met Jon – when we all first met him, I mean?'

'Of course! That was such a fun holiday.' Erika smiled at the memory and sipped her cocktail. 'Oh, my God, do you remember that Rob he used to work with behind the bar? He was so funny. They never kept in touch, did they?'

Darcy shook her head. 'You know what men are like. Actually,' Darcy laughed, 'Jon did bump into him at a festival a few years later, totally randomly. They still didn't bother to swap numbers. It was all, "good to see you, mate, take care," and then they went on with their lives without any curiosity or anything.'

Erika laughed. 'Women can't do that. We'd have to know everything, friend each other online and carry out a postmortem of the past twenty years or whatever.'

'Exactly. That's why I find it so strange that Alex has just slipped back into our lives after however long, and we don't know anything *real* about her. But the thing I wanted to ask you,' Darcy hesitated and took a fortifying slurp of her Hugo, 'is whether you remembered Alex having a thing for Jon back in the day?'

'Alex? Oh shit, yeah!' Erika nodded. 'Right at the start. Oh, my God, I'd totally forgotten about that. She used to get me and Libby to keep you away from the bar so that she could see him more than you. She was paranoid that you'd want him as well and then he'd be bound to go for you.' Erika laughed as she realised what she'd said. 'Not paranoid, at all, of course, because that's what happened!'

'I was an idiot then. If it weren't for Bradley – what an enormous waste of time *that* was – I would have locked things down with Jon from the start.'

Erika held her gaze. 'I think Alex thought you were only flirting with Jon to wind her up.'

Darcy scoffed. 'As if! She always had to make everything about *her*, didn't she? Massive drama queen.'

Erika smiled but said nothing.

'What?' Darcy prompted.

'Ah, no,' Erika said with a shrug, concentrating hard on her cocktail rather than meeting Darcy's eyes.

'No, go on.'

Erika sighed. 'I guess it's OK to say this now; there's so much water under the bridge and we're all adults. And Alex – Alex is like a totally different person to the one we knew back then.'

'OK.' Darcy nodded. 'Spit it out.'

'I don't think you really knew how much power you had back then. Not in a bad way!' Erika hurriedly added. 'I'm not saying you were malicious with it, but you were so popular and all the boys fancied you and you just always got your own way on everything.' Erika risked making eye contact with Darcy. 'Looking back, I think Alex wanted one thing that was hers. Something that you couldn't take away from her.'

Darcy sat back heavily against the bar. 'But I wasn't doing anything to spite her. I was just living my life. I can't help it if things were going better for me than they were for her.' And Alex has certainly turned the tables now, she thought.

'But I think it's fair to say that you liked being queen bee. I think – well, Libby said – that sometimes Alex felt you looked down on her. You used to tease her, you know, not always so nicely.'

'We all did!' Darcy frowned; Erika was making it sound like she'd actually bullied Alex, but she'd never seen it like that at all. 'And Libby said this to you? When?'

Erika shifted uncomfortably. 'Well, I guess she said it at the time but recently, as Alex has reappeared, we did talk about it again. Just, you know, about the . . . sort of *bad feeling* between you two.'

'Oh.' Darcy imagined the two of them sitting up in their hotel room having a good old gossip about nasty Darcy picking on poor little Alex when she was younger. That wasn't how she remembered it. Alex had been so annoying when they were kids, with her lies and her attention-seeking stories. And the very idea that the young Alex would have been a serious rival for Jon's affections back then was laughable.

Darcy looked over towards the pool area where her husband was being treated to the sight of Alex in her immaculate swimsuit. It wasn't so funny now.

'It's not such a bad thing, Darce. We all said and did stupid things back then. I just think that's maybe where some of this awkwardness stems from. I don't suppose she feels that way now, though,' said Erika with a little laugh.

The implication being that Alex's life was so much better now, there's no way she would care about anything that I could say or do, Darcy thought. She felt even more ridiculous for imagining that perhaps Alex was still interested in Jon. Why on earth would she want him when she could have almost anyone?

'OK, no offence taken.' Darcy climbed down from her stool and reached for Jon's beer with her free hand.

'Hang on, was that all you wanted to say?' Erika looked at her quizzically. 'You just wanted to ask me if I remembered that Alex used to fancy Jon back in the day, right?'

'Yeah.' Darcy nodded, avoiding eye contact by sipping her drink. 'That's all.'

Erika squinted at her. 'Really?'

'Really.'

'But why?' Erika slid down from her stool. 'Unless –
you, you don't think that perhaps *even now*, she . . .?'

'No! Of course not!' Darcy forced a laugh. 'Don't be
ridiculous.'

But she knew it sounded hollow. And she felt Erika's
curious eyes on her all the way back to the pool.

10

2017 – Darcy

'Alex, this place is fantastic! How did you find it?'

Darcy heard Libby's excited voice ahead of her as she descended the final steps, clinging on to the handrail and checking on Freya who was behind her, being helped by Jon. The others were ahead, not at all daunted by the cliffside staircase that led from the road down to sea level, but Darcy had felt vulnerable as she was about to put her foot on the first step, especially when Alex said, 'Take care, Darcy, it's a long way down from the top. One wrong move and . . .'

Alex made a chopping motion with her hand, then laughed to show that she was joking, before bounding down the stairs ahead of the rest of them, clearly not perturbed by the vertiginous structure. Darcy swallowed; suddenly it did look precarious and she instructed Jon to help Freya down, despite her protesting that she wasn't a baby and she wanted to run ahead with Tatty and the others.

'Libs, this place is in all the guidebooks and travel blogs. Didn't you do any research before you came here?' Alex teased, looking back at Darcy as she caught them up and rolling her eyes conspiratorially. 'It's like everyone has forgotten that this is meant to be a hen do!'

Was that a dig? Darcy wasn't sure. 'Libby said she didn't want any fuss,' she said quietly to Alex, her voice defensive even as she wondered whether they should have been making more effort. Truth was, she'd been in her own head too much to really think about planning anything special for Libby on this trip.

Instead they'd all followed Alex's suggestion of visiting the Cave Bar, a funky hotel bar, a short walk along the Lapad coast. 'Look, it's built onto the side of the cliff like ours is, but just wait until you see inside!' Alex built up the suspense as the group followed her around the waterside bar to enter the hotel from sea level. 'Ta-dah!'

Inside was a hidden natural cavern interior featuring exposed rock and twinkly lights highlighting the gleam of the stalactites above. Libby looked so delighted as she took in her sparkling surroundings and Alex beamed with pride at her obvious pleasure. The cave walls glittered and Darcy watched as Libby spun around like she remembered her doing when they were kids and exploring somewhere new.

'This is so cool,' Jon said to Freya, who agreed enthusiastically, and Darcy had to admit it was beautiful, reluctant to do so when it had been Alex's idea.

'It's handy having someone who knows the cool places to go.' Erika looked impressed but Darcy sensed she was toning it down; perhaps she also felt bad that they hadn't organised any treats for Libby. 'Did you come here when you were in Croatia before?'

'I didn't stay in Lapad, or even Dubrovnik, last time. Kyle chartered a boat and we toured the islands. It was gorgeous, wasn't it?' she said to Tatty, who agreed with a smile.

'Still, it helps when you have been to a country before,' Darcy interjected, still sore about the implication that she'd been a bad friend. 'You have some local knowledge.'

Alex laughed. 'That's like saying if you've been on holiday to Cornwall you must know your way around London really well.'

'Anyway, the point is that it is gorgeous and I am so happy we are all here.' Libby made the peace, as always, and everyone nodded in agreement.

After admiring the cavernous interior, Alex suggested they sit outside on the squashy sofas at the water's edge and watch the sunset. When Tatty said that she and Freya would prefer to stay inside and look at all the bling, Darcy heard Alex tell her they could get their own table and charge whatever they ordered to her card. When Alex saw Darcy watching on, she added, 'If that's OK with your mum and dad, Freya?'

'Please, Mum?' Freya looked at her hopefully and once again Darcy sensed that Alex had trumped her. With a glance at Jon, who nodded, she acquiesced despite her reservations, and the two girls hurried back inside, their sandals clip-clopping on the stone floor.

The adults made themselves comfortable in a semi-circle on the squashy sofas facing out to the twilight view over the water. The fiery orange glow Darcy had enjoyed on the walk from their hotel had faded into sleepy pinks and purples; a lone fisherman rowing back towards the shore completed the picture-perfectness of the horizon, and for a minute, Darcy allowed herself to relax and take it in. She was in unique surroundings with her family and her oldest friends, there to celebrate Libby's forthcoming marriage, and she resolved to make a proper effort.

'They're getting on well,' Darcy said to Alex, gesturing to the bar behind them as a peal of laughter rang out from the girls' table. 'Thanks for letting them charge things to your card, although do let me pay for Freya's half.'

Alex waved the offer away. 'My treat. It's nice for them to have a bit of independence away from us oldies.'

'Well then, thank you.' Darcy told herself that Alex was being generous, not flash, and she should accept her kindness graciously. 'Though don't come running to me if they order a whole bottle of Slivovitz!' she added with a laugh, pointing it out on the menu.

Alex laughed along and Darcy felt herself lighten. She was starting to relax a little more as Alex leaned forward and added, 'Darcy, I love your dress.'

She looked in surprise, first at Alex and then down at her dress. It was flowery and feminine in cute pinks and purples; she'd been quite pleased with how it looked. 'Thanks,' she said with a small smile.

'No, I mean it. Bold patterns are a really brave choice when you're, you know . . . *curvy*, but I think you've just about pulled it off.'

Darcy's face flushed crimson immediately. She looked around to see if anyone else had heard what Alex had said, but Jon and Erika were debating the beers on the menu and Libby had disappeared. Swallowing hard, Darcy forced herself to look at Alex again. She had no idea of a comeback, none whatsoever.

Alex smiled and excused herself to the Ladies, leaving Darcy glowering.

'What would you like, babe?' Jon slid closer to her and pointed at the menu.

'Um, I don't know.' Darcy glanced at the immaculately arranged text, but the words were a jumble. 'Where's Libby?'

'Loos,' said Erika. 'Or so she reckons. I wouldn't be surprised if we found her back inside the cave, still twirling around!'

Darcy pretended to laugh but couldn't shake the image of Alex following her up there to have a good bitch with Libby about what a useless friend Darcy was; fat, broke and devoid of any initiative or effort to make Libby's hen holiday fun.

When Alex and Libby reappeared, Darcy felt the vibe shift. Libby kept looking at her when she thought Darcy wasn't watching, confirming her suspicions that the two of them had been talking about her. And Alex was seemingly full of concern for Darcy's wellbeing all of a sudden.

'You want to take care of this one,' Alex said to Jon, shuffling along the sofas to sit a little closer to him. 'Looks like she needs a little TLC.'

Jon lifted an eyebrow in surprise. 'Darcy? She's fine.'

'Oh no, do please keep talking about me as though I'm not here.' Darcy was incensed. What was her problem *now*?

Darcy watched as Alex gave Jon a matey dig in the ribs. 'See what I mean? She's a bit . . .' Alex pursed her lips and mouthed the word, 'Touchy.'

Jon laughed, then recovered himself when he saw Darcy's stony expression. 'Oh, she's fine, aren't you, babe?' Before she could answer, he added, 'Maybe just a bit tired?'

Darcy knew he didn't mean to be disloyal but it felt like a slap in the face to hear him agree with Alex.

'She's lucky to have such a lovely husband to take care of her. Still,' Alex flashed a smile in Darcy's direction, 'I bet she tells you that all the time, right?'

Darcy drained her glass. 'Let's settle up and move on, shall we?' She simply couldn't take any more. She sensed Libby's eyes on her again. 'What's up, Libby?'

'Nothing, really,' Libby said, putting on a bright smile as Alex gave a condescending twitch of her lips at Darcy's tone. 'Sorry, I'm just away with the fairies tonight.'

But Darcy knew she wasn't being paranoid. Was it more than badmouthing that had gone on between her and Alex? What if Erika had told Libby about the conversation they'd had at the poolside bar, about Alex having a thing for Jon when they'd first met? And then what if Libby had told Alex? Could that have been what they were talking about for all that time when they disappeared earlier?

Then, when Jon stood up to go and fetch the girls from their indoor table and Alex said she'd go too, to settle the bill, Libby suddenly jumped up and said that she would *also* go.

'Why?' Erika asked, clearly wondering (as Darcy had been) what it had to do with her.

Libby hesitated. 'I just . . . fancy having another look at the interior. I might take some photos.' Then she hurried off after them.

'Bit weird,' Darcy risked saying to Erika, wondering if she was picking up on the strange atmosphere. It couldn't all just be in her head.

'Probably going for another twirl around.' Erika smiled indulgently. 'You know Libby.'

Did she? Darcy was beginning to wonder.

The girls were laughing their heads off as Jon walked them back outside, with a smirking Alex and frowning Libby close behind. 'What?' Darcy asked. 'What's so funny, sweetheart?'

'The lady thought we were sisters!' Freya was clearly delighted, laughing up at Tatty.

'What lady?' Darcy could feel her voice turning to ice as she looked from the girls to Jon and then over to Alex.

'Just the waitress,' Jon said, grinning. 'She said to me, "Your daughters are lovely girls." Isn't that nice?'

'That makes us sisters,' Freya said, slipping her arm through Tatty's.

'Come on then, my lovely daughters, let's find us some pizza!' Jon linked his arm through Freya's free one and led the two girls off towards the steps back up to the path.

Darcy swallowed hard. 'Well, that's tickled them.' She wasn't sure why it bothered her. If it had been any other child, then it probably wouldn't have. In fact, she was sure that if Jon had been called the father of any of Freya's other friends, she would have laughed along with them. It was because Tatty was Alex's child. It all seemed so . . . icky.

'They do look quite similar,' Erika observed, watching the three of them take the steep steps ahead of them. Darcy looked at them again. Annoyingly, Erika was right. They had the same dark hair and long limbs. Neither girl looked particularly like their mother, Darcy thought. They could definitely pass as a family. She swallowed down a shudder, trying to banish that lingering sensation of ick.

'I'm starving,' Libby blurted out, in a hurry to get going all of a sudden. 'Come on, how far away is that pizza place?'

'It's about this far again from the hotel,' Alex said. 'Ten minutes, max. You're right, though,' she added, turning to Erika. 'They do look similar, don't they?'

As Alex smiled at the lively trio ahead of them, a cold prickle of fear trickled down Darcy's spine.

11

1997 – Alex

I steeled myself for the start of sixth form, preparing to see Darcy for the first time in weeks. We'd had different induction days so I'd managed to put off the inevitable until the first day of term. I'd spent the rest of the summer camped out by the phone, jumping whenever it rang and inevitably crashing back down to earth when it wasn't Jonny.

I wrote him a letter at the caravan park, worried that my kohl pencil scrawl had been unreadable and wanting to catch him before the season was over and I lost touch with him altogether. I kept it light and didn't mention Darcy at all. I told him about my summer job at the local pub – I was only waitressing of course, and wasn't allowed behind the bar, but I thought it sounded grown up and gave us something in common. But I'd had no reply.

Erika tried to get us all together for an end of summer party at her house but I cried off, inventing a story about going up to London to lay flowers for poor Princess Diana, whose tragic death had shocked the world.

It was something I'd have liked to do for real if I hadn't been too busy sat at home, scowling at the phone. Diana was the poster girl for romantic dreamers like me.

As far as I knew, Libby still went, along with Darcy and Bradley and a few other people from our year at school, or college, as I should get used to saying now, but I made a point of not asking about it.

It felt so grown up to say, 'I'm off to college!' as I left the house. Being able to wear my own clothes, not a scratchy uniform, and take the bus made it feel like an adult adventure.

Darcy was getting a lift from Bradley, Erika told us, and as we walked from the bus stop to the college entrance, there was Bradley's battered Volkswagen Beetle pulled up in the entranceway, the two of them eating each other's faces. 'Hasn't he gone to uni yet?' I asked the other two, turning my nose up at the sight of them going for it in full view of everyone.

'Middle of the month,' said Erika, as eventually Darcy came up for air and greeted us as she closed the car door behind her. She was dressed in bootcut jeans, slung low around her hips, with an expensive-looking grey jumper and her hair loose around her shoulders. I felt sick with envy taking in her cover-girl appeal.

Suddenly the grungy sweatshirt I'd chosen felt inadequate and unfashionable so I took it off and tied it around my waist, my vest exposing my clavicles.

'Alex. Long time no see.' Darcy smirked. 'Goodness, have you been ill? You're so *bony*!'

'Thanks,' I said, determined not to let her get to me. She could have said slim, she could have even said skinny, and I might have interpreted it as a back-handed compliment, or even genuine concern. But no, she chose the word *bony*, a horrible word conjuring up images of gnarly old hags and starving children, just to make me feel self-conscious. The other two were hovering awkwardly between us so I decided to be the bigger person, metaphorically speaking. 'That's a lovely jumper.'

She ran her hands along its sides, luxuriating in its softness. 'Yes, Bradley bought it for me, bless him.'

'You're still together then?' I couldn't help myself.

'Well, obviously.' Darcy gestured in the direction in which his old banger had limped away and smiled her infuriating smile. 'I told him all about Jonny and he totally understood.'

The sound of his name jolted me, particularly coming as it did from her treacherous lips. Before I could say anything further, we were interrupted by the sound of people calling Darcy's name. I was amazed at how many new people Darcy had already befriended. I was dying to ask more about exactly what she'd told Bradley but didn't feel I could in front of so many strangers.

It wasn't until the bus ride home that the conversation could return to my favourite topic: Jonny. Darcy took the bus with us as Bradley was working at Pizza Hut, cramming in as many hours as he could before going off to uni. The four of us squeezed together upstairs at the back and, before I could think of a way into the conversation, Darcy beat me to it.

'So, guess who I saw yesterday?'

She was grinning at us all expectantly, but no one gave her a guess.

'OK, I'll tell you. I saw Jonny.'

I thought I was going to be sick. She'd seen Jonny. How was that even possible?

'Jonny?' Libby looked at me, concerned, before flicking her eyes back to Darcy. 'How come?'

'He's back in Guildford. His contract just finished on Saturday and he's got two weeks at home before he goes back to uni.'

'But . . . how come you saw him?' My voice was croaky, but I didn't care. I was desperate for her to tell me they'd just bumped into one another.

'He called me. We met up for coffee. Just *as friends*.' She drawled the last bit at me playfully, rolling her eyes as if I were some terrible killjoy. As if it were totally fine to have a devoted boyfriend but also toy with guys who other people were in love with.

'How did he have your number?' Libby asked, as I tried to articulate all the things I wanted to say. My heart was hammering; I was breathless as I felt my throat clogging up. 'Did you give it to him on holiday?'

'No, I thought I'd better not in case I gave him the wrong idea. You know, after we kissed.' Darcy looked at me again, her eyes glinting, and I had to remind myself she didn't know he'd kissed me too.

'So how did he get it?' I needed to know. For weeks now I'd been waiting for him to call *me*, when I knew he had my number, and I'd written to him and waited every day for a reply. Yet she was the one to get a call from him and she – I still couldn't believe it – had met up with him.

'Directory enquiries.' She shrugged. 'There aren't many Starrs in Thorsley, are there?'

Somehow the fact that he'd sought out her number was even more of an insult than him meeting up with her. It showed a level of care, effort and interest that so far he'd entirely failed to show me. I could barely meet Libby's eyes for fear that the sympathetic look on her face would make me cry.

That night, I shut myself in my room and let it all out. Mum knocked on my door every five minutes, but I yelled at her to go away and leave me alone. I refused two phone calls from Libby and all the pleading that both my parents could muster for me to come down for dinner.

I stared for hours at one of the photos I'd had Susie colour photocopy from Libby's holiday snaps. It was one of me at the bar with Jonny. I thought I'd looked so cool that night, but Darcy was right. I was bony. I looked like a stick insect and I hated myself.

It reminded me of when Darcy told everyone she thought I had anorexia. Everyone looked at me strangely for weeks after that, monitoring everything that went into my mouth, making me hideously self-conscious and nervous. I was lucky she didn't cause me to have an eating disorder for real after that. The truth was, I was just one of those annoying fast-metabolism people who could eat what they liked and still be thin; I couldn't help it – yet of course when I told people that, they were shitty to me as well, as if I was boasting or thought I was special in some way. I couldn't win.

I stopped staring at myself and looked at Jonny. It hurt to look at him, he was so gorgeous. I ached to push his floppy fringe out of his face and have him kiss me again like he did on that last night. To have him whisper sweet words to me like the Jonny of my fantasies. How could it be that someone so perfect and amazing could have his head turned by that total bitch Darcy? I wanted to scream. I hated her. I hated her and I hated myself for not being more like her.

Yet, despite my heartbreak, time marched on and I slipped into the rhythm of my new sixth-form life. I still thought about Jonny every day but keeping busy with college and work at least stopped me wallowing and gave me less time to sit in my room listening to music and poring over my tear-stained photos.

At the end of term we went to a Christmas party at Splitz, a cheesy nightclub that usually we would have to lean hard on our fake IDs to get into, but the event was organised by the college particularly for sixth formers. We couldn't buy alcohol without genuine ID though, so Erika and I went to get loaded at Libby's beforehand. Darcy was off with some of her new friends and planned to meet us there.

'Is she still meeting up with him, do you know? Jonny?' I asked, too keen to know the answer to be cool about it.

Erika nodded. 'They went out twice before he went to uni and they've met up once more since. I think she's seen him more than she's seen Bradley, but she swears they're just friends.'

'I don't believe for a minute they're just friends. I know what she's like,' I muttered, swigging my Hooch. 'She's stringing them both along.'

Later at the Splitz party, after we'd worn ourselves out jumping up and down to 'Tubthumping' and 'Born Slippy', we slumped down on some seats in the corner and I found myself next to Darcy.

'I'm having a party the Saturday before Christmas, you can come if you like,' she said without any niceties. I looked at her in surprise; that was the first I'd heard of it.

'But you should know that Jonny will probably be there and I don't want any drama.'

Drama. That's how she dismissed my feelings. Still, my foolish little heart leapt into my mouth when she said his name and the thought of seeing him again was too tempting an opportunity to turn down, so I nodded. 'All right.'

'Cool. Bring a bottle.' She swept away without looking back, leaving me wondering if I'd imagined the whole conversation in an alcopop-induced high.

When the day of Darcy's party came around, I started to get ready around lunchtime, choosing a powder blue dress and white platform shoes that gave me a bit of a Baby Spice look. I decided not to confide in Libby about how excited I was to see Jonny again because I knew she'd discourage me, but I was choosing to be positive. If Darcy was going to stay with Bradley then perhaps Jonny would accept there was no point wasting time on her anymore. Maybe he'd take a fresh look at me.

Libby and I went to the party together, each clutching a carrier bag of clinking delights that our local corner shop had happily sold us. Libby looked fantastic, all in black with slim-fitting hipster trousers and a velvet top, her curls left natural but for a mistletoe Alice band perched on top. 'Are you OK about seeing Jonny tonight?' she asked, as we duck-walked in our huge platforms up the path to Darcy's parents' house.

'Of course!' I trilled, not even convincing myself. I decided to take it down a notch. 'Really. It's ancient history.'

'OK, well, just don't let him get in your head again. I don't think he's good for you, Alex.'

Erika answered the door; she'd gone over early to help set up and looked half-cut already. 'Darcy's here somewhere,' she said, with a funny little burp.

A steady stream of people started to arrive; most I recognised but some I didn't. Bradley turned up alone, already looking different after one term away. He'd let his hair grow, along with the sideburns and fringe. It had a Liam-slash-Noel Gallagher look about it.

'Does everyone have hair like that in Manchest-*arrr*?' I joked as Bradley looked baffled. 'Mad for it!'

'Hey.' Another man appeared beside us. It took a moment for us – me – to recognise him.

'Jonny!' Libby exclaimed, too startled to filter her reaction.

'Yeah! Hi,' he said with a smile, and I realised he didn't remember her name. If indeed he ever knew it. I remembered how he kept calling me *sweetheart* that night in the squashed caravan. 'Darcy invited me, but I can't see her anywhere and then I recognised you girls – ladies,' he corrected himself. 'You're all looking very lovely, by the way.' He nodded at Erika and then at me. 'Alex,' he added, a special greeting just for me. So he did remember my name now. I couldn't help but feel gratified.

He still looked as fit as ever. I noticed his hair was different, shorter with less of the floppy fringe. He and Bradley nodded at each other without recognition in that blokey way. There was a moment of loaded silence and I saw Libby and Erika tense as we looked between the two of them. Here we go.

'Jonny, this is Bradley. Darcy's boyfriend back from uni,' I said with a bright smile. I watched the two of them reappraise one another warily as they each twigged who the other was. 'Bradley, Darcy's probably told you about Jonny. We met him on holiday this summer.'

'Right, yeah. She did mention.' Bradley hesitated and then stuck his hand out to Jonny. 'Good to meet you at last.'

Jonny shook Bradley's hand, looking less sure of himself than I'd ever seen him. The silence between them was deafening and I could see Libby reaching for something to say to break the tension, but I for one was enjoying it. *Reap what you sow, bitch*, I snarled to Darcy in my head.

'I wonder where Darcy's got to?' Erika said, looking around. The house was packed now and it was difficult to even get from one room to the next without pushing through clusters of strangers.

'I'm gonna go look for her,' Bradley said eventually, clearly relieved to get away from our circle of awkwardness, shuffling off to squeeze through the crowd.

Jonny pulled his cigarettes out of his jacket pocket and fumbled for his lighter, but Erika stopped him. 'Darcy's folks don't allow smoking indoors.'

'Ah, Jesus. I can't drink, 'cos I'm driving and now I can't smoke.'

'Come with me, I'll show you somewhere you can smoke,' I said automatically. I knew I'd never get a better chance than this.

As I opened the front door onto the street Jonny huffed impatiently. 'I could have found my own way out here. I thought you knew somewhere better than standing outside in December.'

Darcy's parents' house had a side return through to the back garden with a light installed to deter burglars. It had a small awning and so was also partially undercover.

'Is this it?'

'It's better than standing in the street smoking like a loser,' I snapped at him. Was it so hard for him to speak to me nicely, like a friend?

He looked surprised and then his face broke into a smile. 'All right, sorry.'

'OK.'

I watched him light his cigarette, declining when he offered me one. I was tempted for a moment, just to have a reason to stay out there with him, but the one time I'd tried smoking, I'd thrown up. I couldn't risk that happening now.

I had to keep the conversation going before he inevitably told me that he was fine on his own and sent me packing. The only topic of conversation I could think of was the one I'd steered clear of the last time we were alone together, but I figured I had to go for it.

'Why Darcy?'

Jonny startled as he took a drag of his cigarette and coughed loudly on the exhale. 'What?' he said eventually.

I shrugged. 'It's a simple question. Why her?'

'I don't know what you mean.'

'Yes you do, and don't give me all that "we're just friends" bullshit.' I looked him in the eyes challengingly, imagining I saw a newfound respect there. 'Clearly, you have feelings for her. You don't come to a party full of strangers for a girl you hardly know, if she's just a friend.'

He took another drag of his cigarette and looked at me as if contemplating saying something. I waited, but after a pause he simply took another drag.

'Well, let me put it another way. You showed me the way Jonny Brooks usually treats girls he's not bothered about.' He made to protest, but I cut him off. 'Come on, Jonny. Look how much effort you're prepared to make for Darcy even though she's got a boyfriend. The two things don't add up.'

He smiled a rueful smile. 'You seem so much more mature than when we met in the summer.'

I smiled at him and was about to say thanks when suddenly a window opened on the wall beside where we were standing.

'It stinks in here. Someone has puked,' a voice said from inside and I realised it was the window of the downstairs loo. 'Can't we go to your room?'

'No! My parents are upstairs!'

I recognised it was Darcy and Bradley at the same time Jonny did. He looked horrified.

'Your parents are here while all this is going on?' Bradley's voice carried loudly through the window into the night air.

'It was the only way they'd let me have a party. So it's here or nowhere.'

'Here it is, then.'

Their conversation gave way to kissing noises, followed by the lid of the toilet seat being slammed down. I looked at Jonny in alarm and he shook his head, taking me by the wrist and leading me around to the front of the house. When he carried on past the front door I wanted to ask where he was taking me but thought better of it.

Around the corner from Darcy's house, we stopped in front of a car I didn't recognise. Jonny's, I realised, as he unlocked the passenger door and opened it up for me.

'Where are we going?' I asked in alarm.

'Nowhere.' He went around the other side and slid into the driver's seat. 'But I'm not going to stand there and listen to them shagging in the bog.'

He wound the window down and finished his cigarette in thoughtful silence while I sat there, wondering what to say. 'Jonny . . .' I began.

'I've been such a mug,' he interrupted, throwing the butt out of the window and winding it up. He swung around in his seat to face me. The look in his eyes was so potent, so intense, I felt my heart hammering against my ribcage as he leaned closer to me. 'Such a mug.'

And so it began, our secret romance, in the front seats of his ancient Vauxhall Viva. And this time, when his hand moved to my breast, I made sure not to flinch or do anything to put him off. I leaned in closer and moaned my encouragement into his ear.

The situation felt so unreal I floated out of my body and watched without feeling anything. I was in Jonny's arms, like I'd dreamed of for months. I watched him recline the seat and climb on top of me. I watched his hand slide up my leg and under my dress. I was jolted back to reality when his cold fingers found their target but I was way too under his spell to accept reality at this late stage, so I simply surrendered to his touch.

He fumbled for a condom without breaking off from kissing me and deftly slid it on, opening his eyes only to check that no one was around before parting my legs and taking my virginity. I tried to hide my grimace as he broke into me, desperate not to do anything to spoil the moment this time; burying my face into his neck as he thrust harder and harder into me. When he came, I was triumphant. *See that, Darcy*, I shouted, ecstatic, in my head. Look how crazy he is about *me* now.

He withdrew and rolled off the condom, exclaiming when he saw spots of blood. 'Jesus! You're not still a virgin?'

'Not anymore!' I tried to make a joke of it, with a teasing laugh. 'Has my dress got blood on it?'

'No, you're OK, it's just a tiny bit.' He sighed, wrapping the condom in a tissue. 'But I wish you'd told me. I'd have been gentler.'

'I thought you knew?'

'Maybe in the summer, but now you seem so . . . different.'

I laughed again. 'It's OK. I'm glad my first time was with you.'

His face fell. 'Oh, hey, I never meant this to be a big thing. I thought it was just a bit of fun.' He rolled back over to the driver's seat and inched my chair into a sitting position as I rearranged my dress and knickers. 'I'm not really looking for anything serious you know. I'm back to uni in January and . . .'

'I'm not looking for anything serious either,' I lied, quickly, before he could withdraw his attention from me once again. 'I just meant I was sad not to have heard from you because I thought you were fit and I hoped that one day we'd . . . fuck.' I was pleased with that last bit; I thought it sounded cool and grown up. 'Honestly, Jonny, I'm not one of those high-maintenance girls who need romance and all that shit. I just want to have fun too.'

I knew now how to get his attention. Be cool, be flirty. Challenge him. Tempt him with no-strings fun. A timid little girl crying over photographs was not going to do anything for a red-blooded guy like Jonny. I had to grow up and be the woman he needed me to be.

We stayed in the car a while longer as he showed me how to give him a hand job, which excited and repulsed me at the same time. I felt so powerful, having him in my hands as he panted my name, but the end result was quite disgusting to be honest.

Jonny didn't want to come back to the party, so he saw me to the house and then left, promising he definitely would call me this time. Libby was frantic, but I assured her that we'd just had a good talk and I was totally over it all.

We'd agreed not to tell anyone what had happened, which I was pleased about because I knew Libby wouldn't approve – she wasn't a prude, but I knew she'd worry about me and I didn't want anyone to ruin this feeling – *and* I knew that if Darcy caught even the slightest hint that Jonny was interested in me now, she'd go after him again, full throttle, just to take him away from me if nothing else.

I gave Libby a huge smile; I felt my face almost cracking with it. I was so happy! Even when Darcy appeared and lectured me about leaving Libby on her own all night, I just smiled my secret smile and let her words wash over me. I was creating a new Alex Rigby, one who had all kinds of sex with gorgeous men and was totally cool about it.

In a funny way I found I understood Darcy better now that I'd had a taste of her power. Seeing the effect I could have on a man was intoxicating and I'd only felt it for five minutes; she'd basked in that power from the moment she hit puberty. It was no wonder she'd let it go to her head. The urge to tell her that I'd had Jonny, the guy I was still fairly certain she was half in love with herself, moaning in my arms was immense, but I knew I'd keep more power for myself if I kept that secret, for now at least.

12

2017 – Darcy

Darcy was relieved to see a couple of benches at the top of the incline and willed herself to push on that far before stopping. Climbing the city walls had been Alex's idea (of course) but, in fairness, they'd all wanted to do it as it was the number one attraction to experience when visiting Dubrovnik, according to all the tour guides.

As recommended, they'd gone first thing in the morning to take advantage of the cooler temperatures and smaller crowds but even so it was still uncomfortably hot as far as Darcy was concerned. She could feel her thighs chafing even with the chub-rub shorts she'd put on underneath her flowery cotton sundress and sweat was pooling in her lower back.

She looked at the others ahead of her and envied their unthinking physicality and the ease with which they all, without exception, strolled up the steps and inclines, happily chatting away to one another. Jon was up front with the two younger girls, talking about *Game of Thrones*, much of which was filmed there. Freya wasn't allowed to watch *Game of Thrones*, to her annoyance, which made the idea of it appeal even more.

Libby, Erika and Alex were in the next grouping, all looking strong and athletic in various shorts and vest top combinations. She'd been walking with them to start with but had told them to go ahead and she'd catch them up, her slightly slower pace meaning that a gap was opening up between them. Once she reached those benches, she was going to stop and have a drink of water, Darcy thought, and she didn't care if they went on without her.

'Do you want to stop here for a rest, Darcy?' Alex called back to her, having reached the benches herself. 'You look like you could use a breather.'

Everyone turned to look at her as she puffed red-faced and sweaty up the final slope. She would have liked to have said a brisk 'no, thank you' and steamed on past, now that Alex had drawn attention to her poor fitness levels in that oh-so-caring fashion, but the truth was, she needed to rest. She rarely exercised anymore and she was really feeling this, especially as the sun rose ever higher.

'Poor thing.' Alex frowned with what Darcy was sure was mock concern. 'You really are quite red. Did you put on sunscreen before we set off?' The other women collected around her as she flopped onto the bench. She was glad that Jon had taken the girls to point at some building in the distance and was taking no notice of her in this pitiable state.

'Yes, thank you,' Darcy muttered, reaching in her drawstring bag for her water bottle. 'I'm just a bit unfit, that's all.'

'Lovely views up here,' Libby said, a touch too quickly, Darcy thought. It *was* beautiful. She had to remind herself to take a moment to appreciate that. It seemed like every time they turned a corner there was a dazzling coastline, azure blue seas and unpretentiously elegant limestone buildings to admire, and yet her head was so full of her own dilemmas that she was barely seeing them.

'Cooling face wipe?' Alex was dabbing her own face and neck delicately even though she wasn't so much as glowing. 'I've got plenty.'

'Ah, no, thank you.' Darcy shook her head. Alex was looking at her almost indulgently, as if she were an elderly granny whom Alex had taken for a nice walk to get her out of the house on a sunny Tuesday afternoon. 'What?'

'Come on, take one – they feel lovely.' Alex wiped hers across her forehead and over her eyelids; Darcy had to admit it was tempting.

'Go on then, thanks.'

Alex pulled a pack of wipes from her bag and handed one to Darcy before turning back to Libby and Erika. She began another monologue about the last time she'd visited Croatia and Darcy tuned her out, gratefully swabbing her face with the wipe.

The cooling effect lasted no more than three seconds before her skin began to sting and Darcy felt her eyes watering. 'Shit! What's in these?'

The others looked towards her, their faces recoiling in horror.

'Oh, my God! Your face – what's happened?' Libby came and crouched before her. 'Alex, what did you give her?'

Panic swelled in Darcy's chest at the burning sensation on her face and her friends' reaction. She scrabbled around in her bag, searching for a mirror to check what had happened to her but the pain around her eyes made her squint and she could barely see.

'Just splash her with water, quick!' Erika instructed. 'Maybe she's allergic to something in the wipes?'

'I don't have any allergies.' Darcy's eyes were streaming now and her face felt red-raw. She fumbled for her own water bottle as Libby found hers first and poured some into her hand.

'Quickly!' Erika cried as Libby apologetically dashed the water into Darcy's face. 'More!'

Darcy inhaled in surprise as the water hit her, making her splutter, but the immediate relief on her skin was worth it. Erika poured some more water onto a clean tissue and handed it to her to dab gently at her face. 'Alex, let me see those wipes.'

Alex, who was standing beside them, opened her bag and handed the packet to Erika. 'I'm so sorry, Darcy, I don't know why you reacted like that. Are you feeling better now?'

Erika took the packet and skim read it. 'Looks OK to me.' She held them up to Darcy. 'Nothing there you're allergic to?'

'I don't have any allergies,' she repeated, doing a double take as she saw the wipes in Erika's hand. 'But . . . but that's not the same packet.' Darcy could feel herself trembling. What the hell was Alex playing at?

'What?' Alex pulled a face. 'What do you mean?'

'That's not the packet you gave me the wipe from. This one is white. The other packet was blue.'

Darcy watched Alex's face closely as realisation dawned and she bit her lip. 'Oh, I'm so sorry, Darcy.' She reached into her bag. 'You must have taken one of these by mistake.'

'Disinfectant wipes!' Erika took them from Alex's hand. 'No wonder they stung!'

'Why did you take one of those?' Alex looked at Darcy as though she was the one who was acting crazy.

'You offered me a cooling wipe,' Darcy protested, incredulous, 'and handed me one from that packet!'

Alex gave a little tut. 'I wish you'd checked first, save you hurting yourself.'

'Why are you even carrying disinfectant around with you?' Darcy couldn't even begin to dial down on her accusatory tone.

'Well, I'm a bit of a germophobe, especially when I'm travelling. I'm so sorry, Darcy, I feel *awful*.'

Darcy couldn't bring herself to say that it was fine. Had it been anyone else, she would have believed it was an accident. Libby found a pocket mirror in her handbag and showed her that the redness was receding. Erika said she had some more sunscreen she could apply once her skin had settled a bit more.

Alex smiled sweetly and tilted her head to one side. 'Do you feel fit enough to walk on again, Darcy?'

'Sure.' Darcy stood up, managing not to let out an 'ooh' sound as she put her weight on her feet again. In as dignified a manner as she could muster, she hobbled over towards where Jon and the girls were. Thank goodness they missed that unedifying spectacle, she thought.

'Mum!' Freya cried as she approached. 'Dad says this is where they filmed King's Landing!' As an afterthought, she added, 'Your face looks, like, totally red!'

At least her daughter was happy to see her, Darcy thought. She was pleased that Freya was having fun, and some bonding time with her dad, but it was a shame Tatty was always there too. No offence, she was a sweet girl and Darcy didn't intend to project her feelings towards Alex onto her daughter, but it would have been nice if Freya and Jon could have discovered this together, father and daughter, just the two of them.

'Yeah, watch out for dragons!' Tatty laughed, pointing overhead. Jon ducked, making both girls laugh.

Darcy smiled at him then, feeling tender towards him as she often did when she recalled how the young Jon had wooed her, rather than seeing the middle-aged Jon who often took her for granted. She longed to bring the romance back into their relationship, to feel wanted and hopeful again.

'You look a bit ruddy,' he said to her now. 'Are you puffed out?'

Her heart sank. 'No, I'm fine, thank you. Let's push on, shall we?'

'Hey, you OK?' He looked concerned at her tone and reached out to place a hand on her back.

'Don't touch me, I'm ridiculously sweaty,' she commanded, willing her legs to move faster so that she could break away from all of them.

'What's up with her?' Alex's voice rang out behind Darcy as she stomped off.

'No idea,' said Jon.

'Disloyal bastard,' Darcy whispered to herself, frustration motivating her to steam ahead.

'Hey, wait up,' Erika called out, catching her up. 'Are you OK, Darce? Libby's worried about you.'

'Really?' Darcy looked back over her shoulder to see Libby hovering awkwardly beside Alex and Jon. 'Why did she send you then?'

'She didn't *send* me.' There was a pause as the two of them kept up the pace along the next section of wall until eventually Darcy slowed down and Erika matched her. 'Libby's in a bit of a funny mood today actually,' Erika continued.

'Yeah, I thought that.' Darcy nodded, a little breathless. 'Is it to do with Alex?'

Erika looked at her strangely. 'Why do you say that?'

Darcy sighed. 'Oh, it all seems so *childish*. I can't shake the feeling that Alex is here to cause trouble. And now Libby's acting like she knows something . . . I don't know what. I just have a hunch there's something else going on here that I can't put my finger on.' She looked at Erika. 'Did you tell Libby about our conversation yesterday?'

Erika coloured slightly. 'Oh, I mean, just in passing.' Darcy looked at her silently. 'You know – you were saying how Alex used to have the hots for your Jon.'

'Erika . . .' Darcy covered her face.

'What? I didn't know it was meant to be a secret. Libby was there at the time. This wasn't new information for her.'

'No, I know,' Darcy whispered, seeing the group approaching them. 'But she's close with Alex, she'll probably say something to her. If she hasn't already.'

Erika looked blankly at her. 'So? Again, Alex was there. She knows what happened.'

'Yeah, but I don't want her knowing that I've been thinking about it.' Darcy paused, not sure how to express it. 'It gives her all the power.'

'Well, at least you're not getting bogged down by all that adolescent he-said-she-said stuff anymore.' Erika raised her eyebrows at Darcy before turning to smile at the others who had now caught them up.

'You didn't get far,' said Alex.

'We thought we should let you catch us up. We're nearly at the end.' Erika indicated the view below them. 'Plus we had to admire the amazing view.'

'Oh wow!' Alex stepped in front of Jon and leaned over the wall, treating him to a fairly spectacular view of his own. 'Oh yes, I see what you mean. You don't get to enjoy this every day, do you?'

'I don't,' said Jon, leaving Darcy to wonder if he was playing along with her flirting or just making an innocent comment. If only Alex would lean a few inches further forward, Darcy thought, and take that peachy arse of hers right over the bloody wall, that would solve all her problems.

Turning back to them with a knowing smile, Alex caught Darcy's eye and gave her the distinct impression she'd read her mind. 'It's a long way down.'

'Better be careful then.' Darcy matched her tone.

Jon looked between the two of them, his discomfort palpable, until Freya broke the silence.

'Can we climb that turret, Dad?' she asked, pointing ahead of them.

'Yeah, *Dad*,' Tatty drawled. Darcy bit the inside of her mouth as Alex laughed loudly at her daughter's joke. Clearly this was going to run and run.

'Of course you can, dear daughters!' Jon laughed along, seeming happy to lift the mood. Darcy was surprised to see that Libby seemed as uncomfortable as she felt. She looked pale, despite the heat, and oddly unsteady on her feet.

'Are you OK, Libs?' Darcy asked her, once the girls had headed off towards the turret.

'Bit too much sun for you?' Alex added, when Libby didn't say anything. 'Tell you what, why don't you and I spend the afternoon in the spa when we get back to the hotel?'

Libby nodded. 'Sure.'

'I might book a treatment,' Alex continued. 'A massage or something. I'm just dying to stretch out almost entirely naked and have someone rub their strong hands all over me.'

Darcy almost laughed at the barefaced cheek of her. She looked at Jon, who was studying the view and pretending not to have heard, before rolling her eyes at Erika, who reciprocated. Libby still didn't look well.

'Come on,' said Darcy, rousing Jon with a poke. 'Let's go find your *daughters* and head back.'

13

2017 – Darcy

When they finally came back down to street level, the tourist crowds had swelled considerably and, after getting caught up in the throng of the third tour group in as many minutes, Darcy heard Alex cry, 'Enough! Let's get a taxi.'

Darcy reached for Freya's hand. 'I'm not a baby,' Freya protested. 'Tatty's mum doesn't embarrass her like this.'

'Bully for her.' Darcy looked for Jon in the crowd; he'd slipped away from them. 'One day maybe you'll appreciate having a mum who cares what happens to you.'

Freya muttered something under her breath but Darcy let it go. She just wanted to find Jon and put some distance between them and Alex.

'This is mad.' Erika appeared beside her. 'I knew it got busy but this is next level.'

Alex's voice reached them. 'We can get a taxi at Pile Gate, just up here.' The crowd parted slightly enough for Darcy to spot her standing on the other side of the pavement. Jon and Tatty were beside her, with Libby fighting her way through a boisterous group of Australian teenagers to reach them.

Darcy turned her head away from Freya and spoke quietly in Erika's ear. 'I don't want to go back with her.' She didn't care if she sounded dramatic or paranoid, she needed some time away from that woman. 'Maybe we'll hang back and take the bus?'

There was a local bus that went to Lapad; they'd all come in on it that morning, much to Alex's disgust. After Alex had shamed them all for not doing any research for this trip, Darcy was amused and impressed when Erika had put her foot down at breakfast that morning and said they were taking the bus.

'There you are!' Alex spotted them as they regrouped. 'We can get a taxi from up there at Pile Gate.'

Libby, Tatty and Jon obediently started to walk in the direction Alex was gesturing towards, but Erika called out, 'We're going to stay a bit longer, actually.'

Alex turned to look at her in surprise. 'Oh?'

'Yeah . . . if you're sure you don't mind me tagging along with you lot?' Erika gestured to Darcy, who smiled gratefully and shook her head.

Alex gave a shrug. 'Fair enough. What about you, Jon?'

Darcy saw Jon hesitate; she hadn't told him that she wanted them to stay. 'It sounds like we are staying here for a bit longer,' he said eventually.

'You sure?' Alex moved a step or two closer to him, ostensibly to dodge a family who were holding a giant map outstretched in front of them and not looking at who they were colliding with. 'You don't want to come back and hang out at the spa with Libby and me?'

Darcy and Erika made eye contact as Jon laughed the suggestion off and Darcy hoped that Erika could see the dynamics as she saw them.

'And me,' Tatty added – pointedly, Darcy thought, realising that Alex often barely seemed to remember she had her daughter with her. 'I'll be there too.'

'Can I go with Tatty?' Freya pulled her hand free and Darcy immediately shook her head.

'Not this time. We'll see them later.'

There was a rush of goodbyes as Alex shooed a torn-looking Libby towards the taxis with Tatty dragging her feet behind the two adults and the rest of them heading back into the throng.

'Hold your dad's hand if you don't want to hold mine,' Darcy told Freya, who was put out at being separated from Tatty.

'Where are we off to?' Jon reached his hand out for Freya. 'Is anyone hungry?'

They all made noises in the affirmative and Jon and Freya led the way, stopping to look at the menu cards outside restaurants as they were swept along in the crush.

'She's really got her hooks into Libby, hasn't she?' Erika said, when enough distance had opened up between the two groups. 'Alex, I mean. I'm sorry but I find her so fake.'

'Thank you! Yes – oh, my God, I thought I was the only one who could see it!' Relief washed over Darcy and she felt the words tumble out of her in a surging roll of frustrations. 'And she definitely did that wipe thing on purpose. She could have blinded me!'

'Ha!' Erika gave a slightly forced half-laugh. 'I don't know about that, that was probably an accident. But I do think she's trying to wind you up, you know,' Erika inclined her head to where Jon and Freya had paused to peer at another menu, 'with Jon, I mean.'

'Everywhere is quite expensive,' Jon called back to them, sensing them looking.

'We'll find something,' Darcy called back, before dropping her voice to Erika. 'Don't mention this in front of Jon, will you? I don't want him to feel awkward.'

Darcy wasn't a jealous type ordinarily, she told herself; but then she'd never been in this situation before. At any other point in her life she'd have told Alex to flirt all she liked – Jon was hers. But this time was different. For the first time in their relationship, she felt genuinely threatened.

'Understood,' Erika said, equally quietly, before announcing that she had an idea for lunch, which Darcy was only too keen to go along with. Erika's research the previous night paid off again and she took them to a bakery that was serving locals as much as tourists and without the inflated price tags. They selected a range of bureks, flaky pastry twists filled with cheese or meat, then took them down to the harbourside where they sat on a bench in the shade, enjoying the view as the various boats came and went in the sunshine.

'I can't believe how cheap these were!' Darcy exclaimed as she brushed crumbs, all that now remained of her pastry, from her top, laughing as Freya mimicked her.

'And so delicious.' Jon unwrapped another paper bag to start on a second one. 'Great find, Erika.'

Darcy wanted to hold him close. Her man. Why couldn't it be like this all the time?

Erika nodded, balling up her wrapping. 'This view, good food, good friends, sitting in the sunshine – what more could you want?'

Darcy couldn't agree more. 'Shame Libby missed it. And the other two, of course,' she hastily added when she remembered that Jon and Freya were listening.

Afterwards, Erika insisted on treating them to a drink at a bar she'd read about online. 'I feel bad going without Libby but we can call this a recce,' she said, leading them off the main drag and up some stone steps to a myriad of back streets that all looked the same to Darcy. 'We'll come back with her another time.'

Just as Darcy thought they must be in the wrong place, Erika pointed at a hand-painted sign, high up on the wall, saying 'COLD DRINKS' and pointing to an archway. 'There it is!' Erika immediately stepped through and beckoned for them to follow.

'What is this, Mum?' Freya's eyes widened and Darcy had to admit that she didn't actually know, but as they looked down, all was revealed. Another amazing Dubrovnik panorama greeted them, this time with the bar itself built into the rocks on the outside of the cliff, each layer stepping down towards the sea. There were more vertiginous stairs to negotiate, same as at the Cave Bar, but Darcy found that without Alex breathing down her neck, she didn't feel anxious.

This was the holiday they were supposed to be having, she thought a while later, as they clinked their glasses and sat in companiable silence, even Freya happy to sit still with the adults, pointing out speedboats and kayaks as they moved across the glittering ocean before them. Darcy felt herself exhale and forced herself to be in the moment, contented and peaceable, and not worry about what – or more accurately, who – was waiting for them at the hotel.

Walking back through the Old Town a while later, Darcy's eye was caught by a market stall displaying flowing summer tops in shades of blue that were reminiscent of the clear seas she'd been admiring all afternoon. She stopped to hold one up to herself, the material soft and cool, as she checked whether it came in a larger size.

'That's lovely,' said Erika as Darcy turned to see if there was a mirror. 'It really suits you.'

'It feels lovely too.' Darcy checked the price and did calculations between the Croatian kuna and pound sterling. 'Jon, what do you think?'

Darcy saw the approval in Jon's eyes as he looked at her, paying her attention in a way he hadn't for a while, and she felt the flutter of something long forgotten as he slowly nodded his head. 'I think you should get it. It's made for you.' They smiled at each other for so long that Erika coughed and went to look at souvenirs with Freya. 'In fact, let me buy it for you, babe,' he added. 'My treat.'

'OK.' Darcy felt herself blush as Jon paid the disinterested stallholder. 'Thank you.'

As they boarded the bus back towards Lapad, Darcy held the neatly wrapped package close; it was her talisman against any unpleasantness that was waiting at the other end.

'I think we might do our own thing tonight, if you don't mind?' Darcy broached the subject with Erika as they approached their stop. 'Maybe we'll just stay at the hotel as we're pretty worn out.' Darcy pointed to the two seats opposite where Freya and Jon were both snoozing, her head on his chest. 'Will you tell Libby and . . . the others? We'll meet up with you all tomorrow.'

Erika smiled and bumped her shoulder gently. 'Totally. I get it.' And Darcy believed that she did.

Back in the room, Darcy hung her top in the wardrobe, smiling as she touched it and remembered the moment with Jon earlier. She gave a gasp as his arms slipped around her and she turned to face him, heart full to bursting. 'Shame we can't have a siesta,' he whispered in her ear.

Darcy laughed; there was no chance of that. Freya was wide awake after her nap on the bus and demanding they play Uno with her. 'We've waited so long, a little longer won't hurt.'

They played cards on the balcony, Darcy posting photos of the three of them together from the best possible angle on Instagram and to the dance school parents' group on Facebook. It wouldn't hurt if Alex were to see them either, Darcy mused.

As afternoon drew into evening, Darcy went for a shower and sang to herself, feeling the happiest she'd been in as long as she could remember. Afterwards, as she sent Freya in, there was a knock on the door.

'Who's that?' Darcy wrapped the bathrobe tighter around herself. 'Will you get it?'

Jon nodded and opened the door, peering around it to protect Darcy's modesty. She heard the low hum of conversation but couldn't make out any words.

'Who is it?' She risked going closer, then pulling up short when she saw that it was Alex standing there, her head close to Jon's as they huddled in the doorway.

Jon straightened up and drew the door wide open. 'Just Alex.'

'Hey, Darcy!' Alex beamed at her and then did a mocking double take as she ran her eyes over Darcy's bathrobe. 'Uh oh . . . I wasn't interrupting something, was I?'

Alex pulled an approximation of an 'oopsie!' face as Darcy and Jon both immediately chorused, 'No!'

'I'm just out of the shower. Freya's in there now.' Darcy knew her tone was short but she didn't care. 'What can we do for you?'

Alex gave an overly cute half-shrug, half-giggle and threw her hands up as if she were simply hopeless. 'I've locked myself out of my room. Tatty's in the pool, she'll be back in a minute and can let me in with her key. I was just looking for somewhere to hang out for five minutes.'

Darcy was sceptical; why would *they* be the first people Alex would turn to? Why not go to Libby and Erika's room? Or just chill at the pool with her daughter? She glanced at Jon, who also looked nonplussed, but Darcy couldn't find a reason to say no.

'Why don't you take a seat on the balcony and I'll put something on?' Darcy was over-formal with the awkwardness of having Alex unexpectedly in her space and she was convinced that Alex was enjoying her discomfort.

'Sure.' Alex giggled, allowing Jon to open the door and picking her way delicately over Freya's foldout bed to reach it.

'What's funny?' Jon asked her, and Darcy knew he was as weirded out by the visit as she was.

'Being with you makes me feel young again,' Darcy heard her say as Jon stood aside to let her pass. What the hell was she playing at?

'Um, I—'

'All of you, I mean,' Alex cut in. 'You and Darcy, the whole gang.'

As they stepped onto the balcony, Darcy struggled to hear any more of the conversation, and she focused on dressing in record time so she could join them. She was breathless as she made it out there. 'Sorry to keep you waiting.'

'That's all right,' said Alex, her tone casual and barbed all at once. 'I've been having a nice chat with Jon.'

'Really?' Darcy looked at him; he didn't look like he'd had a *nice chat*. He looked distinctly uncomfortable.

'Yeah, I was saying that Tatty is getting really grown up now. She's just been getting some careers advice from Erika.'

Darcy wasn't expecting that. 'When did you see Erika?'

'Not too long ago, in the bar.' Alex smiled. 'She let Tatty borrow her laptop – before she went in the pool.'

'Why?' Darcy knew she was silly to feel betrayed; she hadn't actually asked Erika to avoid Alex and she could hardly expect her to be mean to a teenager, but the thought of her best friend hanging out with them really stung, especially since Darcy had told her that Alex was getting under her skin.

'Tatty couldn't connect to the Wi-Fi, and was going to simply *die* if she didn't get on Snapchat or something.' Alex chuckled and made a dismissive gesture with her hands. 'Well, you understand, don't you – you're always online. I saw your photos from this afternoon, by the way.' Alex looked Darcy square in the eye. 'Cute.'

Darcy noticed Jon's gaze moving between the two of them; he seemed unsure of himself, which was really not like him. Eventually he excused himself and went back into the bedroom.

'Yeah, Erika was really good with her actually. Tatty found the idea of working in the City quite appealing. Erika's going to sort her out some work experience, maybe even an internship later on.' Alex smiled at Darcy. 'I didn't know you two used to work for the same company.'

'Oh, years ago, not for long.' Darcy waved her hand. 'Before Freya.'

'You stopped working there when you were pregnant, did you?'

'Ah, no, I went back for a bit.' Darcy broke eye contact and stared out over the railings. She did not want to be having this conversation but felt trapped; if she told Alex to get lost then the ensuing awkwardness between them would be seen as her fault. Alex would paint it to Libby as though it was Darcy who was causing a rift in the group.

She sighed, and decided to play along. 'The commute was just too much with Freya to consider and Jon thought, well, we both thought that something closer to home would be better.'

'It must have been a real wrench to give up on such a great career.'

'Kind of. It had lost its appeal before that, to be honest.'

'When Erika was promoted over you, you mean?' Alex tilted her head sympathetically.

Darcy swung around to look at Alex in surprise. Erika had told her about that? 'Well,' she faltered, 'that didn't help. Neither of us would have been comfortable being the other's boss.' She turned to look over the railings again. 'If I'd got the job, I'm sure Erika would have found it hard too.'

'But you didn't.' Alex sighed. 'And Erika's doing *so well* there now, isn't she? A director?' Darcy nodded but didn't say anything. 'Do you ever wish you'd stuck with a proper career rather than giving it all up for a man?'

'Fucking hell, Alex, say it like it is, why don't you?' Darcy almost laughed. Why did she keep letting her guard down when Alex was always ready to stick the knife in?

Alex shrugged. 'How would you put it?'

'I don't know.' Darcy shook her head. 'I wanted to build a home and be a good parent.' She was getting angry, her face flushing red. 'There's nothing wrong with wanting that. *You* obviously wanted it.' She looked at Alex accusingly.

'I didn't say there was anything wrong in wanting that.' Alex was infuriatingly calm and reasonable. 'It's just that Darcy Starr was always the girl most likely to do something spectacular with her life. I guess I'm just surprised to find out that you gave up all your potential, all the brilliant things you could have done and the fabulous life you could have led, all for . . . Jon.' Alex shook her head, as if disappointed in her.

For a terrible moment, Darcy thought she might cry. She couldn't bear to do that in front of Alex. Eventually she said, 'I chose the life I wanted. Jon, Freya and our home life together are the most important things in the world to me. Jon's a great husband. Dependable. Faithful.'

Alex smiled at that, and Darcy grew more indignant. 'I understand that perhaps you're bitter because *your* husband doesn't want you anymore.' Darcy took a breath and wondered if Jon could hear them. She hoped he could. 'I have absolutely no regrets about the choices I made, Alex. I love my life.'

Alex pursed her lips. 'You don't have to convince me. As long as you believe it.'

Darcy took a step back as Alex walked towards her, but Alex simply looked over the balcony rail and pointed to the terrace below where they could see Tatty climbing out of the pool. 'Ah, it looks like Tatty's finished,' said Alex. 'Thanks so much for letting me hang out here, it's been really fun chatting.'

Darcy didn't move as Alex went back inside; she was shaking and she didn't trust herself not to tell the bitch what she really thought of her. Even when she heard Alex talking to Jon, she decided not to intervene. Think of Libby, she urged herself. It was only a few more days. Plus, she trusted Jon even if she didn't – couldn't – trust Alex.

A few minutes later, Jon appeared in the balcony doorway and Darcy heard the click of the bedroom door. 'She's gone.'

'Good.' Darcy paused. 'What . . . what was she saying to you?' It looked like Jon was similarly affected by Alex's visit. He opened his mouth to answer just as Freya appeared in the doorway.

'I'm done in the bathroom. Was Tatty's mum here?'

'Yeah, just for a bit,' said Jon, forcing a smile. 'I'll go and get my shower now.'

'Hang on. What were you going to say?' Darcy stopped him.

Jon looked at her and then to Freya and back again. 'Nothing,' he said. 'Nothing.'

14

1998 – Alex

After getting together at Darcy's party, I'd met up with Jonny once more in the new year before he went back to uni. True to his word, he phoned and said he had a free house that coming Saturday. After telling my parents I was off to Guildford to spend my Christmas money, I took the train and let him walk me back to his place, where we spent all afternoon making love in every possible way I could have imagined. Sometimes I thought it would have been nice just to cuddle up and talk, but I was flattered by how hot he was for me.

'You're amazing,' he panted in my ear as we finished yet another marathon session. I could have purred.

'Do you want to have a shower before you go home?'

That took me by surprise; he was turfing me out. 'Oh, yeah, I suppose I'd better.' I started to gather up my discarded clothes.

'I mean, I'd love for you to stay, but my parents will be getting back soon.'

'And you don't want them to see me?'

'Not like this,' he joked, indicating my nakedness. 'But honestly, with me going back to uni soon they'll be on my case about starting a relationship now and how it'll impact on my studies *blah blah*.' I stopped to look at him as he said *relationship* and he quickly added, 'They won't understand that we're just having some fun. No strings, like you said.'

'I get it,' I said lightly, allowing him to hand me a towel and direct me to the bathroom. My mood felt flat as I showered, although I couldn't put my finger on why. Fun was what we'd agreed; I knew I couldn't ruin things by getting all clingy after the event.

He walked me back to the station and said he'd be in touch next time he was home. I gave him a bright smile. 'That's cool. Just whenever you fancy some fun, like today.'

He grinned at me and shook his head. 'You're so horny. I've never known a girl like you, Alex.'

He certainly remembered my name now, I thought, as I waved him goodbye and boarded the train. I hoped he might call me during term time but resolved to be cool and trust that he would get in touch when he was ready. January and February always dragged, but that year I had the memories to keep me warm.

Then came the catastrophe that no one saw coming; the drama to end all dramas. It was Valentine's, but Darcy and Bradley were over.

She'd been so loved up all term, after reuniting with him at Christmas. She'd planned to surprise him, even persuading her parents to drive her up to Manchester, but her dreams for a romantic idyll had backfired when she found him with another girl.

'I honestly can't believe it. Bradley was so in love with you.' Libby scrunched up her features, unable to comprehend that he was capable of cheating on Darcy, as the four of us sat on the floor in Erika's bedroom.

'He was! He was always keener than I was!' Darcy sniffed, hugging her knees. 'But he said he's been feeling insecure since last summer, since that thing with Jonny.' She looked at me briefly and I kept my face impassive; she still didn't know about me sleeping with him. Twice. None of them knew. 'He said he didn't think my heart was really in our relationship.'

'Was it meeting Jonny at your party that rattled him?' Erika was unboxing a Sara Lee chocolate gateau, breakup comfort food *du jour*, preparing to cut it into quarters with a butter knife from downstairs.

'Maybe,' Darcy admitted.

'He was threatened.' Erika handed us each a plate with a pillow-soft wedge of chocolate squidgy-ness, which none of us could resist. Before she could go around again with a fork for each of us, Darcy stuck her finger into the creamy frosting and held it aloft, contemplating it.

'I bet you're right. And I barely even saw Jonny that night.' She sucked the chocolate cream off her finger and sighed. 'So unnecessary.'

'Well, better to know now than waste any more time on him,' Libby said, through a mouthful of cake.

'And you're free to go after Jonny now!' Erika grinned as I looked on in alarm. I hastily covered my expression by shovelling in a forkful of cake and keeping my head down. Please no, don't let her go after him again, I prayed silently.

'I think I might have burned my bridges with him after the party. I tried to call him at his parents' house a few times over the holidays and I sent him an email at his uni address but he never got back to me.' Darcy shrugged and stuck her finger back into her cake. 'Never mind.'

I took another big forkful to keep my face busy while I processed the fact that she had his home phone number and his email address whereas I had neither and was completely reliant upon him getting in touch with me if he decided he wanted to see me again. I'd had to physically restrain myself from trying to get in touch with him at uni, trusting that playing it cool would pay off in the end. Yet all that time, she'd had his bloody email address.

Well, of course she had, I thought. Princess Darcy always had everything – but had she been to his home? I didn't think so. And had she had sex with him, multiple times, in his childhood bedroom? Almost certainly not. So there. I stuck my tongue out at her in my head. I would have liked his email address, though. We had email on the computers at college. Libby and I sent each other jokes back and forth whenever we logged on. I would have loved to send him sexy love letters to read while he was away from home.

'I don't think I want to rush into another relationship anyway,' Darcy mused. 'Kitty says I should concentrate on myself, and I think she's right.'

Erika frowned at the mention of Darcy's other friends. 'Guys are rubbish anyway.'

'They're good for some things,' I teased, with a knowing smile, fed up with the conversation being all about Darcy again.

'How would you know?' Darcy eyed me speculatively.

'You'd be surprised what I know.'

Her lips twitched. 'Oh really? Like you know Hunter from *Gladiators*?'

'You're never going to let me forget that, are you?' I shook my head as Darcy and Erika fell about laughing. It was just a little white lie. So what – occasionally I'd embellished stories to make my life seem more interesting. It wasn't a massive deal, but Darcy always seemed to find out and roundly take the piss out of me for it, over and over again. 'I don't know why you're laughing, you're the one who just got dumped!'

The laughter stopped abruptly and all of them looked at me in surprise. I shrugged. 'It's true.'

'No, it's not, I dumped him *actually*.'

'Only because he shagged someone else.'

'Don't talk like you know anything about it. You haven't even got off with anyone.'

There was an awkward moment when Libby and Erika looked at me, remembering that I had kissed Jonny on holiday. Darcy never had found out about that.

'That's what you think.' I put the remains of my cake down on the floor and folded my arms. I wasn't going to be patronised by her yet again. She wasn't the only one who'd become a woman.

'Al?' Libby looked at me questioningly. 'Tell us?'

'She's bullshitting. Again,' Darcy sneered.

'I'm not.' I smiled at her; it was gratifying to wind her up if nothing else.

'Who then?' Erika was looking interested too. I wasn't sure that she believed me, but she was definitely concerned that I'd left her behind in the experience stakes.

'I can't tell you.'

Darcy laughed nastily. 'Because he's not real?'

'No. Because he's married.'

I regretted it the minute I said it, but the lie just fell off my tongue as a convenient way to throw them off the scent.

'No!' Libby was appalled. 'Not really? Al?'

I nodded. I hated lying to her but if I admitted I'd made it up, I'd never live it down with Darcy and Erika. Plus, it occurred to me, thinking on my feet, that this could be a good cover story for meeting up with Jonny in future. A mysterious married man who I had to keep quiet about would be a perfect foil for sneaking away without anyone knowing where I really was, or who I was really with.

'I don't believe you,' said Darcy, looking at me through narrowed eyes. She wasn't entirely sure though, I thought. There was part of her that realised it could be true. 'Who is it, if so?'

'Well, I can't tell you, that's the whole point.'

'Convenient,' mumbled Erika.

'Not particularly, but we can't help how we feel.' I gave her a sarcastic smile.

'Where do you even know him from?' Libby obviously believed me but was devastated by my lack of morality. And, in truth, I felt awful.

'Work. And that's all I'm telling you.'

I thought work was a safe bet because they didn't really know anyone from the pub, and so many customers came through the place that it would be easy to invent a mysterious drinker who had caught my eye.

'But you've had sex with him?' Erika was as blunt as ever.

I gave her as patronising a smile as I could muster. 'We prefer to call it lovemaking, but yes. We're having an affair.'

Darcy looked somewhere between horrified and impressed. I still courted her approval, despite the fact that she treated me like rubbish, humiliating and sniping at me. I couldn't help but feel pleased.

'Did you bleed?' she blurted out suddenly. Erika recoiled, looking properly disgusted.

I understood that she was testing me. 'A little bit, the first time, but otherwise it was fine.'

'What's your favourite position?' She looked at me challengingly, as if I couldn't just make up the name of one. We'd all been avid fans of *More* magazine's 'Position of the Fortnight' since we were twelve.

I resisted the urge to show off, instead saying, 'Grow up, Darcy,' and enjoying watching her blush as I shook my head at her.

Of course, feeling like top dog didn't last long, as was always the case in my relationship with Darcy. She settled into her new persona of Tragic Heartbreak Girl, wearing all black to college, listening to Alanis Morissette on repeat, sitting out on the green with the grebo crowd, pretending to enjoy smoking and talking about morbid films that I didn't even think she'd seen.

Guys were queuing up to be the new Bradley but she would put on her brave Princess Diana (rest in peace) face and tell them earnestly that she was, 'just, like, in a place right now where I so need to focus, like, on *me*, you know?' in that affected way she'd recently adopted as a result of overexposure to *Friends* and *Clueless*. She was often to be found trailed by a slow-moving entourage as she mooned around the college grounds like a sad teenage ghost.

Then, one morning in April, she bounded into the library wearing a red sweater that I hadn't seen on her since before Valentine's, her cheeks flushed with excitement. I felt a sense of foreboding as she approached the table where I was on a free period, studying with Libby and Erika, even before she bounced up and down and stage whispered, 'Jonny called me last night!'

My stomach rolled over in that familiar way that I was growing used to. I still hadn't heard from him but I'd been sure, really sure this time, he would call me when he was home for the Easter holidays.

'Oh yeah, what did he say?' Erika was still a bit pissed off with Darcy for swanning off with her new friends.

'Well, I'd emailed him a few weeks ago to let him know what had happened with Bradley and apologise again for Christmas. I hadn't meant to lead him on,' she said solemnly, her voice growing a little louder with her protestations.

'Right,' I said, deadpan. She gave me a double take, unsure whether I was being genuine or not, and decided to believe I was.

'Anyway, I didn't hear from him for ages, but then all of a sudden he called me last night from his parents' place. He's home for Easter and wants to clear the air.' She was practically jumping up and down on the spot; I felt sick watching her. 'I honestly can't wait to see him.'

'Er – silent study please, ladies!' shouted the old dragon at the front desk, while Darcy giggled.

'Sorry. I've got to go to English but I just so had to tell you guys!'

I waited for her to make a pointed barb at me about Jonny having called her first, but she just gave us another grin and scooted off, waving cheekily at the desk dragon as she skipped past her. She'd totally forgotten about me liking Jonny, I realised.

I'd always thought that Jonny was in a love triangle, as they said in my magazines, with Darcy and me. But I understood then that in Darcy's head, *she* was the centre of a love triangle between Jonny and Bradley. I didn't figure in her story at all, so unimportant and irrelevant was I. It was insulting.

'You OK?' Libby whispered, taking in my expression. I hastily rearranged my face into a smile.

'Of course. Ancient history.' I waved her concern away. 'Just feeling a bit sad I can't spend Easter with G.'

G was the codename we'd developed for my mysterious married man. They'd pressed me for a name and eventually accepted an initial when I refused. I'd chosen G as it had a similar sound to the J of Jonny's name.

'Well, that's the price you pay for sleeping with a married man,' said Erika, without looking up from her books.

'All right, Mary Whitehouse!' Libby elbowed her with a grin. 'He's the one who's married, not Alex. I'm not saying I approve,' she paused to give me a mock-stern look, 'but it's not our place to judge.'

'Thanks.' I smiled at her, a genuine smile unlike the sarcastic ones I treated everyone else to. Libby was such a great mate. I wished I could tell her the truth.

When I still hadn't heard from Jonny by the end of that Easter term, I started to spiral again. I hatched plans that involved taking myself to Guildford and seeing if I could find my own way to his parents' house again, before accidentally-on-purpose colliding with him on the street. On the Friday, as we took the bus home, Libby mentioned – believing that I was well and truly over him – that Darcy was going to meet him on the Saturday lunchtime.

'Good luck to them,' I said, making a big deal of looking out of the window so that Libby couldn't see my face.

So that was it then, I thought. Game over. Once they were reunited they were bound to fall in love for real this time. I had to face the fact he hadn't called me in three months, despite our afternoon of passion the last time we met.

On the Saturday, I stayed home, not in the mood to socialise. All I wanted to do was wallow in my misery and torture myself with images of him and Darcy talking, laughing, touching . . .

I was disturbed from my gloomy fantasies by Mum calling me to the phone. 'A *young man*,' she said, in a Harry Enfield voice that she thought was funny, but I wasn't in the mood to appreciate.

It was Jonny, asking to meet up. Caught between delighted and confused, I couldn't help but ask about Darcy; in response, he insisted they were just friends. She was getting over Bradley, he said, and seeing as we were just fooling around and having fun, no one could object to that, could they?

I wanted to ask him if he'd told Darcy he was going to call me but I suspected I knew the answer to that. Still, I wasn't going to quibble. As long as I was still in the picture, I had some power. I wasn't going to scare him off with a tirade of needy questions.

We arranged that he would pick me up after my lunch-time shift at the pub the next day, which fitted in well with my lies about the mysterious G. I told different lies to my parents, seeing as Mum had picked up the phone, saying that Jonny was a boy from college who'd asked to take me to the cinema. She was really excited about me being 'taken out', as she called it, and I couldn't help but think she'd be less enthused if she knew what we were likely to get up to.

After my shift on the Sunday, I freshened up and took a moment to remind myself to be cool. I sashayed out to Jonny's car and leaned in the open window. 'Hey, you.'

'Hey.' His eyes roamed my body, reminding me how alive he made me feel. 'Get in.'

I walked around the front of the car, watching him watch me. When I slid into the passenger seat, he reached over and kissed me, hard. I could feel that it was a hungry *I want you now* kiss. And it was nice to be wanted, and wanted by him in particular.

'Where are we going?' I panted as he released me.

'I thought we'd go for a drive.' He flashed me a wolfish grin as he fastened his seat belt before turning to start the engine.

'Oh.' I nodded, a little disappointed. After all, he'd taken Darcy for lunch, which made it seem like a proper date, with some effort involved. He and I had never actually been out together anywhere.

He turned to look at me in surprise. 'There's not much else to do at four o'clock on a Sunday afternoon, babe.'

'I know,' I said, more brightly, smiling at him. 'A drive is cool.'

He smiled and eased the car out onto the road. 'I just want to be alone with you.'

I smiled back, genuinely this time. 'Me too.'

15

2017 – Darcy

Stepping carefully down into the toilet cubicle at the front of the boat, Darcy wobbled on her sandals and accepted that the wine had gone to her head. The facilities were so tiny that she could barely turn around once she'd closed the door, but she knew there was no way she could make it to the next island stop without a wee.

Alex had apparently suggested the day trip around the Elafiti Islands to the rest of the group the previous night when they'd gone back into the Old Town for dinner. Erika had messaged Darcy from a Bosnian restaurant, incongruously named the Taj Mahal, to tell her the plans.

Darcy, who'd enjoyed not having to spend time with Alex as she, Jon and Freya stayed at the hotel for dinner, would have happily opted out but forced herself to be sociable, telling herself that a beautiful spring day cruising around the unspoilt islands would be worth having to be in Alex's company. And the islands were indeed spectacular; it was just a shame that nothing could make her relax when Alex was around.

The day had started badly, when Darcy couldn't find the new top she'd bought the day before. 'I hung it up in here,' she said to Jon, pointing into the wardrobe. 'Remember, you came up behind me and . . .' she raised her eyebrows, 'you know.'

Jon laughed and had a rummage through the hangers but he couldn't see it either. They asked Freya, who claimed to know nothing about it. Darcy remembered the only other person who'd been in their room in the past twenty-four hours, but knew she'd sound crazy articulating her concerns.

Then, unbelievably, when they met up with the group at breakfast, there was Alex wearing her top. 'You utter psycho.' Darcy hadn't been able to stop herself. She shook her head, adrenaline and – yes – fear pumping through her body as the shock of realisation hit her. 'You took that from my room and now you're . . . wearing it in front of me?'

The others all looked on in horror. Even Freya was staring at her doubtfully, but Darcy was too strung out to register their reactions. She turned to Jon, imploring him to say something, but he was ashen-faced and silent.

Eventually Alex laughed. 'This is my top. I don't know.' She broke off to laugh again. 'I don't know what you're on about.'

Darcy's hands clenched into fists. 'Bullshit. You were in our room and mine has gone missing. I only bought it yesterday.'

'I only bought mine yesterday too!' Alex held her hands up to protest her innocence and Libby nodded.

'She did, Darce. I was with her.'

'When?' Darcy snapped, regretting it immediately as Libby recoiled.

'Last night in the Old Town.'

Darcy swung around to Erika. 'You let her buy the same top as me?'

'I didn't see her buy it, honestly.' Erika shook her head. 'I don't know what's going on here, but—'

'She bought it when you were tasting the liqueurs,' Libby said to Erika. Turning to the rest of the group, she added, 'Erika was trying samples of the Croatian plum brandy thing at the next stall. Tatty was there, she knows.'

Tatty nodded and the group fell silent.

'But mine has gone missing,' Darcy repeated. She refused to let Alex gaslight everyone about this. First the little digs, then burning her skin with that wipe – and now stealing her stuff and parading it in front of her.

'It's probably not even exactly the same top.' Alex twisted to reach around and pull out the label. 'Is it the same brand? And,' she paused, 'mine is a small. Was yours a small?'

Darcy's insides plummeted. There was a clear 'S' on Alex's label. She knew hers wasn't a small, and she knew that everyone else could easily work that out. What the hell had happened here?

'Maybe yours is in the wardrobe, babe. I only had a quick look.' Jon tentatively reached for her arm, the physical embodiment of him saying 'calm down, dear'. It made her want to shake him off, but she couldn't bear the others seeing her angry with him.

'Maybe it fell off, like mine did?' Freya piped up. Darcy saw now that Freya looked concerned and, actually, she was right – the hangers were fiddly and they'd found two of Freya's T-shirts lying on the bottom of the wardrobe since they'd arrived.

Darcy took a deep breath and forced herself to face Alex. 'I'm sorry, Alex, clearly I'm wrong.'

Alex bestowed her most benevolent smile on Darcy. 'No need to apologise, we all get things mixed up sometimes.'

From then on, Alex had been niceness personified, making Darcy even more embarrassed about her behaviour. So far she'd survived the morning by keeping her head down and indulging in the open bar, hence the need to visit the cramped loo.

'Where's Alex? You didn't leave her on her own with Jon, did you?' Libby's voice reached Darcy from the deck outside. Who was she talking to? And why would she be worried about leaving Alex with Jon?

'The girls are there,' Darcy heard Erika reply. 'She's hardly likely to jump him with them watching.'

The boat lurched and Darcy put her hands out to steady herself. She could reach the walls on either side of her without fully extending her arms. She felt her stomach pitch and roll; she wasn't sure if that was due to the ship's motion, the freshly grilled fish they'd had for lunch or the fact that her friends were speculating about Alex Rigby wanting to 'jump' her husband. She suspected the latter.

'You joke, but I wouldn't put money on it,' said Libby.

Darcy held her breath, unsure whether to go out and confront them or wait and see what else was said. She'd known something wasn't right with Libby for a couple of days now, but after the chat on the city walls with Erika, she'd convinced herself that it wasn't anything to do with her. Perhaps she just had pre-wedding jitters? She hardly mentioned Pete, and she didn't seem that excited about the wedding anymore. Other friends of hers talked of nothing else when their weddings were approaching, but Libby was so laid back, sometimes Darcy even forgot that this was meant to be her hen do.

'Do you know something?' Erika said after a pause. Darcy tensed; she needed to flush but didn't want to miss Libby's response. 'Like, has she said anything to you?'

There was, what seemed to Darcy to be an agonisingly long delay before Libby eventually replied. 'Not really. I know she . . . *liked him* before but that was twenty years ago.'

'Have you spoken to her about it?'

Another long pause. 'Kind of. Not really. She says it's ancient history.'

'You *do* know something!' Darcy heard Erika exclaim, wincing at the animation in her friend's voice. Darcy knew her friend liked a gossip, but this was her marriage they were talking about.

It was true that she and Erika sometimes talked about Libby and Pete's relationship, especially since their shit-or-get-off-the-pot approach to getting engaged. Darcy had even talked about Erika's work romance with Alex, of all people.

Darcy had always maintained it wasn't bitching; it was an essential facet of female friendship. Still, it felt hard to take when the tables were turned.

'What's ancient history?' Erika continued. 'Did something happen between them before?'

'I only know what you know,' Libby said quickly, far too quickly in Darcy's opinion. She took the chance to flush the loo and started to wash her hands.

'Did you know about her secret Facebook page?' Darcy heard Erika say over the noise of the running tap, immediately turning it off so that she could hear better.

'Whose? Alex? I have her on Facebook. So do you, don't you?'

'That's her Alex Rigby page. It's only been set up a few months and you know it's pretty sparse. I'm talking about her Lexie Kaplan page.'

'What?' Darcy could hear the confusion in Libby's voice, a sentiment she echoed herself. 'Who's Lexie Kaplan?'

'It's Alex. Kyle Kaplan is her ex-husband – she must have gone by the name Lexie when she was with him. She'd always wanted to reinvent herself. Remember that year she insisted we all called her Sandy?' Darcy heard Erika laugh and she half smiled herself.

Darcy remembered teasing her the whole time, calling her Sandra Dee. 'It's Sandy, short for Alexandra!' Alex would shout, when Darcy had sufficiently wound her up about it. Darcy had made sure the name Sandy never caught on. Perhaps she *had* been a bit of a cow to her at times, she reflected. But Alex had been so annoying with stuff like that.

'How do you know this?' Libby demanded, bringing Darcy back to the present.

'Tatty borrowed my laptop yesterday and I didn't realise she was still logged in,' Erika explained.

'So?'

'So, I wasn't snooping – I wasn't, I promise, it just took me a moment to understand what I was looking at. And on her page there was a photo of Alex, but with the name Lexie Kaplan.' There was a pause. 'Obviously I had to have a little look!'

Darcy dried her hands and wondered what to do. She was aware that there was only so long that she could hog the single toilet on a boat full of tipsy tourists but she really needed to hear the rest of this. She doubted they would keep talking as freely if they knew she could hear them.

'Ah well, it's not surprising that she might want a new account, away from all the people who knew her when she was married to that Kyle,' Libby reasoned.

'Yeah, but I could only see that page when Facebook thought I was Tatty. When I logged her out and went back in as me, I couldn't even find a Lexie Kaplan on there.'

'Let me try.'

Darcy knew that she'd have to vacate the cubicle before anyone sent out a search party for her. She edged out as quietly as possible and could see Erika and Libby on the deck just above her, Libby tapping away on her phone. 'I can't find her either.'

'So, either she has some kind of ultra private, top secret account or she's deliberately blocked us from seeing it. Why would she do that?' Erika was clearly excited to have been doing a little detective work, Darcy thought. 'And that's not all,' Erika continued. 'Were you aware that Tatty is seventeen? Not fifteen, *seventeen*.'

Darcy saw Libby's eyes widen but before Libby could respond, the boat rocked as it passed through the slip-stream of another vessel. Darcy put her hands out and smacked into the railings at the bottom of the steps. Libby and Erika turned to look as she exclaimed in pain.

'Darcy!' Erika rallied first, putting on a bright smile. 'What are you doing down there?'

Darcy rubbed her hand. 'Just been to the loo. In the world's tiniest cubicle. What are you two doing up there?'

Erika and Libby passed a look between them. 'Just came up to stretch our legs.'

There was a silence. Darcy decided to let them off the hook; she knew it wasn't personal. If others had been acting the way she and Alex had been, Darcy knew she'd have plenty to say about it too.

'Well, I'll get back to the others.' She gestured in the direction of the table at the back of the boat where everyone else was sitting. She could see Tatty and Freya taking selfies together on Tatty's phone while Jon and Alex chatted. There was a respectable distance between them and nothing untoward in their body language, but Darcy still felt that familiar, lurching dread when she thought of the two of them together.

'Great, cool, yeah, we'll be back in a minute,' Erika called to her with forced jollity. Darcy gave them a brief, unconvincing smile and then tottered back towards the table.

As she approached them, Alex reached and plucked something from Jon's collar. He looked at her quizzically and leaned forward to say something before he noticed

Darcy and sat back again. 'Hey!' His voice was hasty, unnatural. 'There you are.'

'Here I am,' Darcy said. 'Sneaking up on everyone today, it seems.'

'Feeling better now?' Alex tilted her head in her condescending way that infuriated Darcy.

'I only went for a wee, Alex,' Darcy snapped. She noticed Tatty and Freya looking at her warily. 'What are you two up to?' she said, still more sharply than she ought to.

'Nothing.' Freya's reply was sulky, picking up on her mum's mood.

'Just taking some photos. It's so beautiful here,' said Tatty, her naturally agreeable personality lightening the atmosphere somewhat as everyone nodded their appreciation too.

'Let's have a look.' Darcy decided to make an effort, not wanting to be the one bringing everyone down again. She hated the thought that Jon might be making a constant comparison between her and Alex. Alex already beat her hands down on looks; she refused to let her win on personality too. Darcy knew she was allowing herself to be cast as the suspicious, nagging wife while Alex was the fun, intrepid, carefree one, but she felt powerless to do anything about it.

Tatty obliged, sliding along in her seat so she could show Darcy the pictures on her phone. Darcy admired shot after shot of the beautiful views interspersed with selfies. She lingered on one of the two daughters together with one of the islands behind them and smiled. 'You two really do look similar,' she mused.

'They really do,' said Alex. Darcy caught her eye, registering the amusement on her face. There was something there; she knew it. Alex was laughing at *her*.

Darcy turned to Jon but he was looking out to the ocean and the islands, a fixed smile on his face that didn't reach his eyes.

Tatty is seventeen, Darcy realised, the full implication of what she'd overheard slamming her with a force so strong that she physically jolted. Seventeen. Older than they'd thought.

It was April, so quick calculations told her Tatty must have been conceived no later than the summer of 1999, maybe a bit earlier, depending on when her birthday was. But Alex was still living in the UK in the summer of 1999. She couldn't have met Kyle Kaplan by then because she said she'd met him in Spain.

So, according to Alex's own story, Kyle Kaplan couldn't possibly be Tatty's father.

Darcy looked again to Alex, who was still smiling at her. Could Alex see the mental calculations she was doing? And surely, Darcy allowed the pernicious thought to creep in, this couldn't have anything to do with Jon? She and Jon were together by the summer of 1999. Since then, Jon had only been hers. He'd been devoted to her. Alex had been nothing more than a trifling annoyance to him, mooning around after him like a schoolgirl stalker.

Darcy sat absolutely still. She refused to join the dots in her head.

She knew it absolutely couldn't be that. Anything but that.

Libby and Erika returned to the table. 'What's the joke?' Erika asked, taking in Alex's wry smile.

I am, Darcy thought.

She looked again at Jon, who seemed to be struggling to hold it together. Had something happened between them? Was that why she kept finding them whispering in corners? And was that what Erika and Libby had been hinting at when they hadn't known she could hear them?

Darcy slipped away to get another plastic cup of the slightly warm Croatian Graševina. She felt them all looking at her but she didn't care. They all had their secrets, why couldn't she have hers? But who could she even trust anymore? Everyone was whispering about her or outright laughing at her to her face. She threw half of the wine back in one gulp and grimaced.

Darcy knew she was spinning out of control but she felt betrayed by all of them, even Freya – although she knew how stupid and unfair she was being – for looking like Tatty and for thinking Alex was a better, or at least a more fun, mum than she was.

'Are you OK, madam?' One of the young crew had appeared beside her. The 'bar' was a serve-yourself affair with two cool boxes set out for people to take from as they wished, but the crew kept an eye on it, topping it up where necessary and making sure no one overindulged.

Darcy looked at him guiltily. Was he here to chastise her for drinking too much? 'Oh, yes, yes. I'm sorry.' She indicated the half-empty cup. 'I've had a bit of bad news.'

'Sorry to hear that, madam.' He reached for the Graševina and topped her up again. 'Please do not worry. Enjoy.'

The young man's kindness made Darcy want to cry. Looking at him, she grieved for her younger self, so buried now under years of responsibility and the humdrum realities of life. She'd had no idea how lucky she was then to be young and beautiful and so full of energy and potential.

What she wouldn't have given to go back now and tell the young Darcy to appreciate her youth, her looks, her power. That power she'd once had over people, when everyone was desperate to be her friend or her boyfriend. Maybe find a way to hold onto it this time rather than throwing it away and settling for such a small, insignificant life; one that could be so easily snatched from her by the reappearance of an old enemy.

Darcy shook herself as the man backed away from her intense stare. She was becoming an embarrassment, she realised; one of those women of a certain age who couldn't hold their wine and got maudlin in social situations, making people uncomfortable. She was one step away from taking out photos of herself when she was younger and asking people to agree that she was lovely back in the day.

Erika joined her at the makeshift 'bar' and opened a bottle of lager. 'Everything OK, Darce?' she asked lightly.

Darcy was desperate to ask her about the conversation with Libby but she couldn't find the words. Yesterday, she'd felt like she and Erika were growing close again but now there was this unspoken chasm between them. Instead, she blurted, 'Are you sleeping with someone from work?'

Erika blanched. 'What?'

Darcy couldn't take it back now. 'Are you sleeping with someone?' she repeated, more softly this time. Erika's love life was way down the list of things she had to worry about, but it still upset her that Erika might have confided in Alex and not her. In her mind it had become tangled up with everything else, adding to the sense that everyone was talking behind her back. That everyone was having affairs, of which she knew nothing, left, right and centre.

'No, I'm not,' Erika said, equally quietly. 'But there's obviously a reason you asked me that so, go on.' She looked at Darcy and set her jaw firmly. 'Tell me. Why did you say that?'

'Alex.' Darcy looked over to their table where Alex was holding court, throwing her head back and laughing uproariously at something. What could be *that* funny?

'Alex told you I was sleeping with someone from work?'

Darcy nodded. 'A younger guy. Someone junior.'

Erika laughed humourlessly. 'She really is a piece of work, isn't she? No, I'm not *sleeping with* anyone, actually,' she continued. 'What I'd said to her was that I'd come dangerously close to it.'

Darcy opened her mouth to speak, but Erika put her hand up to stop her. 'Nothing happened. It was a flirtation that got out of control. I stopped it.'

'Who?'

'No one you know. Honestly,' Erika added, as Darcy went to speak again. 'He's only been there a few months and, really, the least said about this the better. It's so inappropriate. I was torn for a while because we clicked and I could tell he wanted more, but I couldn't risk my job. That's it; end of story.'

Darcy looked at Erika, who now had her arms folded and was looking at her confrontationally, like she was daring her to say more. 'I'm not going to judge you,

Erika,' she said eventually. 'Your private life is your business. I just felt a bit sad that you confided in Alex but not me.'

Erika sighed. 'I should have known.' She picked up her beer and swigged it before chuckling sadly to herself.

'What?'

'You're not interested in my life, or what I might be upset about. You're just bothered about me talking to Alex. It always comes back to you, doesn't it?' Erika took a second bottle of lager from the cool box and turned to go back to the table. 'You know what? I'm sick of it. You're both as bad as each other.'

Darcy watched her go. 'Fantastic,' she said, to no one in particular.

16

2017 – Darcy

'Oh, you guys . . . I said I didn't want any fuss!'

Darcy saw Libby blush as she accepted the glitzy, plasticky tiara that Alex handed her. The table was festooned with hen party paraphernalia, everything pink and penis-themed, all the result of Alex's handiwork.

'It's your hen do, missy, and unlike me, you're only going to do this once!' Alex laughed at her own joke. 'We are halfway through the week, and tonight is the girls' night!' She popped open a bottle of prosecco that was sitting in an ice bucket and gave a whooping, joyful cheer, which Darcy made an effort to join in with.

The four women were in the hotel restaurant that opened out onto the patio bar beside the pool. Alex had booked the table, wheedling, 'Be there for Libby,' when Darcy was tempted to tell her to stick it. Erika also seemed unimpressed but, Darcy acknowledged, that might have been more to do with the conversation on the boat. It had been deeply awkward between them for the rest of the day.

Darcy was annoyed that once again Alex had taken over everything, but also felt too bogged down by her own demons to stop her. Despite offering for Jon to take care of the girls, Alex had insisted that he have a night off too, telling him to chill out in the room and get food ordered in – a suggestion he was only too happy to agree to. Then she'd set up Tatty and Freya in her room with a pile of snacks and her permission to order any pay-per-view movie they wanted, as long as it wasn't rated 18 – or 15, she added with a glance at Freya.

As she got changed for the evening, Darcy had raided the wardrobe, looking again for the missing top. She eventually found it scrunched in the corner; theoretically it could have fallen down and got pushed to the side when they were searching for it, but Darcy thought it looked far more like someone had deliberately tried to hide it. She couldn't wear it anyway, she decided, not now everyone had seen Alex sporting her smaller version.

No one actually wanted to be there, Darcy thought, as Alex poured the fizz. They'd spent all day together and everyone had their own issues going on. The atmosphere was tense and the conversation was stop-start.

'Erika, thanks again for talking to Tatty about work experience. That was really kind of you,' Alex said, injecting lightness into her voice

'She's a good kid. Well,' Erika amended, squinting at Alex, 'she's not really a kid, is she?'

Darcy's tummy turned over; she really didn't want to hear anything about this again.

'Yeah, I believe you all thought she was a bit younger than she is?' Alex smiled.

Libby looked at her aghast and Darcy shivered as the atmosphere turned a few degrees cooler than it had been, even beforehand. Erika gave a sarcastic tilt of her head. 'I guess I was just confused as to how you'd managed to meet Kyle before you went to Spain.'

Alex's smile didn't budge. 'Kyle's not Tatty's biological father.'

Darcy saw Erika's face fall as Alex laughed, adding, 'Don't worry! Both of them know that; it's not a secret.'

'But she refers to him as Daddy?' Erika frowned.

'He *is* her daddy as far as she's concerned. He's been in her life since she was a baby and they adore each other.' Darcy speared an olive, wishing spitefully that it was Alex's face, poking it repeatedly as Alex continued. 'He wanted to adopt her but that would have meant me getting in touch with her biological father to request his permission and that would have been . . . complicated.'

'Alex.' Darcy heard the warning tone in Libby's voice.

'Oh, that reminds me, I haven't taken my pill.' Alex jumped up, and Darcy risked a glance at her. Her cheeks were flushed with merriment, while the rest of them looked more like they were attending a funeral than a hen do.

'I'll check on the girls while I'm up there. If the food comes out, don't wait for me – it's not like my salad will get cold!' Alex laughed heartily at her own joke and then strutted off towards the lifts.

'So.' Darcy broke the silence left in Alex's wake; Libby was fiddling with her handbag and Erika was staring resolutely into her glass. 'Kyle isn't Tatty's father.'

Darcy noticed the other two share a quick glance and felt her own face flame with irritation. 'That's a bombshell, don't you think?'

Erika opened her mouth, hesitated, then closed it again.

'Yeah,' said Libby eventually, her eyes still focused on her bag strap. 'Bit weird.'

Darcy dropped her hand on the table, making the olive bowl clatter on its saucer and forcing Libby and Erika to look at her. 'No, it's not a *bit weird*. It's huge. And I think you'd both be saying a lot more about this if you thought I couldn't hear you.'

'We—what?' Erika frowned as Darcy sat back in her seat, taking a long draw on her wine. 'What do you mean?'

'I heard you two on the boat.' Darcy's voice wavered and she shook herself to recapture her composure. 'When I was in the toilet. You were making . . .' she took another sip, reaching for the right word, 'insinuations.'

Libby put her head in her hands.

'What did you hear?' demanded Erika.

'The stuff about Lexie Kaplan and the secret Facebook page which, by the way, I searched for myself when we got back and I couldn't find it either. And,' she paused meaningfully, 'the fact that you two didn't think Jon could be left alone with Alex in case she – what was the word?' Darcy eyeballed Erika. 'Jumped him.'

Erika laughed unconvincingly. 'That wasn't serious.'

'Really?' Darcy wasn't laughing at all.

'Really. I just think Alex is a terrible flirt. It's about her, not specifically about Jon.'

Libby looked up from clasping and unclasping her bag. 'It's nothing, Darcy. Jon is fine.'

Darcy turned her attention to her. 'Who said he wasn't?'

Libby floundered, shrinking under Darcy's glare. 'I just mean . . .'

'See, I think you know something.' Darcy reached for the prosecco bottle and topped herself up. 'I think that's why you're being so quiet.'

'I don't. I—'

'You said something on the boat about ancient history.' Darcy pointed at Libby with the little silver olive spear, and watched as her friend shifted uncomfortably.

'Can we just take this down a notch?' Erika put her hands out to Darcy, but the appeal for calm had the opposite effect.

'You don't need to tell me how to behave.' Darcy took another gulp and almost shouted, 'I'm not the liar here!'

'I'm not lying,' Libby whispered eventually, looking at Erika, a sheen of tears in her eyes.

'We all knew she liked him back then, if that's what you're talking about,' said Erika.

Darcy shook her head. 'It's more than that.'

'OK, ladies, I have the pasta?' The waiter arrived with a charming smile.

Libby nodded and they all accepted their dishes with quiet thanks, looking at Alex's salad as the waiter retreated.

'She's been gone a while.' Darcy reached once more for her glass.

Erika shrugged. 'She said not to wait for her.'

They sat in silence for a full minute. 'This is ridiculous. What's she playing at?' Darcy stood up, wobbling slightly as the effect of the last few glasses took hold.

'Where are you going?' Libby asked, her face a picture of concern.

'I'm going to find her.'

'Don't, Darcy.'

'Just leave her, she'll be back in a minute,' Erika added.

'I'm going to find her,' Darcy repeated, looping her bag over her shoulder, mumbling to herself as she walked away. 'And I'm going to find out what the hell she's playing at.'

With the stunned silence she'd left at the table weighing heavily on her, Darcy made her unsteady way to the lifts and rehearsed her opening line in her head. *Is all this about me?* That was what she wanted to say, but feared it sounded pathetic, and she needed to be strong. She needed to find a way to regain control and establish something more like the dynamic they'd had at school. 'When I always won,' she muttered out loud as she stabbed the lift buttons repeatedly, earning herself a sideways glance from the other people waiting.

When she reached their floor, she squared her shoulders and took a deep breath, striding to Alex's room on a wave of wine-enhanced assurance. 'Just what is your problem?' she rehearsed to herself as she rapped her knuckles on the door. Her hand was tender from where she had slammed the table earlier, so she massaged it with the other hand as she waited for the door to open.

'Just what is your problem?' she repeated, as the door swung open.

'Mum?' Freya looked up at her, concerned. 'What's wrong?'

'Oh!' Darcy took a step back. 'Oh, Freya, love. I was . . .' She shook her head. 'Is Alex here?'

Darcy noticed Tatty's head peering curiously round the corner from the end of the bed, surrounded by half-empty crisp bags and chocolate wrappers. On the TV, *Titanic* was blaring out and Jack was about to draw Rose like one of his French girls. Tatty reached for the remote and pressed pause, Kate Winslet's boob on the screen distracting Darcy as she shook her head again.

'Sorry, Tatty, is your mum here? It's just . . . the food has arrived and she's been gone ages.'

Tatty shook her head. 'She was here but she went a while ago.'

Then Tatty wrinkled her nose in a way that reminded Darcy of Freya when she was feeling uncomfortable or awkward about something. Was she Jon's? Darcy couldn't believe she was even asking herself such a question, but she had to admit that the evidence was mounting. *Complicated*, that was the word Alex had used. Jesus. The thought was unbearable, overwhelming.

'Are you OK?' Tatty said eventually, shaking Darcy from her introspection.

'I'm . . . yes. Yes. I'm fine, thank you. I probably just crossed over with her on the way here.' Darcy backed out of the doorway. 'Freya, are you having a nice evening?'

Freya glanced at the boob frozen on the screen, then to Tatty and back to her mum. She shrugged. 'Fine.'

Darcy forced herself to smile at the girls before bidding them good evening and soon found herself back in the hallway, discombobulated, with the door closed in her face.

She dithered on the spot; should she stop by her own room and talk to Jon? They were becoming like strangers. She needed his reassurance. Yes, she decided, heading in that direction. They needed to hold each other and be honest. She wasn't going to let paranoia get the better of her.

Yet . . . she hesitated. She was tipsy and riled up and very likely to start an argument if she charged in there the way she felt at that moment. She changed her mind and pivoted in the other direction.

No. She stopped again. This needed sorting now. She wasn't going to let Alex, or anyone, drive a wedge between them. She, Jon and Freya were a family and that connection between them was precious. She swung around again, vowing to keep it positive. No accusations or recriminations. Anything that might have happened in the past would be a hard pill to swallow, but in no way did the past compare to what they had now.

Darcy swiped her key card and swung open the door. She was halfway across the room when she registered the moving shapes on the bed, her bed. Their bed.

'Darcy!' Jon saw her first. 'Fuck.'

Darcy froze, her eyes locked on his, lying flat on their bed as Alex rode him. His hands, which had been gripping Alex's arse, were now working on pushing her away.

Darcy couldn't tear her gaze from Jon's but she was aware of Alex rolling off, treating her to a view of her smooth, unblemished body and augmented tits pointing proudly at her.

'Oh, my gosh, Darcy, I'm *so sorry*.' Insincerity oozed from Alex's voice as she bit her lip theatrically, and slowly – slowly – reached for a sheet to cover herself.

Darcy finally met her eyes, feeling her own burning with hate. She was frightened to open her mouth and say anything in case she vomited over the pair of them.

Then, Alex laughed. She laughed and laughed, Darcy and Jon both staring at her, appalled, as she rolled back onto the bed, hooting with uncontrolled, uproarious laughter.

'You fucking psycho,' Darcy spat out, eventually.

'Darcy, please talk to me. I can explain.' Jon finally gathered his senses, slid away from Alex and swung his feet onto the floor, scrabbling around for his pants.

Darcy turned her glare back to him. Tears pinpricked her eyes, sparkling diamond-hard. 'I hope that bitch was worth it.'

She turned and fled, Alex's mocking laughter still ringing in her ears.

17

1999 – Alex

I hadn't wanted to go to the Leavers' Ball; it was the last thing I felt like doing. Two years of sixth form were already over and I didn't feel I had much to show for it. I was fairly sure I'd failed all my exams; all I could think of was Jonny moving home from uni and making his choice between me and Darcy.

It had been over a year that we'd been meeting up whenever he came home. I knew he met her too, but he said they were still just friends and I was happy to keep our relationship quiet in case it motivated Darcy to go after him.

Until recently, I was sure he would be coming home to me, despite them spending so much time together. It was still me he came back to, over and over, to kiss and hold and make love with. It had to count for something, didn't it?

I'd never been happy about the fact they'd stayed friends but I was playing it cool, being the non-demanding, happy-go-lucky girl I knew he needed me to be. We were still young and I wasn't going to tie him down. As long as he kept returning to my arms, I knew I still had him.

But that last time, when he'd been home for Easter, it had been different. I sensed a shift in the way he spoke to me, in his reluctance to hold me. Then he shattered my dreams. He told me that he was seeing Darcy and they were going to go public as soon as he was back home.

This was it, I'd thought. It was time to put my heart on my sleeve and tell him it wasn't just sex – I really did love him. Perhaps he'd gone to Darcy because he thought I didn't care enough? So I told him and I waited for the relief on his face and for him to say he'd always loved me too, but he'd been scared to show it. I waited and waited. He seemed unable to find the words.

When he told me that he didn't feel that way about me – told me that I was a great girl, but he'd always thought we were just having fun – the bottom dropped out of my world. I'd been everything he'd wanted me to be, trusting that eventually he'd accept that I was the one, and in the end, it meant nothing. It counted for nothing. And worse than that, the person he *did* love, the one he *did* think was worth the effort, was the person I hated most.

Red mist descended and I'd told him in no uncertain terms that if he finished things with me, I would make damn sure that Darcy knew all about us. I'd tell her every filthy detail. All the times he'd been at her house for tea and cakes with her family before driving straight over to my house and shagging me in the back seat of his car. The time she'd phoned him and he couldn't pick up because I was going down on him; her stupid, stuck-up voice ringing through his parents' house, amplified on the answer machine, rambling on about some film they were going to see together, all while I was sucking him off.

'Do you think she'd want you then? Do you?' I'd snapped, all pretence of being cool and laid back completely washed away.

He looked terrified. It occurred to me, perhaps he was just scared of being caught out and made to look the bad guy. So I told him if he kept seeing me, she'd never need to know. I needed to keep hold of him somehow. I hated the idea of sharing him with her, but to lose him entirely was unthinkable.

I knew he wasn't convinced but I used every weapon in my arsenal to work on him. He was reluctant when I moved towards him, which hurt like hell, but I pushed on; I hadn't spent the last year and more being shown exactly how to please him without learning a trick or two about how to turn him on. In the end, he surrendered himself to me and I was victorious. As long as I could make him feel like that, he was mine. Partly, anyway.

Since then, I'd been a coiled spring of anxiety, waiting for Darcy to announce they were a couple, although she'd said nothing to me. And as if that wasn't stressful enough, we'd all had coursework deadlines and revision and university applications and exams – *and* then my parents decided that was the moment to sell up and retire to Spain, just as the absolute cherry on the cake.

'But where will I live?' I'd blurted out, too shocked to notice I was bursting their bubble of a big, happy announcement.

They'd patiently explained to me that the family home would be in Spain and I would go and see them there in the holidays – 'Won't that be nice?' – but as I'd be off to uni soon, there was little point them staying around when they were keen to go.

'Your dad's sixty next year, Ally, and I'm not far behind. We want to go while we can still enjoy ourselves.' Mum looked sad and I didn't want to add 'pissing on my parents' dreams' to my list of woes, so I'd had to accept it. I was aware they were that bit older than all my friends' parents but recently I'd been too wrapped up in my own dramas to pay them much attention.

Mum was keen to spend some time with me before they went and insisted on taking me shopping for a dress to wear to the Leavers' Ball. We spent an afternoon in Guildford (me constantly looking out for Jonny, even though I knew he was still in Southampton), perusing the department stores and eventually choosing a tight-fitting floor-length gown in scarlet that only someone as skinny as me could pull off. It had tiny spaghetti straps that suited my shape but would have looked obscene on

Darcy, so I knew there was no chance of her choosing something similar.

After Mum bought me the dress as a *well done for passing your exams* gift (I didn't have the heart to tell her not to count her chickens on the exam front as we were having such a nice day), we went for coffee and, over our massive *Friends*-style mugs, she gently interrogated me about whether I'd be going to the ball with 'the boy I was seeing' or not.

'Mum! I'm not seeing anyone.' I blew on my coffee to avoid her eyes.

'Ally, I'm not stupid. I know you're going out with that boy with the car. And I know you don't want to talk about it!' she added quickly, as I started to protest. 'You don't have to tell me your business; you'll be eighteen soon.' She gave me a little smile. 'But just promise me that whoever he is, you make sure he treats you right. OK?'

I gave her a nod and looked away again, mortified by the whole conversation.

'I mean it, Ally.' She was sterner now. 'For a long time I was worried that you didn't know your own worth. You deserve a decent young man.'

'Shudurrrp.' I covered my face.

'All right, that's all I'll say. Just know that any young man would be lucky to have you for his girlfriend, and if they don't appreciate that, then they're not right for you.'

I dismissed her words, sweet and well-meaning as they were, because she didn't understand what the world was like nowadays. It might have been different in her day, when men were gentlemen and women were ladies and everyone waited until they got married before they had sex and everyone stayed faithful forever, but it wasn't like that anymore. Girls had to be everything; they had to have it all. They had to be funny and fit and brave and have *girl power*, but they were also supposed to be vulnerable and virginal and fragile so men wanted to protect them. They had to be ladettes but also ladylike. It was exhausting.

Getting dressed for the ball – a laughably grand title – I thought again about how I didn't want to go. I'd never fully embraced the social scene at sixth form, staying close to Libby rather than making many new friends (unlike Darcy, who seemed to be friends with our entire year group), and with my head so full of Jonny, I was never interested in meeting any boys. The same went for my studies; I'd coasted the classes, never fully engaging, just doing the bare minimum so my mind was free to go to its happy place – imagining me and Jonny together away from everyone else.

Annoyingly, I was relying on Darcy for a lift that night. She'd offered to drive us all during a lecture about how she didn't need to drink to have fun, but mainly she wanted to save her money for uni. We'd all been learning to drive, but with her September birthday, she'd had the head start and was the first to pass her test.

I was the last to be collected even though my parents' house was only a few streets away from Darcy's. That was her way of showing me that I was the lowest on her pecking order and also that she didn't want to be in the car with me for any longer than was necessary. The feeling was mutual. When she pulled up in her old but well-maintained Mini Metro, I saw that Kitty, one of Darcy's new friends, was in the front; Erika was sitting, arms folded, in the back, Libby with her big dress bunched up against her in the middle seat so that I had room to take the final place. My dress was so tight I had to go in bum-first and then swing my legs around, which made everyone laugh, even Libby, although hers was good-natured.

'My goodness, Al, how can you breathe in that dress? It's gorgeous by the way,' she added, from under a lap's worth of chiffon.

'Yours too,' I said, straightening out a few of her layers so I could see the top half of her. She looked particularly radiant, despite being buried alive under her own dress, and I wondered if she was hoping to see any particular boy that night. With a stab of guilt, it occurred to me that I knew almost nothing about her love life. Lately, all we'd talked about was the fictional G and how I thought it was over because it looked like he was going to make a go of things with his wife. It was the only way I could vent about Jonny without breaking my cover. She knew I was upset and was always there for me to talk to, yet I'd rarely reciprocated. I didn't even know if she liked anyone. I was a bad friend, on top of being the girl that nobody wanted. I despised myself.

Arriving at the venue, it soon became clear just how low budget an event this 'ball' really was. The planning committee had decided on a big blowout with low ticket prices to save more money for booze. So here we were in the function room of the local cricket club (decorated with tissue pompoms), looking at a buffet consisting of twiglets and a cheese-and-pineapple hedgehog and with someone's big brother on the decks as entertainment.

Darcy and Kitty were swept away to see Dazza's new tattoo, whoever Dazza was, as soon as we walked in. The rest of us hovered in the doorway.

'I'm really glad I bought a new dress for this,' Erika said, looking around her like she could smell something nasty.

'Ah, come on, it'll be a laugh.' Libby dug her in the ribs. With her huge taffeta number, Erika's formal jade green gown and my floor-length satin sheath, we did look as if we were going to the opera rather than a low-budget teenage party. 'Let's get drunk.'

I was still underage, with my eighteenth not until the following month, so the plan was for the others to get my drinks while I held us a table. There was little chance of my fake student ID passing muster in here with so many tutors around. I thought fondly of it though, as I found us a table, because it reminded me of when we first met Jonny and my life had changed. I was a girl then and I was a woman now. I'd spent my whole time at sixth-form college being in love with him.

Maybe if you hadn't been, you'd have had a better time of it, a treacherous voice in my head said. That voice had snuck through a few times since Easter when Jonny declared himself in love with Darcy. That voice told me I'd wasted my time and that he wasn't worth it. I ignored it of course, because I didn't know who I would be if it weren't for Jonny. I'd created a whole persona based around what I thought he wanted me to be. I couldn't go back to the girl I was before; she was long gone.

I simply couldn't lose him, or I'd lose myself too.

Libby and Erika returned from the bar clutching three bottles of Smirnoff Ice and three shots of something green. 'Shots are a pound each!' Libby declared happily, as they offloaded the drinks onto the table before me.

'What are they?' I took a sniff of one and was none the wiser.

'I dunno, apple something.' Libby picked one up. 'Happy Leavers' Ball!'

She tipped her head back and downed it before I had even finished repeating her toast, wincing as she slammed the glass back down on the table.

'It's going to be one of those nights, is it?' Erika grinned. 'Fine by me. *Prost!*'

'*Prost!*' we chorused back, making sure to make eye contact with her because she'd told us so many times if you don't do that when you toast in Germany, they say it's seven years' bad sex. None of us were prepared to risk that, even though to my knowledge, the other two were still virgins and I only knew how to have sex with one man, and how could that ever be bad, when you loved someone as much as I loved Jonny?

Libby made a start on her Smirnoff Ice as she'd already downed her shot and I started to wonder how soon it would be before they'd need to go up to the bar again at this rate. Luckily, Darcy made herself useful for once, coming by with a bottle of Bud and a glass of something clear which she set down in front of us. 'People keep buying me drinks even though I've told them I'm driving,' she explained. 'Help yourself.'

'What's in that one?' Libby pointed at the glass of clear fizz.

I sniffed it. 'Archers and lemonade?'

'Yeah, I think so.' Darcy started to turn away from us and back to her fans when some other guy I didn't recognise came over to her with a glass of red wine.

'For you, Darcy.' He seemed nervous as he handed it over, shifting from foot to foot.

'Thanks, Tobes.' She put it down on the table with the others and gave him a smile.

'I was wondering if, erm, you were . . . ah.' The guy Darcy called *Tobes* hesitated. 'If you were seeing anyone?' he blurted eventually.

'Oh!' Darcy seemed caught between surprised and amused. 'Well, it's complicated, but yes.' I saw her expression change from unsure to sure. 'Yes, I am actually.'

Tobes' face fell. 'Ah. Oh well. Cool. Good for you. I was just gonna . . . *you know*, but that's cool, that's cool.' The shifting from foot to foot ramped up a notch and Darcy nodded uncomfortably. 'I'm just gonna . . .' Tobes pointed towards the bar and, after one last, painful hesitation, bounced off towards it.

'Oh God!' Darcy exhaled as he left and we all laughed.

Erika shook her head. 'Another one bites the dust.'

'So were you letting him down gently or are you seeing someone, Darce?' Libby had already finished her Smirnoff Ice and was eyeing up the free drinks that Darcy had bestowed on us, her fingers hovering over the Bud, then across to the wine, and then back to the Bud again.

'Bit of both.' Darcy gave a coy, secretive smile. I wished she would pull up a chair and sit down; with her standing, and us looking up at her, I felt like she was some sort of visiting celebrity whose every word we were hanging on to.

'Don't tell me that you and Jon are properly going for it at last?' Erika exclaimed, taking the red wine for herself and pushing the Bud towards Libby, and the Archers towards me.

I tensed. Would she tell them? I really hoped not; I wasn't ready for it to come to a head. Also, I'd noticed that Darcy had recently been referring to him as Jon, rather than Jonny, as if he'd grown out of *Jonny*, and now Erika was doing it too. I didn't like it.

'Kind of.' Darcy was nonchalant at first, then a slow smile split her face in two as she failed to conceal her happiness. Erika gave a little gasp and Libby's eyes widened with surprise. I necked my drink so they couldn't see my face. 'I mean, it's not official yet, but it will be when he comes home from uni. We're going to be together, properly.'

'Oh, Darcy, that's great news. I'm really happy for you.' Libby's enthusiasm was genuine and for a moment I couldn't believe she was being so callous. I stared at her, horrified, before I remembered, of course, she had no clue about anything. She believed G was a totally different man who I'd been seeing all this time, and not just my way of talking about Jonny. I threw back what was left in the glass of Archers and reminded myself to keep my story straight.

'Me too.' Erika was notably less excited, but even in my tense and rapidly becoming tipsy state, I knew this was because Darcy hadn't confided in her. They used to tell each other everything. With becoming so popular and seeing Jonny on the quiet, Darcy had really neglected her recently and Erika was getting more and more fed up about it.

Darcy smiled again; it was like she couldn't help herself. And I hated to acknowledge it, but these smiles were not the nasty, sarcastic ones she threw out when she was jibing at me or generally being unpleasant. She was bursting with genuine happiness. My gut twisted and I looked for something else to drink but everything was finished.

'I'll go.' Erika picked her way to the bar. Darcy slipped into her seat.

'She seems pissed off with me,' Darcy said to Libby. If either of them had noticed I was the only one not to congratulate Darcy on her news, then neither of them were showing it.

'Ah, maybe she was a bit gutted not to know about you and Jonny until now?' Libby voiced what I'd been thinking. Darcy's face fell.

'Of course. I've been so wrapped up in him – Jon – that I haven't really been thinking about much else.'

'You seem really happy.' Libby smiled and squeezed Darcy's arm, making me flinch. I looked around, willing Erika to return with the drinks.

Darcy laughed. 'I am, honestly. I should've been brave enough to ditch Bradley and be with Jon from the start. Me and him together, it's unlike anything I've ever experienced.'

I closed my eyes and willed myself to stand up, go to the loo, go anywhere away from this conversation, but I was rooted to my chair. I had to hear it, torture though it was.

'He's just so loving. He calls me every night now that he's got a mobile. He says he can't wait until we can be together properly.'

I clenched my fists under the table so hard I could feel my nails cutting into my palm. I hadn't even known he'd bought a mobile phone. He'd only ever called me from his parents' house when he was free and wanted to see me, never for a chat. Libby made 'awww' noises and Darcy basked in her admiring attention.

'He told me he's never felt like this before and that he really loves me. He literally says "I love you" every single day on the phone.'

'He's a keeper.' None of us had noticed Erika return but she gave Darcy a smile that didn't quite reach her eyes and unloaded the tray of drinks she was carrying.

Darcy nodded and stood up, indicating that Erika should have her seat back. 'Well, I'd better get back over there.' She indicated to where a gang of people I hardly knew were congregated. 'Kitty wants me to meet her new bloke Tommo; he's one of Doorknob's mates?' Her voice went up at the end of the sentence as if we should

know who Doorknob was. I certainly didn't but I nodded along with everyone else, just so she'd leave quicker.
'Erika . . . do you want to come and hang for a bit?'

Erika looked surprised but nodded and followed her;
Libby gave Darcy a thumbs-up as they departed. Everybody was happy. Everybody but me.

'And then there were two!' Libby said, raising a bottle.
'Cheers!'

'Cheers,' I mumbled into my glass.

18

2017 – Darcy

Returning to the restaurant, it seemed impossible to Darcy that it was less than ten minutes since she'd gone in search of Alex. The room looked as it did when she had left it, the same waiter who'd served them gave her a little smile as she careered past him, and the table was still laid with their plates of barely touched food, adorned with the absurd frippery of a hen night, yet the axis of her world had shifted. How could it still all look the same?

A few moments earlier, as she'd stood in the hallway, unable to process what she'd seen, Darcy's first instinct had been to take Freya and run, to get herself and her daughter as far away as possible from the scene of so much ugliness. Then, as she'd marched back towards Alex's room, she'd faltered. She couldn't let Freya see her like this. Freya deserved at least one parent who considered how their actions would impact her. So Darcy had kept going, heading back to the only people who could perhaps help her make some sense of what she'd just witnessed.

'There you are!' Libby's face was tense and she jumped up in her seat as Darcy staggered towards them. 'Oh, my God, what's wrong?'

'Did you find her?' Erika reached out to take Darcy's arm.

Darcy spat out a laugh and shook away Erika's hand. 'Yes, I found her.' She swayed, looking across the table before spotting her abandoned glass.

'Is that a good idea?' Libby said quietly as Darcy reached for it.

'To be honest,' Darcy paused, picking up the glass and throwing the contents down her throat in one go, 'I don't care if it's a good idea or not.'

Erika tried to reach for her arm again. 'Shall we go and get some air?'

'She was fucking him.' Darcy avoided Erika's hand and spread hers out wide as if conducting the London Philharmonic. 'Congratulations, you two. You were right about that slag jumping him at the first opportunity. She was fucking my husband – in *my* bed. WELL. DONE.'

'Is everything OK here, ladies?' The smiling waiter had appeared, his smile a little more anxious now. Darcy noticed everyone was looking their way.

'Not really, fella.' Darcy smiled back, even in her shock and inebriation registering that she'd called someone *fella* for the first time in her life. 'I've just caught my husband in bed with a sla—'

'We'll go outside,' Erika interjected, gesturing for Libby to help guide Darcy out as the waiter discreetly nodded his understanding.

Trailed by intrigued looks from neighbouring tables, Darcy allowed herself to be shuffled out onto the terrace, past the alfresco diners enjoying the cool evening air and down to the edge of the seating area by the coastal path. Darcy looked up to the balconies of the hotel behind them, trying to work out which one was hers, theirs – what did *theirs* even mean now? She couldn't go back to that room tonight, so where would she sleep? Where would Freya sleep?

'Freya,' she blurted, breaking the silence. 'How am I going to tell Freya? She can't stay in that room tonight, not after . . . that.'

'We'll sort something out, don't worry about that now,' Libby soothed. 'Is she still with Tatty?'

Darcy nodded, tears springing, unbidden, once again. 'Oh yeah.' A brittle laugh. 'She just loves her new half-sister.'

'Darcy!' Libby's voice couldn't hide her shock.

'Well, let's face it, they'd all be happy if I just fucked off and let them be a lovely, happy, *beautiful* family together.'

'You don't mean that!' Erika took Darcy by the shoulders and attempted to lock eye contact as Darcy turned away. 'Freya loves you, and nothing will change that. And no matter what her mother has done, remember Tatty is blameless in all of this.' Erika finally found Darcy's begrudging eyes. 'Surely we're not really thinking that Tatty is Jon's daughter, are we?'

'I don't know, ask her.' Darcy inclined her head towards Libby, who was averting her gaze out to sea. 'You never did answer my question before.'

'Libby?' Erika turned to her. 'Do you know something? Like, really know something? From before?'

Libby took her time, sitting on the edge of the wall around the terrace. When she finally raised her eyes to face the other two, they were awash with tears.

'Libby?' Erika repeated. 'You're scaring me now.'

Darcy laughed, a violent 'hah!' that reverberated around them in the starlit darkness. 'You're scared?' She turned to Libby. 'Tell me, right now, what you know. And tell me,' Darcy moved to stand over her, 'why you've sat on her secrets for all this time.'

'Because I forgot!' Libby blurted out, her hot tears drawing lines of diluted mascara down her face. 'I didn't even know if it was true.'

'What was true?' Erika looked between the two women.

'Which was it?' Darcy demanded at the same time. 'You didn't know, or you forgot?'

Libby gulped her tears and rubbed her face with the backs of her hands. 'Both.'

'Oh! Classic Libby.' Darcy gave another bitter laugh. 'Of course I couldn't expect a straight answer, even about something as important as this.'

'Stop it, Darcy.' Erika spoke quietly, but firmly. 'I know you're upset but can't you see she is too?'

Erika moved and sat on the wall next to Libby. 'Just tell us what you know, Libs. No one's blaming you.' She gave Darcy a steely glare and indicated a chair from an empty table at the edge of the terrace.

Sighing, Darcy, dragged it over and sat opposite them. 'Come on then.'

Libby took a deep breath. 'Apparently, or so she told me, years ago at the Leavers' Ball, remember at the end of sixth form?' The others nodded. 'She told me that night she'd been sleeping with Jon.' Libby's voice faltered as she registered Darcy's expression. 'That's why we fell out that night. I was standing up for you.'

'She was sleeping with him then?' Darcy's face was ashen, ghostly in the dim lights of the terrace. 'At the Leavers' Ball? We were together then. We'd been together for a while.'

'Was it a one-off, do you know?' Erika probed. 'Or was she . . . were they . . .?' She tailed off, looking at Darcy and then back to Libby.

Libby looked helpless. 'I genuinely don't remember much of the conversation, I was so drunk that night, we were doing shots, drinking all those random drinks guys kept buying you – you have to believe me, Darcy,' she implored. 'The only reason I've never said anything is because I'd blanked it out. Alex reminded me about it the other night.'

'When?' Darcy and Erika spoke together; at any other time they would have laughed and called 'Jinx!', Darcy thought, but not then.

'At the Cave Bar.' Libby rummaged for a tissue and blew her nose.

'That's why you've been so suspicious of her.' Erika nodded. 'And it means that—' She brought up short, horror on her face.

'That Tatty really could be Jon's.' Darcy sighed again, resignation on her tear-stained face. 'I knew it. I just had a feeling, seeing them together.'

Erika hesitated, then added, 'I had a feeling too. The dates didn't add up when we found out that Tatty was older than we thought and when I saw the Lexie Kaplan profile on Facebook. Tatty was a flower girl when Alex married Kyle.'

'That doesn't mean she's Jon's.' Libby was still hopeful, Darcy registered, despite the evidence that was piling up, and she didn't know whether to envy her optimism or despise her for it.

'Tatty told me, when we were talking about work experience, that she'd just turned seventeen. So she must have been conceived in the summer of 1999.'

'And if *she* was sleeping with Jon at the Leavers' Ball then the dates would add up perfectly.' Darcy sat back in her chair. 'So not only have they betrayed me, not only have they *fucked* on this holiday, but my husband has had another daughter all this time.'

'Do you think . . .?' Erika hesitated, and then added, 'No.'

'What?'

'Do you think he knows? Has it been . . .?'

'Has it been going on all this time, do you mean?' Darcy shook her head. 'I don't know what to believe anymore.'

'No,' said Libby. 'It can't have been. She's been out of the country. If she'd been back, I'd have known about it.'

'Oh, grow up!' Darcy slammed her hands on the arm of her chair, her right one still tender from where she'd bashed it earlier. 'Alex Rigby only does something if it suits her. Stop imagining she's some great friend to you, Libby, she's used you as much as any of us. Why do you think she wanted to come on this holiday?' she demanded, jumping out of her seat now and leaning in towards Libby's tearful face. 'To celebrate your wedding, because she's so loyal to you? So loyal, she fucked my husband and then fucked off into the sunset for the best part of twenty years, only to come back and . . . fuck up absolutely everything.'

'Stop it, please,' Libby whispered. 'People are looking.'

Incandescent, Darcy spun around and saw the diners at the rear of the terrace, bathed in the warm light of the restaurant behind them, trying and failing not to look interested. 'Sorry to interrupt your dinner!' Darcy called to them in an icy *Downton Abbey* accent, with a regal little wave. 'I've just found out that my husband has been cheating on me since we first met and has a daughter with another woman. You'll excuse me for being somewhat peeved!'

Erika put her hand on Darcy's arm. 'That's enough.'

'I'll say it is!' Darcy agreed, turning to stride back towards the hotel.

'Where are you going?' Erika was swiftly following behind, leaving Libby on the wall, head in hands.

'I'm going to get my daughter.'

'Please, at least calm down before you speak to her, Darcy. *Darcy!*' Erika repeated as Darcy strode ahead, past the tables of diners pretending to study their plates.

Inside, Darcy pivoted back to face her friend. 'You always say there's nothing more annoying than being told to calm down.'

Erika acknowledged that with a tilt of the head. 'Yes. But in this case I'm thinking of Freya. Please don't go to her like this.' She slipped her hand into her jacket pocket and withdrew her key card. 'Go to my room, sit and breathe for a minute. Maybe have some coffee?' She looked pointedly at Darcy, who was swaying slightly. 'I can get Freya and bring her to the room once you've had a chance to decompress a bit?'

Darcy considered Erika's words. 'You're right, I know you're right. Oh God.' She slumped against the wall and ran her hands over her face. 'How can I tell her?'

Erika sighed. 'Maybe you don't need to, not everything? Not tonight anyway? We could concoct something plausible, later.'

Darcy winced at the word *concoct*. 'More lies? No.' She shook her head. 'My daughter deserves better. I'm going to have to get it over with.'

'I'll come with you then.' Erika made to follow her, but Darcy put her hand out.

'Go to Libby, she's on her own out there.'

'You sure?'

'Honestly. It will be OK, I won't say anything to upset the girls. I just need to get Freya out of there.. And tell Libby I'm sorry I shouted at her,' Darcy added, as Erika nodded her understanding but still seemed reluctant to leave her.

'Go.' Darcy insisted, propelling her friend towards the terrace and watching as she disappeared into the darkness. 'I need to be with my daughter.'

19

2017 – Darcy

Darcy headed to the lifts, retracing the journey she'd made a short while before in not exactly blissful ignorance, but certainly without the weight of despair that was dragging her down this time. Pressing the button for her floor was an effort, stepping into the lift's bright light was an assault on her senses. She wanted to crawl into bed and never come out again.

Outside Alex's room, Darcy took a moment to wipe under her eyes and run her fingers through her hair. She knew she mustn't frighten Freya by steaming in with all her naked hurt and anger blazing across her features. 'Calm,' she said quietly, forcing herself to regulate her breathing. 'You can do this.'

Steeling herself, she rapped the door, half imagining that she'd find Jon and Alex in there with them, all sitting on the bed, laughing like a happy family. Laughing at *her*. But when the door swung open it was Tatty, a quizzical look on her face. 'Hi again?'

Behind her on the screen, the *Titanic* was about to go under and Freya was at the edge of the bed, knees hunched up to her chest.

Darcy nodded at Tatty and pushed past her, unwilling to look too closely at her face or engage with her in any way. 'Freya, love. Come on, we need to go.'

'Go where?' Freya didn't take her eyes off the screen.

'Back to our . . .' *Shit*, thought Darcy, she should have sorted out another room before coming for Freya. 'Back to the, erm, the room.'

'Nooo, I wanna see the end of this!' Freya groaned. 'It's nearly finished.'

'There's still about an hour left actually,' Tatty dead-panned. 'This is one long-ass movie!'

Darcy ignored her. 'Come on, Freya, I mean it. You can finish this another time.'

'Why?' Freya dragged out the word with a whine in her voice. 'It's not fair!'

'Well, life isn't always.' Darcy gathered up Freya's trainers that were kicked off at the side of the bed and prodded her arm to prompt her to move.

'Ow! What is wrong with you tonight, Mum?' Freya swung angry eyes at Darcy. 'Why are you being like this?'

Darcy bit her lip; she couldn't lose her temper. 'I'm not being *like* anything,' she said eventually. 'I just need you to come right now, so stop arguing and get your arse off that bed.'

'Is everything OK, Darcy?' Tatty asked.

Darcy forced herself to look at the girl. She'd asked politely enough and with none of the attitude that Freya was giving her, but Darcy felt the urge to scream at her all the same. When she registered her delicate features and creamy complexion, all she could see was the horror that she'd walked into earlier. Tatty was here because Alex had done *that*, with her husband, and she couldn't help but resent the girl.

'Not really, Tatty, as you ask. I've got to give Freya some bad news.'

'Is Dad OK?'

She had Freya's attention now. Wide-eyed and worried that something terrible had happened to her father, she was now looking at Darcy for reassurance.

Darcy opened her mouth and then closed it again with a sigh. Was this going to hurt Freya even more than the scenarios her daughter was currently imagining? If he'd hurt himself or was ill – nothing life-threatening, obviously – Freya would be scared for him, but ulti-mately rally, and his position as top number one guy in her world would remain unsullied. She could deal with that. But this was going to break her daughter's heart in a totally different way.

'He's fine,' said a voice behind them. Darcy jumped in surprise. Alex had let herself in.

'Mom, what's going on?' Tatty looked concerned.

Alex's eyes were downcast, her face a picture of contrition. 'It's OK, hon, nothing to worry about. I just need to talk to Darcy for a moment.'

Darcy had recoiled as soon as she'd seen Alex enter the room; upon hearing this, she immediately shook her head. 'No. No way. Come on, Freya.'

'Darcy, please.' Alex held her hands up. 'I'm so sorry about . . . before. Please would you just give me a few minutes to explain?' Her eyes were wide, imploring; the expression on her face made Darcy want to slap her.

'Please,' Alex repeated. 'I totally understand how you must be feeling but maybe talking about it will help? Freya can stay here with Tatty.'

Darcy hesitated as Freya looked between the adults, one foot on the floor ready to follow her mum, frozen in confusion. The last thing Darcy wanted was to spend more time with Alex, but she *did* want answers.

'Mom? What are you talking about? What happened before?' Tatty hovered between them. 'You're freaking me out.'

'I'll tell you later, sweetie.' Alex squeezed her hand. 'I promise it's nothing for you girls to worry about, but I did upset Freya's mum earlier and I just want to talk it out with her.' She turned her beseeching eyes on Darcy again. 'Maybe a chance to apologise, and try to explain?'

Darcy sighed. She needed to keep it together for Freya. It would be so easy to lay into Alex and tell their daughters everything that she'd found out that night, but someone had to be the adult in the room. Someone had to keep some dignity. The girls would be hurt enough when the truth came out; right now, the least she could do was try and minimise their pain. 'OK.'

Relief washed over Alex's face. 'Thank you, Darcy.' She gave Tatty's hand another squeeze. 'We'll go and chat somewhere quiet, and you girls stay here and finish your movie, yeah?'

'Mum?' Freya double checked with Darcy, who nodded, unable to speak.

'Where will you be if we need you?' Tatty was still troubled.

'Down in the terrace bar?' Alex raised her eyebrows at Darcy, who shook her head.

'Libby and Erika are down there.'

Understanding dawned in Alex's expression. 'OK, the coffee bar up in reception?'

Darcy shrugged her acceptance.

'Right then, that's where we'll be. And honestly, girls,' Alex added. 'Don't worry. We'll sort it out; you just chill here.'

Darcy dropped a kiss on Freya's cheek as the girls returned to staring at the screen. Alex held the door open, but Darcy dodged around her, the thought of being near to Alex making her balk. She could barely bring herself to step inside the enclosed space of the lift, imagining she could smell Jon if she stood too close to the woman.

The ride between floors seemed to take forever and Darcy felt claustrophobic for the first time in her life. When Alex caught her eye and gave a little half-smile, her expression unreadable, it made Darcy shiver. Suddenly, giving Alex the benefit of the doubt seemed like a very bad idea.

Darcy willed the doors to open and, when they finally did, Alex politely stood aside for her, making Darcy wonder if she'd imagined things.

At the coffee bar Alex immediately had the attention of one of the young male servers and gave him a warm smile. 'Espresso macchiato, please.'

He returned the smile. 'Yes, miss.' Turning to Darcy, he added, 'And you, madam?'

Darcy's heart sank. Insult to injury, she thought, acknowledging that every man in the vicinity seemed to prefer Alex to her. She was tempted to walk straight back out again.

'Cappuccino?' Alex suggested, as Darcy shrugged and the waiter hurried off, no doubt wondering what he'd said to upset her.

'He didn't mean anything by it.' Alex slid into a chair and indicated the one opposite.

Darcy felt her face flame at the thought of Alex noticing her reaction. 'I don't give a shit what coffee we order – this isn't a social occasion,' she snapped. 'What are we even doing here?'

Alex sat back in her seat. 'I thought we should talk about what's happened.'

'You say "what's happened" as if you had no control over it.' Darcy's face twisted with the pain of reliving the moment she found them together. 'As if you didn't engineer it.'

'It wasn't all on me, you know.' Alex gave her a sympathetic look. 'Jonny and I have ties that go way back, as I suspect you've worked out by now.'

Darcy said nothing. Was it nothing more than sex between the pair of them? She could almost understand Jon having his head turned with Alex looking like *that*, offering it on a plate, and with there being so little sex in their marriage these days. It was a depressing cliché, but one that Darcy could at least understand; it was a tale as old as time.

The idea of them being *in love*; the very thought of Alex having a connection with Jon that spanned the decades, just as she did, was something else entirely.

Eventually Darcy spoke. 'If you're working up to dropping your big bombshell about Tatyana then save your breath. Everyone's worked out that she must be Jon's kid. *As I suspect*,' she repeated Alex's earlier words, 'you wanted us to.'

'Oh!' A change came over Alex's expression, the conciliatory warmth that had been in her voice now stripped away as she added, 'It's like that, is it?' She gave a little laugh, designed to infuriate. 'You did the math.'

'It's maths, plural, you pretentious—' Darcy broke off, shaking her head with exasperation. 'You grew up in Surrey, same as me, so stop pretending you're from New York; you sound like a dick.'

The waiter arrived with the coffees and, after a quick glance between the two women, placed them down and backed away without a word.

'Now, this is the Darcy I remember from school.' Alex pushed the cappuccino towards her. 'You used to talk to me like this all the time before your boring life left you with nothing to say for yourself.'

'My life is—' Darcy stopped, correcting herself. 'My life *was* just fine before you came back and blew it all up.' Her voice cracked and she put her head in her hands. Rage and loathing gave way to sadness. 'But it was all a lie, wasn't it?'

'Well . . . yeah. That's what I wanted to tell you.' A hint of defiance crept into Alex's voice. 'Jonny was sleeping with me from the start. All the time you were together at college, he was also seeing me.'

'I know,' Darcy mumbled beneath her hands. 'Libby told me.'

'Oh.'

Darcy raised her head, face awash with angry tears, her red-rimmed eyes aflame with hatred. For once it seemed like Alex had nothing to say.

'Don't worry, she kept your secret all these years.' Darcy pulled a tissue from her handbag. 'She only spoke up tonight after I told her what I'd seen. You and him, in my bed,' she clarified, as if Alex could have been in any doubt.

'And this is why it's time for you to know the truth, no matter how painful this must be for you.' Alex tilted her head, her face full of regret. 'We were together back then, and he still wants me now. You're never going to be enough for him, Darcy. I'm sorry.'

Darcy stood up, still a little unsteady from the drinks at dinner, and backed away towards the hotel reception. 'You're not sorry. You're enjoying hurting me. And part of me wants to know why, and why *now*, but to be honest I'm more concerned about my little girl and how I'm supposed to tell her about all this, so I'm going to get her and take her home.'

Alex jumped up and followed her, gripping her arm as she tried to put distance between them. 'I'll tell you why.'

Darcy hesitated. The sensible thing would be to go to Freya and start the painful task of finding their way through this mess. Yet, Alex was looking at her with such intensity, Darcy couldn't help wanting to know the truth. The full truth.

'Darcy! There you are!'

Darcy swung around to see Erika striding towards her, Libby's tear-stained face peering worriedly over her shoulder. They both stopped short when they saw Alex.

'What are you—?' Erika shook her head and turned back to Darcy. 'Are you all right? Jon's been trying to get hold of you.'

'Freya's gone back to your room – I mean, his room. You know, whatever,' Libby added, flashing a look of pure disgust at Alex. 'He's putting her to bed and will wait there for you. He wanted you to know she was OK.'

Darcy took her phone out of her bag and saw the sixteen missed calls. 'It's on silent. I did tell Freya where I was going,' she added, defensive now.

'Of course you did. I guess Jon didn't expect you and . . . *her* to be up here together. I mean.' Erika ran her hand through her hair as she tried to find the words. 'Like, what the fuck?' There was a pause, as no one had a response to that. 'Oh, and Tatty's fine as well, she stayed in your room,' Erika added, projecting her voice in the direction of Alex but without looking at her. 'If you give a shit.'

Alex waved away Erika's jibe. 'She's a big girl.'

'Yeah, seventeen, as it turns out.' Erika's eyes glinted and Darcy knew what was implied. Even after all she'd seen and heard that evening, Darcy still couldn't make herself believe that Tatty could be Jon's. That there'd been another woman, and another child, all these years.

Alex stood up straighter, locking eyes with Erika. 'You're very holier-than-thou tonight, aren't you? Shame you weren't so keen on honesty back in the day.'

Darcy's stomach plummeted. Her best friend? 'No,' she whispered. 'Not you as well? You knew?'

'No!' Erika was indignant. 'I knew nothing about any of this.'

'Liar! You knew he kissed me, that night at the caravan park,' Alex cried. 'Did she ever tell you about that, Darcy?'

'The caravan park? The first night he kissed me?' Darcy put a hand out to steady herself as Libby stepped forward to support her. Darcy tried to make eye contact with her instead. 'You knew this too, I suppose?'

Libby sighed. 'Alex said there was no point upsetting you. Back then we never thought we'd even see Jon again anyway.'

Darcy pushed Libby away. 'But you should have told me when we got together. And you,' Darcy snapped as she pointed at Erika. 'You definitely should have.'

Erika faltered. 'I don't know. To be honest, it didn't seem that important. It was a teenage kiss at a caravan park. It was obvious you were the one he wanted,' she said eventually. 'By the time you guys were properly together I'd kind of forgotten that Alex was ever involved.'

Alex bit out a laugh. 'As always!'

'Meaning?'

Darcy swallowed hard as Alex turned her attention from Erika back to her again.

'Meaning,' Alex said, 'that Darcy's relationships and feelings were always so bloody important to you all, but mine never were. Mine were a joke, they meant nothing to you. And you were meant to be my friends too.'

Libby shook her head and made to object, but Alex cut over her.

'It might have been Darcy who picked on me, but none of you ever had my back.'

'Picked on you?' Darcy was incredulous. 'Did I do anything like what you have done to me this week, huh? Not just tonight.' Darcy could feel herself flush as her voice grew louder. 'When you called me fat. When you hurt my face with that chemical wipe. When you did . . .' she threw her hands up, 'whatever it was you did with my top, because I *know* that it was you. When you—'

'Ladies, excuse me. Is everything OK?' the woman on reception called over, peering at them, concerned at the noise.

'Oh, yes, all fine.' Alex quickly switched to charming mode. 'Sorry about my friend.' She looked pointedly at

Darcy, daring her to respond and make an even bigger scene. 'We'll chat outside.'

Alex gestured for everyone to follow her and the woman on reception gave her a thankful nod.

'Really?' Erika muttered, reluctantly shuffling towards the entrance. 'We're going to do this on the street?'

Darcy didn't care where they talked; she just wanted it over with so that she could get back to Freya. 'I've been humiliated in every part of this hotel tonight,' she said, grimly, 'it makes no odds to me.'

As they stepped out into the moonlight, Darcy could hear the faint whisper of the sea far below them. The road was silent and as she looked down at the coastal path, she found the rich blues and greens that usually greeted her were now swallowed up by inky blackness.

Along one side of the hotel was a stone staircase that led all the way down the cliffside to the beach entrance below. Darcy could see that the lights of the terrace bar and restaurant were still on. It felt like an age since they were down there, beginning an evening of what was meant to be hen-night fun and silliness. But of course, Darcy realised with hindsight, Alex had orchestrated it all, so that she had everyone where she wanted them. Where did she even begin with unravelling all of this?

Libby rubbed her arms as the cool night breeze made its presence felt. 'Please let's not do this now. We all need time to calm down and decompress.'

'But she wants to know *why*.' Alex jabbed a finger close to Darcy's face, making her recoil. 'And I was about to tell her.'

'This I'd like to hear.' Erika folded her arms.

The glow from the hotel entrance highlighted Alex standing before them, reminding Darcy of when they were children, using a torch to make scary faces as they told ghost stories on sleepovers.

'Good. Because all this . . .' Alex took a pause to appraise each of them in turn. 'This is about so much more than Jonny.'

20

2017 – Darcy

Darcy deliberately kept her face impassive as Alex described, in lurid detail, how she'd first slept with Jon at her party – in the front seat of his car; *spare us, please* – and how they'd continued to hook up whenever they could through their college years. The years that Darcy had always fondly looked back on as the halcyon days of her romance with Jon, now forever tarnished by the knowledge that he'd never been the sweet, loving, devoted young man he'd presented himself to be.

Occasionally she would be jolted by Libby's sharp intake of breath or a tut from Erika, reminding her that her friends were also party to her humiliation and had even played their own roles in this grand deception. She managed to control her facial expressions by focusing on a fleck of spittle in the corner of Alex's mouth and imagining this was all simply a horrible, drunken nightmare she would soon wake up from.

Alex went on and on, telling her that Jon – or Jonny as she still insisted on calling him – was hers first. 'You were with Bradley, and you chose him. What gave you the right to decide you were going to have Jonny too?' Alex's voice was losing some of its seductive affectations; she was starting to sound more like her petulant teenage self. 'And let's not forget, you were only with Bradley because you decided to steal him off Erika!'

Erika scoffed. 'That wasn't what happened! He was just a mate.'

'I didn't steal anyone *off* anyone.' Darcy's eyes never left the fleck of spittle that was now almost dried out. She'd never thought that Erika minded her going out with Bradley, even if they had been close first. 'No one can be taken who doesn't want to go.'

'True.' Alex smiled smugly at that. 'Jonny didn't need much persuading tonight.'

Darcy remained silent.

'In fact, he never did where I was concerned. Maybe if I'd stayed around, things would have turned out differently.'

The fleck had disappeared, Darcy could no longer see where it had been. Reluctantly she met Alex's mocking expression. 'But you didn't, did you? You ran away and never told any of us you were pregnant.' Darcy's eyes narrowed. 'You could've used your pregnancy as leverage, but you didn't. Why was that?'

Alex shifted her stance and put a hand on her hip. 'What do you mean?'

'You could have forced Jon's hand, made him be a father to, to . . .' She faltered, 'Tatyana.' Darcy swallowed and reminded herself it wasn't the girl's fault. 'You had a solid gold reason to keep yourself in his life, but you didn't.'

'Alex?' Libby appealed. Darcy wondered if she was still hoping to find an explanation to any of this that would mean Alex wasn't to blame after all. Libby always did look for the positive. But Alex ignored them both.

'In fact, you've taken pains to tell us what a wonderful, amazing life you've been having all these years, first in Spain and then in New York.' Darcy took a step forward, picking up on Alex's reticence. 'And it's taken you, what? Nearly eighteen years to be bothered enough to come back and mess with us. I don't get it, Alex, why now?'

Alex fiddled with the strap of her expensive watch; Darcy sensed she'd rattled her. 'Or maybe you'd prefer I call you Lexie – Lexie Kaplan – like they do on your secret Facebook account?'

Alex suddenly dropped the watch and it clattered onto the pavement. For a moment she looked like teenage Alex, withering under the glare of super-confident Darcy as she bent awkwardly to retrieve it. 'So what?' She shrugged. 'So you know I have an account in my married name? You can't blame me for wanting to leave that behind now Kyle and I have split up.'

Erika barked out a laugh. 'Is that what this is about? You're angry about your divorce so you've come home to settle old scores?'

Alex avoided her eyes and Darcy saw that Erika had hit the jackpot. 'Oh, my God, that's it, isn't it?'

'Shut up!' Alex spat, as Darcy matched Erika's harsh laughter. 'You've no idea what you're talking about.'

'I do actually,' Darcy managed as she wiped her eyes. 'All this heartache just because Alex Rigby is still the same deluded drama queen she was when we were at school.'

'And you're still a bitch, and a bully.'

The two women stared at each other; twenty or more years' worth of hostility festering between them like a suppurating sore.

Libby put her hands out between the two of them. 'Please, can we—'

'Bully? Really?' Darcy ignored Libby's protests. 'You call me that after everything you've just done to me?'

'And have you never wondered why?'

'Why what?'

'Why I am the way I am with you?'

Darcy frowned. 'Because of Jon, obviously. You were jealous.'

Alex ran her hands through her hair, frustration evident in every move. 'This goes back way before Jonny. You were beyond vile to me at school. You were, Darcy,' she added as Darcy made to object. 'You belittled me and mocked me and destroyed my confidence. I was the butt of all your nasty, lowdown jokes.'

'It was banter!'

'It was bullying.'

Darcy felt the silence descend upon the group. 'Surely you agree this is nonsense?' She looked first to Erika, who was uncharacteristically quiet. Darcy suddenly remembered the conversation they'd had by the pool a few days before, when Erika had mentioned the power Darcy used to wield when they were younger.

'Libby?' Darcy turned to her instead.

Libby squirmed, keeping her eyes fixed on the ground. 'Maybe not bullying exactly. But yeah, there was teasing and stuff, I suppose.'

Darcy thought for a minute. 'I don't think it was as bad as you're making out. Alex used to slag me off as well, remember.'

'I got the odd pot-shot in when the chance arose, but it was nothing compared to how you treated me.' Alex stood up straight and forced eye contact. 'Just think back to some of the things you said to me, Darcy. My clothes, my body, my voice, the things I liked – you picked at every-thing. Including the things I could do nothing about.'

Darcy thought back. She could remember some of the jibes she threw and yes, perhaps some were a bit mean, but they were teenagers; it was par for the course, wasn't it? And Alex was constantly looking for attention back then, she deserved to be taken down a peg or two else she'd become insufferable.

'Imagine someone treating Freya the way you treated me.' Alex raised an eyebrow.

Darcy's whole body shifted in discomfort. For a moment, she couldn't speak.

'You'd call it bullying then, wouldn't you?' Alex added, her voice entirely neutral.

Darcy imagined Freya being mocked for her clothes, her body, her very sense of self, and she found she could barely breathe. If someone spoke to her little girl like that, they would deserve to be torn apart. It wasn't the same with her and Alex; it couldn't be.

'But you were always telling lies and making stuff up for attention. Like the DJ and, and . . . Hunter from *Gladiators* and . . . that married man! G, wasn't it?'

Alex smiled like she knew all of Darcy's secrets and then some. 'G was my codename for Jonny.'

Darcy felt her face drain of colour as it finally hit her that what Alex was saying was true. Her whole relationship with Jon, their history, their family – it was all built on lies and deceit. And had she really been such a relentless, crowing bully? She felt like her whole body might buckle and fold in on itself in shame.

'No,' she heard Erika say as if through a dense fog. 'You told us he was married.'

'I could hardly tell you the truth, could I? It was just a way of talking about him without giving the game away. Anyway,' Alex gave a casual one-shouldered shrug, 'we're getting off topic.' She pointed at Darcy again. 'Do you remember when I bled on my skirt?'

Darcy swallowed. She did remember. Alex had her first period at fourteen, quite late compared to the rest of them. The first time she tried to wear a tampon she didn't have it in properly and so she leaked onto her skirt during geography. Libby had taken Alex aside and lent her a jumper to tie around her waist and cover the stain, but Darcy had told everyone anyway.

'Do you remember?' Alex repeated, eyes gimlet-hard.

Darcy nodded stiffly, trying to banish the unwelcome picture of it being Freya in that bloodied skirt, vulnerable and embarrassed. And so very young. She knew Libby and Erika would remember too; she couldn't lie.

'Ben Taylor lifted the sweater up, and everyone laughed at the stain. Remember that?'

'OK, I'm sorry, I didn't think it was a big deal.' Darcy rubbed her temples and wondered if her hangover was already kicking in. She needed to defend herself. 'I was a stupid kid. But if you're telling me that a bit of teasing at school equates to what you've done then—'

'It wasn't *a bit of* teasing!' Alex exploded. Darcy jumped, surprised at the outburst. She wasn't quite sure how she'd gone from being the one with righteous anger to the one being held to account. 'You have no idea how deep some of that stuff cut. And you were always, *always* the one to get what you wanted. No one would ever say no to you. It was so, so unfair.'

Darcy looked at Alex's face, her cheeks flushed, features twisted – all that beauty she had worked so hard to attain now distorted by her fury and her memories.

'And then, when I finally met someone who meant something to me, for the first time someone who saw *me* and was interested in *me*, you had to have him.' Alex glared at Darcy. 'Jonny could have been mine if you would've just kept away. And then none of this would have happened.'

'You're deluded.' Darcy rubbed her head again, wondering if she had any painkillers in her handbag. 'It wouldn't have mattered if I'd kept away from Jon. *He* sought *me* out; he made it clear he wanted to be with me. He married me, for Christ's sake. I didn't force him into any of those things.'

Alex shook her head, as if in sympathy for Darcy's misunderstanding. 'Then why was he sleeping with me on the side?' Her tone was turning triumphant. 'Because he was so bored after doing crappy good-girl stuff with you. He needed me for intimacy and love, he—'

'He used you for sex.' Darcy sniffed. 'That's what your big love affair was as far as he was concerned. A long-term booty call. Good enough for a shag, nothing else.'

Alex shook her head but Darcy imagined a lightbulb brightening above her own, easing the tension as she joined the dots from their past.

Darcy laughed bitterly. 'There you have it.' She tilted her head and returned to Alex one of those condescending smiles that Darcy had been taking from her all week; a smile of self-satisfaction designed to provoke. 'He fucked you, and he married me.'

Libby abruptly turned on her heel. 'I can't take any more of this. Erika?'

Erika nodded and gestured back to the hotel. 'Please will you two call it a night?'

Alex ignored them. 'It was much more than that,' she insisted, but Darcy could see the certainty had gone from her eyes. Alex's hands were trembling, clenching and unclenching as she started to pace. 'It *was*.'

'Give it up, Alex, have some respect for yourself.' Darcy leaned back against the railings and noticed that the tightness pulsing in her head had eased somewhat. 'I think on some level you've always known, or you'd have stayed and fought for him when you realised you were pregnant.'

'How are you *still* so smug?' Alex stared at her in disbelief. 'You've just found out that your whole marriage is built on a lie and you're standing there giving me a lecture on self-respect.' Her voice cracked. 'You're going to stay with him, aren't you? This whole fucking shitshow has been for nothing.'

In the silence, Libby and Erika looked on helplessly, stopped in their tracks once more, and Darcy decided to be honest; she'd had enough game playing. 'I don't know.'

Alex spat out a noise that might have been a laugh, tinged with tears, which she blinked away furiously. 'You two think you can carry on playing happy families after this? Just carry on like I never existed – *again*?' She rubbed her eyes, the tears were coming readily now as she resumed pacing, trying to shake them off. 'Talk about having some respect for yourself! He's treated us both like shit, Darcy, both of us. He might have married you, but what kind of marriage is it if he'll cheat on you so easily? If he'll lie to you from the off?'

'He's Freya's dad.' Darcy sighed, then pulled up short as another thought occurred to her. 'But – shit – he's Tatty's dad, too. I guess we'll have to address that at some point.'

Something flashed in Alex's eyes. Darcy saw the change for a fraction of a second before Alex wiped her face and turned away.

'He *is*, isn't he?' Darcy pushed. 'Alex?'

'Alex?' Libby repeated.

Alex turned back to face them, awash with messy tears now. 'He's not,' she whispered between gulps.

'He's not?' Darcy couldn't take it in.

Alex took a deep breath. 'Jonny isn't Tatty's father. I was fucking with you.'

'Jesus.' Erika shook her head. 'On purpose?'

Alex nodded, her usual artificially smooth veneer replaced with the tumult of raw emotion.

'But you were sleeping with Jon back then?' Libby's eyes were wide. 'The dates add up.'

'Not quite.'

'I don't believe it.' Darcy was incredulous. 'Why would you – how could you exploit your own daughter like that?'

'I didn't!' Alex was up and shrieking in Darcy's face, pushing her back against the railings. 'And I'm not taking another lecture from you!'

Erika rushed to action, attempting to prise Alex away as Libby froze, watching helplessly. 'What the fuck are you doing?'

'Get off me!' Alex shook her off and leaned over Darcy, pinning her against the railings. 'All of this is on you.' She jabbed her finger into Darcy's shoulder. 'Tatty is the result of a cheap one-night stand with some creep I don't even know the name of and none of it would have happened if it weren't for you and Jonny. You, you fucking smug bitch, you ruined my life!'

Darcy was unable to move, terrified by the force of Alex's outburst. As she tried to think of a response, she noticed a movement over Alex's shoulder. 'Alex, stop.'

'Don't tell me to stop! YOU stop telling ME what to do!' Alex shouted in her face. 'Of course I would have preferred for her to be Jonny's rather than a mistake I barely consented to.'

Erika followed Darcy's gaze and gestured over Alex's shoulder. 'Alex. Stop!'

'What?'

Alex spun around. 'Oh no. No, no, no. That's not what it sounded like.'

She was face to face with Tatty, flushed and tearful, emerging from the hotel entrance.

Tatty looked as if she were about to turn and run but Libby put out a gentle hand. 'Are you OK?'

'What did you hear?' Alex demanded, striding away from Darcy, who slumped with relief. She grabbed Tatty's other arm. 'It's not what you think.'

'Be kind!' Libby admonished as Tatty flinched. 'You're frightening her.'

'I heard you say that I was a mistake you barely consented to.' Tatty spat out the words as if they tasted vile in her mouth. A fresh tear trickled down her face and, despite her own turmoil, Darcy's heart went out to her; suddenly, it was easier to be compassionate towards her now that she knew the truth.

'I didn't mean that the way it sounded. You're not a mistake.' Alex reached for Tatty again but the girl pulled away and walked over to the stone staircase, looking down towards the beach. The lights in the terrace bar were off now, Darcy noticed. Everyone else had called it a night and it felt like they were the only people still awake.

'You always said my real dad was your teenage boy-friend.' The pain in Tatty's voice cut through the darkness and Darcy and Erika shared a look, each knowing what the other was thinking. Had Alex never grown out of her fantasies and lies, or was this a more innocent act of wishful thinking on her part?

'The truth is,' Alex said as she took a shuddering breath, 'I was so sad about Jonny – Jon – ending things with me for Darcy. And one night when I was upset, I met this guy who made me feel good for a moment.'

'Who?' Libby interjected.

Even in the half-light Darcy saw shame flood Alex's face. 'Just some guy. I never saw him again.'

'A one-night thing?' Tatty's face was scrunched up in disgust and misery. 'A mistake?'

'Did you even know his name?' Erika's voice was hostile.

'Look, I know it doesn't sound good, but it was one of those moments in time that I think happen for a rea-son. I was so pleased when you came along.' Alex tried again to move closer to Tatty. 'I know you're angry and you're right to be, but nothing has really changed.'

'Except you used me to settle old scores with your friends. How could you, Mom?' Tatty's voice cracked. 'How could you lie about something as important as that? As if I were a toy to be passed about between you all!'

'I didn't lie.' Alex insisted, ignoring Erika's noise of dissent. 'Not really! I never said Jon was your dad, Tatty, and everything I said about us being together when we were young was true. He was with me before Darcy.'

'Or *at the same time* as Darcy,' Erika muttered. Darcy appreciated her efforts; she didn't have the energy to defend her relationship anymore. There was no point fighting over Jon. He wasn't the man she'd thought he was.

Tatty shuddered. 'The whole thing is so gross, I just can't even.' She backed away further from Alex. 'And you and him . . . tonight? Is that true?'

'Listen, please, I will answer all your questions I promise, but let's just go back to the room, huh?' Alex gestured to Darcy. 'I think we're done here.'

Tatty wiped her eyes and shook her head. 'I want Daddy to come get me. I hate being here with all this – whatever it is – going on. And after what you just said, I don't want to be near you either.'

Alex was immediately incensed. 'Absolutely not! You think darling *Daddy* is going to fly all the way out here and get you?'

'Alex!' Libby urged. 'Stop shouting at her.'

'He will! He's in Amsterdam this week, it's only a couple of hours away.' Tatty lifted her chin defiantly at her mother and for the first time Darcy noticed a resemblance between the two of them. 'I've been messaging him.'

Darcy risked another glance at Erika and wondered if she knew about that from when Tatty had logged into her laptop.

'I told him everything was weird with you two.' Tatty turned to face Darcy for the first time. 'And Jon.'

Darcy didn't know what to say. She wished she could comfort the girl but she had nothing left; she just wanted to get back to Freya.

'So I guess that's because you're having an affair with Jon, right?' Tatty turned back to Alex. 'Is that what this is all about?' When Alex didn't reply, Tatty continued. 'Because it wouldn't be the first time you cheated, would it, Mom?'

Darcy was stunned. She could see that Erika and Libby were too. Hadn't they been under the impression that it was Kyle who'd ended things?

'With Jon?' Erika rallied first.

'No, some guy at Daddy's work,' Tatty said, her voice heartbreakingly impassive. 'That's why they split up.'

Alex clenched her hands into fists. 'Enough.'

'I'm not coming with you.' Tatty backed away again as Libby edged forward to appease Alex. 'I hate you.'

'Alex, leave her be tonight. It's so much to take in.'

'She can crash with us if she wants,' Erika added.

Alex gave a brittle laugh. 'Oh, you'd love that, wouldn't you? Especially you.' She pointed at Darcy. 'My daughter hates me. My friends hate me. Jon is going to stay with you, even after everything.' Alex pulled at her hair and made an awful howling noise; Darcy realised she was sobbing. 'I've lost everything again, because of YOU!'

Alex lurched forward, Libby unable to restrain her as she swiped her arm towards Darcy, who made her escape towards the steps. Erika stepped between them but Alex shoved her out of the way as Tatty cried, 'Mom, please!' and put her hands out to stop her.

Darcy saw Alex coming for her again and ducked down beside the railings as Alex launched herself forward once more. In a blur of pushing and shouting, Darcy heard the thud of Alex's hands making contact, followed by a shriek, and she instinctively covered her face.

'Tatty!' someone screamed; Darcy wasn't sure who. She realised that it wasn't her who Alex had hit and rose from her crouching position to see Libby and Erika running down the stone steps. Alex was standing a few feet away from her at the top of the staircase, her hands over her face.

'Tatty?' Erika called. 'Tatty, can you hear me?'

Darcy looked down and in the darkness could make out a shape on the first landing point of the staircase. Libby shone the torch from her phone as Erika kneeled beside the shape.

It took Darcy a moment to register what she was seeing. 'Oh, my God, what have you done?' she gasped, as Alex jerked, sobbing, beside her.

On the steps below, Darcy could see that Tatty was motionless, blood pouring from the side of her head. 'What have you *done*?' Darcy repeated, louder this time. 'I'm going to get help,' she called down to Libby and Erika, turning to run back into the hotel.

As she passed Alex, her face still frozen in a silent howl at the top of the steps, Darcy paused. 'You stupid, selfish woman.'

'Hurry, Darcy, she's in a bad way,' Erika shouted up to her. 'Please hurry!'

21

1999 – Alex

The evening was dragging, despite Libby's best efforts for us to have fun. Drinks came and went; Erika never returned, so we drank the shots she had bought for herself as well as our own and Darcy floated past a few more times dropping off various beers and other delights. We were mixing like crazy, but nothing was lifting our spirits. Or mine, at least.

'Do you want to dance?' Libby asked. I shook my head.

'Want to get something from the buffet?'

I pulled a face. Buffet was too generous a description for the sad collection of cheap party snacks they'd put out and they were even less appealing now they'd been sitting out and pawed over for a few hours.

'No, maybe not,' Libby agreed. 'Well, do you want to go and mingle a bit? We've been sitting here all night.'

I shrugged. 'I don't really know anyone.'

Libby was clearly losing her patience with me and I felt bad for ruining her night.

'I'm sorry,' I said eventually. 'I'm feeling a bit down. Shall we get some more drinks?'

Libby swayed in her chair as she turned to look at the bar. Perhaps she was drunker than I'd realised. 'I can't go up there again, it's only been five minutes since I bought these.' She waved the empty shot glasses. 'They'll think I'm an alky-whatnot.' She burped delicately. 'Pardon-ay moi!' Libby giggled and I couldn't help but smile. 'Why don't you try? They're not checking IDs anyway.'

'OK.' The previous however-many drinks made me brave, but it was only as I stood up that it hit me just how many we must have downed already. I shuffled over to the bar in my too-tight dress and smiled at the nearest server. He had dark, floppy hair like Jonny did when I first met him. He returned my smile and came straight over.

'Yes, gorgeous?'

I was taken aback by his flirtatious tone. 'Oh. Thank you.'

He laughed and I was mortified. 'I mean, yes please, may I have two Smirnoff Ices please, and two, no, four, of those green apple shot things, please? Thank you. Please.'

He looked at me for a moment and I held my breath waiting to see if he would ask for ID, but instead he just smiled again before going to get them. As he placed the bottles in front of me, he leaned in. 'Are you here with someone tonight?'

Leaning on the bar with one hand for support, I used the other to point to over where Libby was sitting, singing along to 'Kung Fu Fighting' and doing the moves even though she was on her own. 'My friend.'

He chuckled at Libby's funky dancing. 'No boyfriend?'

A wave of sadness hit me. 'No. No boyfriend.'

'How is that possible?'

He *was* flirting with me. I looked at him properly and he raised an eyebrow; it was quite sexy. I never found any other men attractive, so this was exciting. He reminded me of Jonny in the early days, what with the floppy hair and working behind the bar, but this guy was like a version of Jonny who really fancied me and was doing all the running.

'I don't know.' My voice came out as a whisper.

The bar was getting busy, so I went to pay for the drinks but he only charged me for the bottles and slipped me the shots for free. He winked at me as I thanked him. 'Come back and see me later,' he called after me, as I tottered back to the table.

I dodged Libby's karate-kicking limbs ('Ha!' she shouted. 'Hoo huh!'), and put the drinks down. 'I need to tell you something.'

As soon as I said it, I wondered what the hell I was doing. I hadn't planned to tell her anything but suddenly, in that moment, I just needed to say it. I needed to tell someone.

'Yeah?' She stopped dancing and looked at me with her open, trusting face.

'Oh, my God.' I downed one of the shots. 'I'm sleeping with Jonny.' Libby looked at me in disbelief; I threw down another shot. 'There was no G. Well, there is but it's Jonny. Jonny is G.'

Libby lurched as if she was going to be sick.

'Are you OK?' I asked.

'I'm fine.' She reached for a shot and then hesitated before drinking it. 'Are you for real?'

'Of course!' I watched her neck the shot, offended that she'd had to ask.

'I assume Darcy doesn't know?'

'Of course not,' I scoffed. 'Do you think I'd still be alive if she did?' I saw the look on Libby's face and saw she wasn't in the mood for joking. Suddenly, I realised I'd put her in an impossible position. I hadn't thought that by unburdening myself I'd be weighing her down and now I honestly regretted opening my mouth.

'Look, they both kept saying they were just friends. I didn't know that they were actually . . .' I found it hard to articulate, so distasteful was the idea of them being together, 'you know, properly, going out or whatever.'

'So you haven't slept with him since you found out about Darcy? That's not so bad then.' Even in her drunken state, Libby desperately wanted to think the best of me.

'Well, just once,' I admitted. 'The night he told me they were . . . a *thing*.'

Libby wobbled. 'You still went with him after you knew they were together?'

I felt a rush of anger at the injustice of it all. As far as I was concerned, I was seeing a single man and waiting for him to be ready to settle down.

'He's the one who's been cheating, not me. And why are you only concerned about how this looks from Darcy's point of view? What about me?'

Libby stayed silent and swigged her last remaining shot, her hands trembling. We never fell out and I hated this feeling that she disapproved of me.

The music changed and I recognised the opening to 'Boy You Knock Me Out' by Tatyana Ali. I had been playing this song on repeat all spring, thinking about Jonny and hoping he was coming home to tell me that we were going to be together. Properly together. The lyrics were so perfect; I'd spent hours singing along with Tatyana's voice on the CD player in my bedroom. I thought of it as *our song*, even if Jonny didn't know about it. Hearing it played now, after Darcy's news, was heartbreaking.

'Did he tell you he loved you, too?' she asked eventually.

Tears came unexpectedly into my eyes. 'No.'

Libby looked at me sadly as she swayed in her seat. 'Did you never worry about him spending all that time with Darcy?'

'Of course I did! I'm not stupid,' I snapped. 'But I figured that as long as I was in his life, I still had a chance.' I softened; I had to try to make her understand. 'I love him so much, Libs, I had to do whatever it took to keep him coming back to me.'

She didn't get it, I could tell. She just kept shaking her head. 'But you were a doormat, you let him walk all over you. That's not love.'

'What would you even know about love? You've never even had a boyfriend!' I sneered, wanting to hurt her like her words were hurting me. I was *not* a doormat! I was just . . . accommodating. Understanding. Cool.

I saw the wave of hurt pass over Libby's face. 'Well, if I'm so crap then why are you unloading all your drama onto me? Now every time Darcy tells me how much she and Jon love each other, all I'll be able to think about is your . . . *betrayal.*'

'I didn't betray anyone!' I was livid. 'And don't pretend that Darcy wouldn't do the same to me, even if I had! I can't believe you're taking her side!' That upset me more than anything. 'If she's so precious to you then go and be her best friend.'

'Fine.' Libby struggled to her feet, the combination of alcohol, the big puffy dress and her new high heels making it difficult for her to stand up with any kind of grace. 'It's probably all lies anyway.'

'It's true! I can't believe you're more worried about her than me.' Tears were pouring down my face now as Libby hobbled away. 'And his name is Jonny, not Jon!'

No one came over to me as I sat and cried. I could feel a few people looking at me, but mostly they were all drunk and caught up in their own lives. I should never have told Libby, I realised, especially not when we were both so drunk. She was bound to react badly. Still, her calling me a liar really hurt. And a doormat. I'd never seen my relationship with Jonny like that. He was a free spirit and I was happy to be there for him whenever he needed me.

'Hey, hey! What are all these tears for?' The guy from the bar was collecting glasses and he looked at me with concern and kindness in his eyes. 'What's happened? Where's your friend?'

I pulled a tissue out of my handbag and dabbed at my face, trying to pull myself together. 'We fell out. She's gone off with our other friends.' I waved in the general direction of where they'd all disappeared off to.

'That sucks.' He sat in one of the empty seats. 'Can I get anyone for you?'

My eyes welled up again. 'I don't have anyone else. I don't even know how I'm going to get home.' I didn't want to have to call my parents and have them see me like that and a taxi from the stupid cricket club would have been far more than I had on me.

'Shhh. It's OK, I'll make sure you're OK.' He snaked his arm around my shoulders and drew me towards him. It felt nice to be held, even though up close he didn't remind me as much of Jonny as I'd first thought. It was strange to be in another man's arms. He smelled different and his limbs were chunkier than Jonny's. 'I can drive you home. Where do you live?'

I told him and he smiled. 'That's not too far. Wait for me at the end and I'll take you home, OK?' He stood up, squeezing my shoulder lightly as he withdrew his arm and scooped up the empties on the table. As he walked away I saw that Darcy was standing watching, a confrontational look on her face.

'What are you playing at?' she snapped. My stomach somersaulted at the thought of having things out with her. 'Libby's in bits over there.'

Libby. 'What . . . what did she tell you?'

'Nothing, except that you'd had a row. She's crying her heart out to Erika over there, so I thought I'd better come and see what was going on. And then I find you snuggled up with him.' She inclined her head in the direction of the barman, who was on his way back to the bar with his arms full of glasses. 'Did you fall out over him?'

'No.' Relief that she didn't know what I'd told Libby made me say it more aggressively than I meant to.

'All right!' Darcy held her hands up in surrender. 'None of my business. But I'm going to make a move now. It's no fun being sober when everyone else is either snogging or crying.' She gave a rueful smile and I sensed she was trying to make the effort, but the thought of sitting in her car with Libby knowing what I'd done was just too awful.

I shook my head. 'It's OK. He's going to take me home.'

'Who?'

'Him.' I pointed at the barman's retreating back.

'Do you even know his name?' Darcy looked at me like I was insane and I felt the familiar urge to slap her smug face.

'He's been kind to me tonight,' I said pointedly, the *unlike my friends* part left unsaid.

Darcy sighed as if I were ridiculous. 'Oh, Alex, don't go home with some random bloke just because you and Libby have fallen out. Look, Kitty's going home with Tommo, so you two don't even have to sit next to each other, you can sit in the front and she can . . .'

'I'm not twelve, Darcy,' I cut in, unable to stand her bossing me around a moment longer. 'You just make sure Libby gets home OK; she's very drunk. Don't you worry about me,' I added. 'Not that you ever do.'

Darcy looked stung. I thought she was going to say something else, but after a moment's hesitation she turned on her heel and stomped off muttering, 'Fuck's sake!'

Bridges well and truly burned, I hobbled over to the bar and perched on a stool, waiting for my knight in shining armour. I wanted to ask his name but I felt silly now, as if it would break the intimacy between us. He came and chatted to me between serving customers and slipped me shots whenever he could.

I assumed the girls had gone ahead and left without me, and when the lights came up at midnight, I saw for definite that they had. As the last few people trickled out and the planning committee members were lurching around with bin bags trying to clear up the bomb site that was the aftermath of a teenage disco, suddenly my barman was beside me with his coat on. 'Ready?' he asked with a smile.

I nodded and followed him out to his car. In the dark I couldn't see where I was going and he reached out to steady me. 'Oops.' I giggled. He stopped and drew me closer to him. In the blackness he looked a bit like Jonny again. I looked up at him and wondered if he'd kiss like Jonny. He must have read my mind because he lowered his head towards me and dropped a tender, questioning kiss onto my lips.

I shivered and he pulled me closer. He kissed me again and I let myself believe it was Jonny. Jonny loved me after all; he was kissing me so tenderly. I let him lead me into his car. It was so familiar to me; it felt natural. I let him guide me into the back seat, my eyes half closed as his hands roamed my body. He was having trouble freeing me from my ridiculously tight dress, so I went to help him but it was too late, the seam had ripped.

I looked at the torn seam aghast; how was I going to explain that to my mum? And in that moment of clarity, I finally appreciated that this wasn't Jonny. It was a stranger. I didn't even know his name. *What was I doing here?*

He continued to pull at my dress and I wished he'd stop but I couldn't find the words. He'd been so kind to me, it would be cruel to say no after letting him get this far. His strange hands worked their way under the ripped skirt of my dress and I bit my lip, willing it to be over. If he sensed the change in me – the fact that I'd stopped kissing him back, the way I'd tensed up – he didn't show it. He carried on and I didn't stop him. It was only when he was thrusting inside of me, my eyes squeezed shut, that I realised I hadn't heard or felt him put on a condom.

Afterwards, he kissed me on the forehead and we climbed back into the front seats. He was good to his word and took me home. I stared out of the window in silence the whole way there. When he bid me goodnight, he didn't ask for my number, nor I his.

I snuck upstairs and took the dress off as soon as my bedroom door closed behind me. I examined the torn seam in my hands and wondered if I could fix it before Mum took it to the dry cleaner's. I noticed my hands were shaking and I sat down on the bed, hugging the dress to me as I cried for all that I'd lost.

22

2017 – Darcy

Darcy braced herself to open the door, unable to shake the images of what had greeted her last time. This time she found a far more benevolent sight, one that would have warmed her heart were it not for the earlier events of the evening.

Freya was conked out in a starfish position on her foldout and Jon, who'd taken the time to remake the bed – the bed Darcy could barely look at – was sitting on the chair, watching over her. As Darcy walked in, he sat up straighter and immediately held up his hands. 'I know I fucked up. Please, Darcy, let's talk.'

'That's the best opener you've come up with while I've been gone?' Darcy curled her lip.

'I've been going out of my mind waiting for you to come back.' Jon ran a hand through his hair. 'Where have you been all this time?'

Darcy almost laughed. How could she sum up what had happened over the past few hours? Her arms ached to scoop Freya up and hold her close, but she forced herself to let the girl sleep. Tomorrow would be hard enough; she needed to let her have some peace now.

'Have you been with her? With . . . with Alex?' Darcy noted that Jon was loathe to say her name. 'Because you need to know that she is crazy. Whatever she's said to you will be bullshit.'

'Oh, I know she's crazy. It wasn't me who needed convincing on that score.' Darcy never took her eyes off the sleeping Freya. She looked so vulnerable, the rhythmical rise and fall of her breathing bringing a lump to Darcy's throat. 'And I've been gone so long because there was an accident. With Tatty.'

Jon's eyebrows shot up. 'Tatty? What?'

Darcy registered the alarm on his face and wondered if he believed Tatty was his daughter. Had he been misled like the rest of them? And if he had, did he want it to be true?

'She fell down some of the stone steps by the entrance. You know, the ones that lead down to the beach.'

'How?'

'It doesn't matter how.' Darcy didn't want to relay it all again. While it might have been Alex who pushed her – a push that had been meant for Darcy – she still felt partially responsible.

Jon bit the inside of his mouth. 'Is she OK?'

'She was knocked out and they've taken her to hospital to check her over. Concussion, possibly, and she cut her face quite badly.' Darcy shuddered as she remembered the blood on the steps. The relief, when they'd realised it came from a gash on Tatty's face rather than from a head injury, had been palpable. 'She'll need stitches and God knows what else.'

'Nasty.' Jon sighed. 'But could have been worse I guess.'

Darcy screwed her eyes shut to banish the image of Tatty lying bloody and unmoving in the stony darkness. 'Yes,' she agreed. 'Could have been worse.'

Alex had still been sobbing and her heightened hysterics were distressing Tatty when she came around, so Erika had travelled with Tatty in the ambulance while Alex and Libby followed on in a taxi. No one had suggested that Darcy should accompany them.

'About . . .' Jon cleared his throat. 'About . . . earlier.'

Darcy put up a hand. 'Please. It's late.'

'Let me explain.'

Darcy leaned over Freya and tenderly stroked her hair out of her face. 'Not now, with Freya here.'

'She's asleep.'

'No.'

'We could talk out there.' Jon stood and indicated the balcony. 'Please?'

With a last look at Freya, she reluctantly followed him and looked out to the dark water's edge. The view, so tranquil and soothing in the sunshine, felt oppressive and threatening now.

'So many people hurt tonight,' she commented. 'I'm not sure how we're all supposed to get up tomorrow morning and carry on from here.'

Jon came towards her again, hands outstretched. Darcy wasn't sure if he was reaching for her or begging forgiveness; either way, she held herself back.

'I know I messed up tonight, but you have to believe me, it meant nothing.'

Darcy couldn't help but laugh. 'Original.'

'I'm telling you, Darcy. Alex was the instigator of all of this.' His eyes were wide, imploring her to believe him. 'She's been on at me for days, since we got here. And I know you were suspicious – don't pretend you weren't – so you know I'm not lying.'

'So what! That doesn't excuse you.' Darcy struggled to articulate it; her mouth filled with bile whenever she tried. 'It doesn't excuse your part in this.'

'I know.' He ran his hands through his hair again. She knew he often did that when she pulled him up on anything; not doing his share of chores, forgetting to put the lid back on the toothpaste. She couldn't quite believe that he was trying it now, with something so serious. 'I was . . . weak. I'm *so* sorry.'

'Another cliché.' Darcy suddenly understood why all the soap operas and reality shows went over and over the same old tropes. This really was how people spoke to each other when the worst happened.

'But it's true. I don't know what else to say. It meant nothing; it was a moment of madness, that's all. Maybe . . .'

Despite herself, Darcy prompted, 'Maybe what?'

'Well.' Jon sighed. 'Maybe it's a mid-life thing, you know? Flattered at being hit on by such a—' He stopped, panic flashing across his face as he realised he was about to admit how attractive he found Alex. 'By someone different.'

Darcy choked a bitter laugh. 'Like a weak-willed moth to the old, irresistible flame.'

Jon looked warily at her. 'What did she say to you? Because that was before you and I got together and it didn't—'

'It didn't mean anything?' Darcy mocked.

'It didn't!'

'You're going to have to come up with something better than this if you want me to take you seriously, Jon. This is our marriage we're talking about.' Tears flooded her eyes again and she couldn't be bothered to wipe them away; she was exhausted. 'Our whole life together has been a lie.'

Darcy sank onto the nearest balcony chair and put her head into her hands. Weeping quietly, she thought of how Jon used to come and spend time with her when she was at college, constantly telling her how special she was, the light of admiration aflame in his eyes when he looked at her. She'd never doubted him then; she knew she was the one in control. Recently of course, they'd taken each other for granted, but what couple didn't after so long together? The young Jon, though, with his Hugh Grant hair and cheeky grin – she'd always had the memories of him to hold onto, the beautiful, innocent moments that made all the so-so days worthwhile.

Knowing that he'd been with *her* back then too was almost worse than what she'd walked in on that night. Alex had even trashed her memories of their perfect young romance, the ones she'd held in her heart and reminded herself of whenever Jon was thoughtless or selfish or indifferent. Darcy wondered how long she'd been in love with a fantasy. It was as if she'd believed she was marrying Hugh Grant in *Four Weddings and a Funeral*, but she'd ended up with Hugh Grant from *Bridget Jones's Diary*. Did she ever know him at all?

'All right, I'm going to tell you the truth.' Jon crouched in front of her and attempted to take her hands, but Darcy pulled away from his touch, too fresh were the images of him gripping Alex's smooth behind. 'What I'm going to say might sound callous, but I hope it'll prove to you that I've always loved you, Darcy. It was always you.'

Darcy wiped her eyes and looked into his, as familiar to her as her own. The ones that Freya had inherited. She said nothing but inclined her head a little to indicate she was listening.

'I did sleep with Alex before we got together *but*,' he added, seeing Darcy's indignant expression, 'it was *before* we got together. Not at the same time, not properly. Not once we committed to each other. You chose Bradley, remember? I was gutted . . . and Alex was, well, she was *there* and she boosted my confidence because it was so clear that she wanted me, even if you didn't.'

'Don't try and put this on me. I've always regretted not finishing with Bradley sooner, but we were kids,' she argued, 'what did we know then?'

'Exactly! The same applies to me and Alex!' Jon's eyes shone; Darcy knew he thought he'd found a loophole.

'But you knew about me and Bradley, I never hid that from you. He was there first.'

'And technically Alex was there first, for me.'

'But you never told me, that's the difference!' Darcy's voice rose and Jon rocked back on his heels. 'And she was my friend, supposedly. It's totally different. You've had almost twenty years to mention it. I wonder why you chose not to?'

Jon stood up and turned away, the slight click in his knees as he straightened his legs reminding Darcy how much time had passed since they first got together. 'I know this sounds bad, Darce, but it was just sex with Alex. For me anyway. I was holding out for you.'

Darcy tutted. 'Doesn't sound much like holding out if you were shagging her at every opportunity.'

He shook his head. 'It wasn't like that, believe me. It was just now and then. And I meant emotionally.' He turned to face her and pointed at his chest. 'In here. I never felt that way about her.'

'So you used her?'

He squirmed and cast his eyes down. 'I . . . don't like to think of it like that. I thought she knew the score. She knew that I used to meet up with you, you know, before we were together.'

'And you told her that it was me you really loved and that she was a placeholder shag? Come on!' Darcy also stood and went to look over to the neighbouring balcony that Alex had once draped herself across; now it stood in blackness. Would she or Tatty be back there anytime soon? Darcy wondered.

Jon took the chance of moving a little closer to Darcy, leaning on the balcony rail and following her eyeline. 'I know it doesn't make me sound good, but I was a young lad, I didn't think about things the way I might do now. I knew you were the one I loved, but while I couldn't have you . . .'

'Love the one you're with?' Darcy's voice was sarcastic, almost poisonous. Jon opened his mouth to protest but before he could, she added, 'And I don't know why you think you're any better now just because you're older, when you've only this minute blamed your own weakness for falling into bed with her tonight as well!'

Jon closed his eyes. 'I don't know what's wrong with me.'

'I think you do, actually.' Darcy turned her back on the view. 'I think you got it spot on when you said you were weak. That's exactly what you are. How do I know you haven't been weak all through our marriage?'

Jon swung around to face her and gripped her arms. 'I swear, I haven't.'

'You know that Tatty isn't your daughter?' Darcy registered Jon's surprise at the abrupt change of subject. 'You must have wondered, everyone else did.'

Jon shrugged. 'I never thought she was. Why would I?'

Darcy wanted to shake him; how could he be so unaware? 'Don't you wonder who her father is? Because I certainly do – Alex was part way through telling me about how she'd barely consented to some guy, on the rebound from you, may I add, when poor Tatty turned up and heard Alex say she was a mistake, poor kid.'

'You can't blame that on me!'

'Well, Alex does. She blames us both. That's what this has all been about.'

Hope flickered in Jon's eyes once again as he pounced on that information. 'See, I told you, she sought me out on purpose. Everything she's done has been about her trying to get between us!'

'But you didn't have to let her!' Darcy cried, her heart splitting in two all over again. 'If you'd been half the man I thought you were, you would have come to me and been honest and we could have faced her together. But you didn't because you're so *weak*, you just took your opportunity to fuck someone you find more attractive than your wife these days.'

'That's not true.' Jon's voice was flat.

'You're not even convincing yourself at this point, Jon.' Darcy hesitated and then added, 'I think . . . I think you should go.'

'No!' Fear spread across Jon's face. 'I'm not going anywhere. I'm staying with you and Freya and we're going to work this out.'

'Oh! You've remembered Freya now, have you? How kind. Were you bothered about her when you were shagging another woman in our bed?' Darcy fought to keep her voice low. 'Now I have to tell her that we're apart because you were unfaithful – on our family holiday, with Mum's friend from school – how do you think that's going to go?'

Jon jumped up, fear livid in his eyes now as he paced the balcony. 'No, no, you can't tell her. It doesn't have to be over, we can work it out, we're a family.' He stopped in front of her. 'You can't expect me to go, just like that?'

'You broke our family with your lying and cheating. Don't blame me for what happens next.'

Darcy hardened her heart as Jon's face crumpled and his anguished sobs rang out through the night. She wondered if people in the rooms either side of them would be woken by his noise as she ignored his desperate pleas and his repeated assurances that this would never happen again.

Silently she picked her way past Freya's bed and put some of his things into a suitcase, while he sat and sobbed on the balcony. She refused to say anything else as he begged her to change her mind. She simply handed him a tissue and guided him out into the hallway.

'Let me at least say goodbye to Freya,' he rasped, once they were both in the corridor.

'I'm not waking her up just to upset her. I'll tell her, calmly, tomorrow and then I'll let her call you.'

'Please, Darcy . . .'

'I won't be unreasonable about Freya but I need you to go now. And don't just get another room, I want you to go home, even if you have to buy another ticket, we'll pay for it somehow. I honestly can't stand to have you here another minute.'

Jon swallowed hard, knowing she meant business. 'And then what?'

Darcy reluctantly met his eyes. 'By the time we get home on Saturday, I'd like you to have found somewhere else to live.'

'But I don't want to leave you.'

Darcy assessed the broken man in front of her, unrecognisable either as the man she'd shared half her life with or the boy who'd stolen her heart. 'You have to take some responsibility for what has happened here – and maybe I do too. But Freya doesn't need to see us falling apart, so please, do the right thing now and give us some space.'

She took a deep breath as finally he turned and walked away from her, the shake in his shoulders telling her that he was still sobbing. Closing the door to their room, Darcy ignored the double bed and slipped fully clothed into the space next to Freya, careful not to wake her daughter as silent tears slid down her face.

23

2017 – Darcy

Darcy swore she hadn't slept at all, but when she jolted awake she noticed the crack of butter-yellow sunshine that hadn't been there last time she looked. She cursed herself for not pulling the curtains properly and rolled over, away from its cheery brightness, only to collide with Freya's elbow, the way she'd done a thousand times in the past when Freya was still small enough to climb into bed with her – them – and would clamber right up to the headboard so that all of her limbs were somehow in Darcy's face whenever she moved an inch.

The memory made her smile until she registered Jon's absence, and the reason she was squashed on a pullout bed with her daughter. Darcy forced herself to breathe deeply in case the weight of that realisation, and what she had to face today, threatened to pull her under. She looked at her sleeping daughter and focused on the reasons why she had to be strong, and calm.

Across the room, her phone beeped softly from within the confines of her handbag. Usually she kept it beside the bed but she hadn't completed her usual night-time routine for obvious reasons. Carefully edging herself away from Freya, she found she was still wearing her dress from the previous night. Excruciating pains in her head and her stomach were competing for her attention and she couldn't be sure which was the most powerful: the grief or the hangover.

Carefully avoiding her reflection in the mirror, she retrieved her phone and saw it was just gone 8 a.m. The message was from Erika: *Let me know when you're awake.*

Darcy replied: *I'm awake now. Freya's still sleeping.*

There was a pause as Erika typed: *Come to my room once you're ready. Let's talk. Or I can come to you?*

Darcy looked over at the double bed, untouched since Jon had remade it the previous night. She didn't want to be in that room any longer than she had to be. She typed: *We'll come to you x*

Erika sent a thumbs-up and Darcy steeled herself to add: *Where's everyone else?*

Erika's reply was immediate: *Still at the hospital.*

Across the room, Freya stirred. 'Mum?'

Darcy bashed out a last reply: *Freya's awake. Let me talk to her first and then we'll come round x*

'I'm here, love.' Darcy hurried over and perched awkwardly on the side of the bed.

'Why are you wearing that?' Freya blinked and pushed herself up to a sitting position. 'Where's Dad? Did you sleep in my bed last night?'

Darcy swallowed hard. 'Yeah, I did, sorry. I hope you don't mind.'

Freya shrugged and blinked again at Darcy, waiting for her other questions to be answered.

'I slept in my dress because, well, because your dad and I had a . . . falling out last night and that's why he isn't here.'

'Where is he?'

'He's . . . he's gone home, I think.'

'You think?'

'I hope . . . I hope he's gone home. That's what we agreed that he would do. Look, Freya,' Darcy broke off, seeing her daughter's eyes, so like Jon's, facing her with confusion and burgeoning suspicion. 'I have to tell you something and it's not very nice I'm afraid. It's bad news.'

'Is this something to do with Tatty's mum?' Freya blurted. 'You two were so deeply weird with each other last night.'

Darcy clenched her fists and told herself to breathe. Focusing on the shard of yellow morning light beaming in through the curtains, she reminded herself it was a big world and this drama was fairly insignificant in the grand scheme of things. Scary and life changing for an eleven-year-old, obviously, but nothing they couldn't overcome.

'Yes.' She nodded. 'I'm afraid so.'

'Are they having an affair?'

Darcy almost laughed; what did Freya know about affairs?

But of course she knew, Darcy reminded herself. Freya watched *EastEnders* and endless repeats of *Friends*. She knew more than Darcy gave her credit for.

'Not exactly, but they did . . . kiss. Last night. That's why we were fighting.'

'Did they have sex?'

'Freya!' Darcy was shocked, before remembering Kate Winslet's frozen boob on the screen the night before. Her daughter knew about sex; she knew about affairs. But to hear her talking about her dad that way, despite the strangeness of the situation, that was a different matter altogether.

'Are you gonna get divorced?' Freya's voice dropped at this terrible word, her bravado dissipated.

Darcy reached over and squeezed Freya's hand. It was warm and small; she looked so vulnerable despite all her big talk, it made Darcy want to cry. 'I don't know yet, love, it's too soon to say. It's all been a bit of a shock.'

'Is he going to live with Tatty's mum?'

Darcy took a sharp intake of breath. 'No, I don't think so. I think it was a mistake.'

'I hate him.' Freya pulled her hand away and folded her arms. 'It's disgusting.'

Darcy closed her eyes and shook her head.

'I mean it. I don't want to see him,' Freya insisted.

'I understand you're angry, sweetheart, I'm angry too. But he's your dad. He's made a mistake, but he loves you very much and he was sad to leave you.' Darcy cursed herself for insisting he go, leaving her to deal with this alone. 'He's . . . he's done the right thing by going home and giving us some space. Try not to be too cross with him.'

'But why didn't he say goodbye?' A single tear rolled down Freya's cheek.

'Oh Freya, love.' Darcy gathered her up in a cuddle, something her daughter rarely acquiesced to these days. 'I asked him to go last night. You were asleep and I didn't want to upset you. Now,' Darcy continued as Freya sobbed in her arms, 'you can be mad at me for that if you want, but try to understand I did it for the right reasons.'

Freya sniffed and Darcy ground her teeth, silently praying for strength. 'I told him you'd call him today, so you can have a chat and see that he's OK. Is that all right with you?'

Darcy forced a smile and Freya nodded.

'Good girl.'

Darcy then had to break the news about Tatty's fall, framing it as an accident and keeping her voice light. 'She came looking for her mum and slipped down the stairs in the dark, but she's going to be fine.'

'Will she need an operation?'

'I don't think so. Maybe a few stitches in her face. Erika can tell us more when we go and see her in a bit.'

'But Tatty's so pretty, she can't have stitches in her face.' Freya's lip wobbled and Darcy worried she was going to cry again. If Alex had been there, Darcy would have happily wrung her scrawny neck for the hurt she'd put them all through.

It was past nine before they were ready to go to Erika's. Darcy forced herself into the shower, the warm rivulets washing her tears away while Freya stayed in bed with Darcy's permission to go on YouTube for a bit of escapism. Usually she policed Freya's internet usage with a diligence verging on paranoia, but that day she figured they both just needed a moment to decompress.

Afterwards, while Freya was in the bathroom, Darcy checked what she'd watched and to her relief saw it was one of those incomprehensibly popular vloggers that Darcy didn't understand the appeal of, but who always made Freya laugh like nothing else. Darcy's insides contracted at the image of Freya sitting in bed, trying to make herself feel better with internet pranksters while she processed what was happening.

As they left the room, Darcy squeezed Freya's hand. 'OK?'

Freya half nodded, half shrugged, and withdrew her hand to go on ahead and open the door to the hallway. Darcy registered the sound of the click and slide as the door opened and shook her head violently to clear the image that popped into her mind, the one she was faced with as she'd opened that door the previous night. Bile rose hotly in her throat and she coughed and turned away.

'Mum?'

'It's OK, come on.' Darcy pushed on and closed the door behind them. Freya gave her a brave smile and she returned it.

The hallway was filled with the early morning hotel smell of coffee and eggs, and Darcy was surprised to see the other residents going about their holiday as if the world hadn't imploded. She swapped greetings with an elderly couple they passed and picked up a hair bobble dropped by a group of Italian teenagers, calling out and handing it to one of them. They said *grazie* but didn't register her, too wrapped up in themselves and their own tanned, long-limbed gorgeousness.

As they approached Erika's door, a family of four walked towards them in the other direction, arms wrapped around one another and laughing at something the dad had said, passing Darcy and Freya in an oblivious cloud of happy togetherness. They were the embodiment of what Darcy always liked to portray her family as, and it hit her that soon she would have to face the other parents at the school gate and at Freya's dance events and admit that they weren't so perfect after all. The idea of changing her status on Facebook from married to single felt more symbolic than taking off her wedding ring; she absolutely couldn't face it yet.

As the cookie-cutter family strolled away, no doubt heading into a beautiful sunshine-filled day of *#making-memories*, Darcy noticed Freya watching them and squeezed her hand again. Freya's face showed her pain as the two of them stared at each other wordlessly, and this time she didn't pull her hand away.

'Hey!' Erika's head poked around the door, making them jump. 'What are you doing standing around out here?'

Darcy managed a smile. 'Are you keeping watch?'

'I'm expecting a delivery.' Erika ushered them in. 'What's going on? How's Tatty?'

Erika gestured for them to sit down on Libby's bed, which hadn't been slept in. 'Her face is a total mess, black and blue, but she's very lucky not to have smashed her skull in.'

Darcy frantically gestured for Erika to dial it down as Freya's eyebrows shot up in alarm. 'Erika is exaggerating, love.'

Darcy saw that Erika understood. 'Oh. Yes, sorry. I shouldn't joke around. But she'll be fine. She's having some scans just to check, and then she'll probably be out soon.' Erika turned back to the door and peered through the peephole. 'Libby stayed with Alex and I got back a couple of hours ago. I've had no sleep and feel rough as anything.'

'Tell me about it.' Darcy gave a wry smile. 'I think we're all feeling like that this morning.'

'Jesus, yeah – sorry!' Erika spun around to face Darcy. 'I didn't even ask how you two are doing after, well, you know. Does Freya . . .' Erika looked between them. 'Have you two had a chat?'

'Yes, we have.' Freya's tone was somewhat salty. 'Mum told me all about my dad getting off with Tatty's mum, so you don't have to keep it a secret anymore.'

Erika's mouth dropped open at Freya's frankness; Darcy almost smiled – it was rare that Erika was rendered speechless.

A knock on the door sent her dashing to open it. 'Thanks so much, we really appreciate it,' Darcy heard her say to the man at the door, before reappearing with a heavily laden tray.

'I didn't think they did room service here, only the buffet?' Darcy peered at the coffee pot and selection of pastries as Erika set it down at the foot of Libby's bed.

'They don't, but I went and chatted up one of the guys downstairs and asked if we could get a few bits to go as we'd had a rough night. He said he'd make us up a tray once the rush had passed, bless him.' Erika's eyes shone and Darcy saw that it was her way of looking after them so she feigned a decent amount of enthusiasm, even though the thought of eating made her feel ill.

Freya swiped a croissant and asked if she could go online. Darcy felt guilty packing her off with YouTube for a second time that morning but also didn't want her to overhear anything distressing, so she agreed. Darcy and Erika poured coffees and took the plate out onto the balcony as Freya flopped onto Libby's bed with Erika's laptop.

The sunlight twinkled on the water below, injecting cheer into the view once again, but Darcy still felt cold and blank. 'It's such a shame that such a gorgeous place will forever be associated in my mind with *her* and all of this . . . awfulness.'

Erika picked at a pain au chocolat and nodded her agreement. 'I don't know if you'll want to hear about this, but I thought I should tell you.'

'Oh?'

'Alex told us who Tatty's father was, or at least, she told us as much as she knew about him.' Erika put the pastry back down on the plate. 'It was some barman at the Leavers' Ball. After we all went, she let him take her home and he . . .'

'He didn't?' Darcy remembered Alex saying that she barely consented. 'You know?'

'She's not saying he forced her, only that she realised midway through that it was a mistake and didn't feel she could say anything.'

'Jesus.' Darcy stared out at the view again, then snapped back round to Erika as something occurred to her. 'I saw him with her! I was driving, remember? I went to get her, told her it was time to come home, but she refused. I TOLD her not to go with him but she dismissed me.'

Erika pulled a face. 'You tried; she can't blame you for what happened if she sent you away.'

'Still.'

Darcy lapsed into silence, wondering how things would have turned out for them all if she'd insisted that Alex come home with her that night. Would she have tried harder if it had been Erika or Libby?

Eventually, Erika spoke. 'What happened with Jon when you got back?'

Darcy recounted their conversation, Erika listening silently until she reached the part where Darcy told Jon to leave. 'He's gone?'

'Yep.'

'I really thought you two would work it out.' Erika took a sip of her coffee. 'You can't forgive him, no?'

Tears sprang into Darcy's eyes, surprising her; she didn't think she had any left. 'No,' she whispered. 'If it was just one moment of madness then maybe I could have, but not with her, and not with all that happened years ago.'

Erika put her cup down and reached across to squeeze Darcy's hand. 'About all that,' she began. 'I honestly only knew about that silly kiss at the caravan site. Nothing else.'

Darcy sniffed and used her free hand to pull a tissue from her pocket. 'I would still have liked to be told about it when Jon and I got together.'

'At the time, it didn't even cross my mind. It was already forgotten. You guys took two years to get it together properly, remember.' Erika shook her head. 'By then Alex was always going on about that G bloke—'

'Who turned out to be Jonny,' Darcy cut in and Erika winced.

There was another silence as Erika released Darcy's hand and they both sat back with their coffee cups. Darcy didn't want to push Erika away, she realised. Her part in all this had been minimal and mostly driven by good intentions. She gave Erika a rueful smile. 'We never really believed her about G anyway, did we?'

'True! There was always something off about the fact that no one ever saw any evidence of this mystery man,' Erika agreed. 'I just assumed she made him up to sound more experienced than she was. To compete with you.'

Darcy took a deep breath; she needed to know. 'Do you think I bullied her? Is this all my fault?'

'No!' Erika was unequivocal. 'If what you did was bullying, then I also bullied her and so did half the people at school. I guess. . .' She tailed off, watching the movement of coffee as she tilted her cup back and forth.

'Go on.'

'Look, you were really popular. Like, a *big character*, you know? If you made a joke, lots of people would laugh.' Erika hesitated and Darcy could see she was trying to find the right words. 'Alex was quite a misfit, always hiding behind Libby. We all teased her a bit and I don't think you in particular were any worse to her than the rest of us, but with you being so popular, maybe . . . maybe it's what these days they would call "punching down", do you know what I mean?'

Darcy considered Erika's words. 'I didn't appreciate back then how easy I had it. I just thought it was the natural order of things.' She gave a little laugh. 'That if people liked me, it must be because I was a good person. And that made me feel that even if I was being a bit of a cow sometimes, that was balanced out by the fact that everyone thought I was funny, so it couldn't be so very bad.'

Erika said nothing and Darcy had another thought. 'Alex said I took Bradley away from you. That's not true, is it?'

Darcy watched as Erika stood to fetch the coffee pot to refill their cups. 'Erika?'

'No, it wasn't like that,' Erika said eventually, cradling her cup as she sat back down. 'I did like him, at the start, but we were nothing more than friends. I never told you because it was just a crush and it was clear he didn't feel the same,' she added hurriedly, as Darcy's face fell. 'Alex must have picked up on the vibes. She was always watching you, you know, even back then. I think she was torn between resenting you and wishing that she could be more like you.' Erika risked a smile. 'She always wanted to be queen bee.'

Darcy took a sip of her fresh coffee. She hadn't felt like a queen bee for quite some time. Probably since college, if she thought back. It was slapped out of her pretty quickly at university when she was surrounded by people who had more interesting backstories or who were better read, wealthier, more glamorous than her. She was nothing special once she stepped out of her hometown, she found, and she'd been grateful to have Jon to come back to, Jon who'd always seemed to appreciate her.

Then there was her career, or lack of one. 'Ben Taylor came into the hotel a few months ago,' Darcy said suddenly. 'Remember, the one who pulled Alex's . . .'

'I remember.' Erika nodded.

Darcy wished she didn't. Since Alex had reminded her of the period stain incident, Darcy kept having flashes of it being Freya in that situation. Images of Freya cowering from body-shaming bullies alternated with the sight of Tatty lying bleeding and motionless on the stone steps and a pertly naked Alex riding Jon in Darcy's bed. She shook her head to clear the pictures from her mind.

'He was on some corporate jolly – I think he's in insurance or something. Anyway,' Darcy continued, 'he recognised me on reception and came over to say hello. He made me feel,' she swallowed, 'so *small*. As if it were the shittiest job ever and he was, like, disappointed in me or something.'

Erika frowned. 'Why? What did he say?'

'Just that he'd expected more from Darcy Starr than to be "waiting on people", as he put it. He thought I would have done more with my life.' Darcy remembered the feeling she'd had in the pit of her stomach as he'd swaggered off with his colleagues and left her standing at the desk, humbled and unable to think of any sort of a retort.

'Ben Taylor always was an idiot.'

'Yeah, but Alex was saying something similar the other day. I know she was trying to wind me up, but maybe there is some kind of karma in the way the tables turned between us.' Darcy's eyes dropped to the floor, registering Erika's feet in her Balenciaga sliders, next to her own knockoff pair from a website in China. She simply couldn't imagine a life where she spent upwards of £300 on pool shoes. 'She was talking about how I gave up working in the City and settled for such a boring life, just for Jon.'

Erika shifted in her seat; Darcy knew she hated talking about when they worked together, but everything had become tangled in her mind and she wanted to straighten it out. She wanted to be a better person going forward, and a better friend.

'I don't regret giving it up, you know. I wasn't cut out for it. And you deserved that promotion, Erika. I'm so proud of everything you have achieved.' Darcy reached over and returned the squeeze that Erika had given her earlier, giving her a small smile as she saw the surprise on Erika's face. Darcy realised that she'd never properly said anything like this to her before. 'And this whole Alex thing has made me determined to shake things up and build a life that I'm proud of. And then you can be proud to be my friend, like you used to be.'

Erika blinked and Darcy thought she might have seen a tear escape, but in true Erika style she shook it off.

'I'm already proud of you, silly. There's more to life than having a flash job.'

'I'm not saying you're flash, just that you have a fabulous life.' Darcy thought of Erika's immaculate flat and stunning social life. 'And you deserve it.'

Erika laughed. 'Society dictates that as a single woman in my thirties, my life is meaningless without a family. I bet a lot of people would rather be in your position. They'd probably look at my life and think that it's sad as fuck.'

'I don't, I think you're amazing.' Darcy stood and opened her arms for a hug.

There was a brief hesitation before Erika stood to join her. Darcy knew that Erika preferred an air kiss from a distance but that moment felt like it needed a hug. As she wrapped Erika in her arms, Darcy murmured into her hair, 'I'm sorry about the other day on the boat. I didn't mean to be dismissive about your love life. I just wanted you to talk to me.'

'No, I overreacted.' Erika said into her shoulder. 'Massively. And I'm sorry for gossiping with Libby about Jon and Alex. I got carried away with the drama of it all and forgot this was your real life we were talking about.'

'Erika!' Freya's voice came from inside the bedroom. 'Your phone is going off!'

Erika released Darcy and hurried inside.

'News on Tatty?' asked Darcy, as she followed her in.

'It's Libby.' Erika picked up the phone and scrolled her messages. 'Tatty's still the same but, oh my God, guess who's shown up at the hospital?'

Darcy's chest tightened and she turned away from Freya's inquisitive eyes. 'Not Jon?' Please say he hasn't gone to be with Alex, she silently begged.

Erika shook her head. 'Kyle.'

24

1999 – Alex

As the plane sped along the runway, my stomach turned over and I took a deep breath, hoping I wouldn't be sick, or at least, not until the seat-belt sign went off and I could pop to the loos and be discreet. I wasn't usually a nervous flyer, but I'd felt sick so often in the past few weeks, it seemed like the prospect was never far away.

Beside me, my parents squeezed each other's hands and grinned like excited children. Mum was in the window seat, looking down at the land we'd left behind as the plane bumped and dipped on its climb through the clouds. My dad, a man of few words, sat between us and must have noticed I was a little green around the gills as he said, 'You OK, love?'

I nodded. I knew what was wrong with me and I certainly wasn't travel sick. After two missed periods, there could be no mistaking it; I was pregnant. One test could have been written off as a maybe, but I'd taken four and they'd all showed the same thing. That, plus the sore boobs and constant nausea had pretty much hammered it home. I'd been to see the doctor, who'd confirmed it, but otherwise I'd told no one.

Mum and Dad had been so busy with the move, so distracted by contracts and flights and removal firms and surveys that my strangeness had flown below their radar. They still thought I was going to uni in September and if I was worried about anything then it was my exam results. I didn't care about my A-levels; I was fairly sure I'd failed them all. The pregnancy made up my mind – I was going to stay in Spain with my parents. They just didn't know it yet.

We'd always planned that I would fly out with them so I could see the new place and help them get settled in over the summer. The new plan, which only I knew about, was that once we were settled in, I would break the news and tell my parents I was staying there with them. And that they were going to be grandparents.

I was deliberately waiting until we were in Spain before I told them about the baby. I knew I was going to keep it; the idea of having someone to love uncondi-tionally and have them love me back was so powerful I knew that, terrified though I was, I wanted this baby more than anything in the world. What I didn't want, however, was any interaction with my baby's father, and if I'd told my parents while we were still in England I knew they would have forced me to confront him and make him take some responsibility.

I didn't ever want to see him, or think about him again. The fact that I didn't even know his name or anything about him filled me with utter shame. I'd given myself to him so easily, thought so little of myself that I hadn't expected any better than sex in a car with a nameless stranger. I didn't feel any anger towards him; he hadn't attacked me or assaulted me, yet it's undeniable that he saw an opportunity, with me in a drunk and vulnerable state, and he'd taken advantage of it. Whoever he was, he wasn't someone I wanted in my life. Or in my child's life.

I'd hoped at first that perhaps the baby was Jonny's, but I knew in my heart that it wasn't. It had been too long; I hadn't slept with Jonny since Easter, plus he'd always used protection. I was extremely tempted to pass the baby off as his, in order to trap him, or at the very least, ruin things with Darcy, but to make the dates work I'd have had to seduce him again and with the way I'd been feeling, I feared he'd be able to see right through me.

Plus, if I'd offered myself to him again, after everything, and he turned me down out of deference to Darcy, I didn't know how I would ever recover from that.

He'd phoned me again – Jonny – the weekend after the Leavers' Ball. I took the call but I refused to meet him; at that point I'd still been too sad about what had happened that night. I wanted to ask him why it had to be her, what did she have to offer him that I couldn't give him? Why did he give her everything that he held back from me, when all I'd ever done was love him?

I knew he was only calling me then to make sure I wasn't going to ruin what he had going with Darcy, so I told him not to worry, his secret was safe. I was going to keep my distance and say nothing. His relief was palpable, even down the cold phone line. It stung. Even at the very last moment between us, his thoughts were all about *her* and keeping *her* happy, protecting *her* from the damage I could do.

I remembered what Libby said to me the night of the Leavers' Ball. I'd been avoiding her calls ever since. She'd tried a few times, but I didn't call back. She even rang the doorbell once, while I hid upstairs, glad there was no one else home to answer the door and blow my cover. It was the week before my eighteenth birthday, and when I didn't answer she posted my birthday card through the letterbox. I opened it as soon as she left, hoping perhaps there was a note inside, which of course there was.

I'm sorry about that night at the ball, I was so drunk. I think you were trying to tell me something and I can't even remember why we argued. Please call me, we should talk about this. I don't want to fall out with you. I miss you. I still want to celebrate your eighteenth birthday. Call me, please.

But I'd been feeling too sick to face her. I did miss her too, but I couldn't quite forgive her for thinking of Darcy over me when I told her what had happened. It made me mad to think that, to everyone else, even my best friend, Darcy and Jonny were the natural couple and I had always been the outsider, the cuckoo in their nest.

Neither Darcy nor Erika had contacted me, not even when my birthday came around. They never did simply call me or want to meet up with me one on one; it was Libby who held our so-called friendship group together. I knew they wouldn't miss me if I stayed in Spain, nor I them if I'm perfectly honest. We'd become toxic, and the dynamics that were swirling around weren't good for any of us.

I hadn't wanted to get into questions about why I wasn't seeing my friends on my birthday, so I'd told Mum that Libby had visited and dropped off her card early because she'd had the chance to go abroad at the last minute and so would have to miss it. I said we'd planned a big celebration for when Libby returned and accepted the offer to go out for a nice dinner with her and Dad instead, hoping and praying that she wouldn't see Libby around town during the time she was meant to be mysteriously 'abroad'. As far as I knew, I'd got away with the lie, as Mum had never mentioned anything.

The seat-belt sign pinged off, bringing me back to the present, as the cabin crew busied themselves with the refreshment trolleys. Mum and Dad were chatting quietly about arrangements for when we arrived and for a brief moment I felt guilty for the worry and responsibility I was going to bring them with my news. An unexpected, fatherless grandchild was not part of their dream new life, nor was a live-in adult daughter. But my parents had always given me everything I wanted, and I knew they wouldn't let me down now.

I'd phoned Libby that morning before we left for the airport. I knew she'd recently started using a pay-as-you-go mobile but I didn't call that as I didn't want to actually speak to her. I called her home number at a time when I knew she was likely to be out at her summer job at the arts centre, and I left a message on the answerphone. I said there'd been a slight change of plan and I'd call her soon to update her properly on what was going on. Maybe I would, I thought, maybe I wouldn't. Maybe a clean break was what was needed. For everyone.

The more I thought about it, the more the idea appealed. I could reinvent myself in Spain, I thought, entertaining fantasies of strolling along the beach holding hands with my as-yet faceless child. People would wonder, who was this mature, self-contained young woman and her beautiful offspring? I'd learn Spanish and make new friends, not even thinking about Jonny or indeed any man. The next chapter of my life was going to be about me and my baby.

And if, one day, a man did come along, I might see where it went, but I was never going to let anyone else into my heart. No one was ever going to be able to match up to Jonny anyway, so I would use them before they had the chance to use me. Money, sex, power – they were all different kinds of armour, I realised, and I knew the only way to keep myself safe was to play these men at their own game.

As for Darcy and Jonny, I had to bide my time. One day our paths would cross again, I vowed, and by then I would be a new woman, one that Jonny saw as worthy of his care and attention. Soon enough he'd see how spoiled and horrible Darcy was, and when that moment came, there I would be, ready to swoop in and be there for him. In the meantime, I was going to work on myself and my transformation.

The stewardess paused beside me to offer us drinks. Mum and Dad considered champagne but then decided not to as they had to pick up a hire car at the other end. I was relieved; I wasn't sure how I could convincingly decline alcohol, now I was legally old enough to order it, without them passing comment. In the end we accepted three diet Cokes and toasted new beginnings in Spain with our plastic cups.

'This is going to be such an adventure!' Mum giggled, looking out of the window again.

I murmured my agreement as I clicked my Tatyana Ali CD into my Discman and pressed play on 'Boy You Knock Me Out'. 'I can't wait.'

25

2017 – Darcy

Lunchtime came and still Darcy couldn't face eating – it was all she could do to pick at the pastries at Erika's that morning – but she thought she should try and create some normality for Freya.

They went down to the coastal path, Darcy careful to make sure they took the lift through the hotel rather than using the outside steps, leaving Erika to catch up on some sleep, or more likely try and press Libby for information about Kyle.

Down by the beach, Darcy took a moment to stop and look back up at the steps, still unable to fully comprehend what had happened – and what could have happened – up there. She'd been surprised at first that the hotel and medical staff didn't insist on calling the police. They'd all agreed to say it was an accident, and Erika had said to Darcy earlier that with the staff having seen them drinking and shouting earlier in the evening, they may have simply put it down to drunken 'Brits abroad' fighting and behaving badly.

It was depressing to think that they should come to that conclusion so easily, but it meant that no one asked any awkward questions.

It was a short walk to the shops and cafés of Lapad, but despite the brilliant sunshine and the amount of carefree people seemingly having a great time on their holidays, nothing appealed to either Darcy or Freya. The brightness of the weather was an assault on Darcy's senses and the happiness of the people around them seemed only to highlight the strangeness and tension of their situation.

They passed the pizzeria where they'd all gone on the second night after the Cave Bar, when Alex was revelling in the suggestion that Tatty looked like she could be Jon's daughter. 'Do you want to go in there again? They do other stuff besides pizza,' Darcy asked Freya, who shook her head. 'You enjoyed it the other night,' Darcy added, trying not to betray how she felt about the place.

'That was then,' said Freya, clearly picking up on her mother's mood. After a pause, she added, 'Is my dad also Tatty's dad?'

Darcy shook her head. 'No, darling, he's not.'

Freya accepted this with an incline of her head, but Darcy could see she was still troubled.

'Do you want to call him yet? He might be home by now.'

'No.' Freya strode off ahead, leaving Darcy to hurry after her.

In the end, Darcy picked up some provisions from the supermarket and they took them back to the hotel. She felt happier being back in their room since the housekeeping staff had been in to clean. Sitting on the balcony in silence, Freya kicking her chair leg as she peeled a satsuma, Darcy tried again to inject some fun into her daughter's day. 'Do you want to play a game? Uno, or something?'

Freya gave her a scornful look. 'With just two of us? That would be rubbish.'

The comment was a gut punch to Darcy, who wondered how many other elements of their lives would be rubbish now that it was *just two* of them.

When Freya had finished eating, Darcy picked up her phone. 'I'm calling your dad,' she announced. 'It's been long enough.' She saw a mixture of emotions play across Freya's face but there was hope among them, so Darcy was sure she was doing the right thing.

Freya pulled her chair around so she was sitting next to Darcy and they could both be in the frame. It gave only two rings before Jon appeared on the screen. 'Hey.' He looked gaunt and bleary-eyed. For a moment Darcy's heart went out to him before her head took over.

'Jon,' she said curtly. The formality felt all wrong but she didn't know how else to talk to him anymore. 'Freya's here to say hello to you.'

'Hey, Frey,' Jon sing-songed with false cheer. 'I'm so sorry for what happened. Are you doing OK?'

Freya's voice cracked as she replied, 'Why didn't you say goodbye?'

'Your mum thought it was best I go right away – and she was right,' he added, hurriedly, seeing Darcy's frosty expression. 'I made a really big mistake and your mum needs some time and space to think about things.'

'But you're not going to split up, are you? Not forever?'

'No,' said Jon, at the same time as Darcy said, 'Maybe.'

'Please, Darcy,' Jon implored her through the screen. 'Think about it.'

Darcy took a deep breath and changed the subject. 'Where are you, anyway?'

'Still at the airport.'

'Not Dubrovnik airport?' Darcy couldn't believe it. 'Are there no flights?'

Darcy knew that wasn't the case as she'd looked online earlier to see which one he might have taken and there had been a couple of options. Expensive, but possible.

Jon hesitated. 'Well, no, I mean, yes, there are flights but—'

'But what?' Darcy peered closer to the screen. 'Oh. Please don't say that you've been waiting, hoping I'll change my mind?'

Freya twisted in her seat. 'Can he come back, Mum? The airport's not far.'

'I could, Darce, if you wanted me to.' His eyes appealed to hers.

'This isn't fair,' she whispered. 'You were supposed to be giving me space.'

Part of her ached to hold him and have their little family back the way they were. The other part felt unfairly guilt-tripped and railroaded in front of Freya.

'Look, on a practical level, all the flights are really expensive at short notice and there's only a couple of days left anyway.' Jon knew he was working on her, Darcy could tell.

'Please, Mum?' Freya joined in.

That was enough. Darcy took the phone back inside the room and told Freya she needed to speak to her dad alone.

'Don't try and emotionally blackmail me in front of our daughter, do you understand? You're the one who did wrong here and the one thing I asked for was a bit of space. I only called you so that you and Freya could have some time to talk.' Darcy was incensed as her indignation tumbled out. 'How dare you use this as an opportunity to wheedle your way back in?'

Jon gave a bitter laugh. 'Hardly an opportunity! I spent last night sitting on an airport bench, not that you care.'

'Don't put that on me.' Darcy heard a knock at the door; Erika had said she would let them know when she was up and about. 'Get on a plane, Jon, and sort yourself out.'

Jon's face sneered into the camera. 'No wonder I went elsewhere, you cold bitch,' he snarled, before immediately disappearing off the screen.

Darcy jerked away from the device as if she'd been stung. Who was this man? Her hands were shaking as she dropped the phone onto the bed. He'd never spoken to her like that before.

There was another knock at the door, more insistent this time. Rattled, Darcy moved to open it, glad to see her friend as that call had really shaken her. But when she swung open the door, it wasn't Erika.

'Hello, Darcy,' said Alex. Her face, free of makeup and blotchy from crying, was twisted into a grotesque semblance of a smile.

Darcy tried to slam the door, but its soft-close feature meant she couldn't do it quickly enough and Alex pushed her way into the room.

'Get out,' Darcy hissed under her breath, not wanting to alert Freya, who was still out on the balcony.

'No.' Alex folded her arms across her chest. Darcy noticed that although she was raw from tears still, Alex was freshly showered and changed, with her hair pulled up into a messy bun. Had she been back here in the hotel for a while? Darcy shuddered, imagining her just a few rooms along while she'd been sitting there, oblivious, with Freya.

'What are you doing here? Where's Tatty?'

Alex's eyes narrowed. 'Still in hospital, thanks to you.'

Darcy choked out an indignant splutter. 'Thanks to me?'

'I told you last night, all of this is your fault.'

Darcy backed away from her. 'You are deranged, seriously. Please get out of my room. I don't want to frighten Freya.'

Alex started to cross the room and Darcy jumped, making Alex laugh, a cold, brittle sound that set Darcy's teeth on edge.

'I've really got you rattled, haven't I?' Alex sat on the edge of the bed and ran her hands along the length of the duvet, inviting Darcy to remember the image of her splayed on top of it the night before. 'What do you think I'm going to do to your darling daughter? Hurt her like you hurt mine?'

Darcy put herself in front of the balcony door. Behind her, Freya was out there alone, suddenly vulnerable, even though she didn't know it.

'You hurt your daughter, not me,' Darcy said in a quiet but determined voice. 'She found out the truth about you, which was bad enough, and then you knocked her down a flight of steps. You. Not me.'

'That was an accident. We all agreed. And anyway, her scans all came back clear and she's had her stitches done. She's going to be fine.' Alex gave a little shrug. 'Me, on the other hand . . .'

Darcy couldn't believe what she was hearing. How could Alex still make this about her at a time like this? 'What about you? Shouldn't Tatty be your priority?' Something else occurred to Darcy. 'Why are you back here if she is still in hospital?'

Irritation flashed across Alex's face. 'Kyle's with her.'

'Oh.' Darcy nodded her understanding. 'Sent you packing, did he?'

Alex thumped her hand on the duvet. 'He has no right to come here and tell me what to do. He reckons Tatty doesn't want me around.' She paused, looking out towards the balcony. Instinctively Darcy prepared herself to block the doorway. 'Oh relax, Darcy, I'm not going to hurt Freya. I'm here because he said if I didn't leave Tatty with him, he'd get his lawyers to make sure I stayed away. One of his flunkies brought me back here to pack.'

Darcy allowed herself to unclench a little. 'Maybe it's for the best, Alex. Let Tatty process everything that's happened. You can trust Kyle with her, right?'

'Oh yeah, he's father of the year. Always has been parent number one in Tatty's eyes.' Alex's tone was ripe with cruel sarcasm. 'That reminds me.' She turned to make innocent eyes at Darcy. 'Where's Jonny?'

Didn't she know? Darcy wondered. Surely Libby must have relayed messages from Erika while they were at the hospital. Or had Alex come here looking for him?

'He's gone,' Darcy admitted eventually, loathe to tell her that they'd separated.

'Gone home?'

'Yes. Well, he's at the airport waiting for a flight.'

'Really?' Alex brightened. 'Right where I'm headed.'

Darcy let the disgust she felt shine openly on her face. 'You are . . .' she began. 'There are no words. You have ripped a family apart, put your own daughter in hospital, trashed your friendships, and yet all you're interested in is point scoring.'

But Alex wasn't listening. Darcy saw her smile to herself as she rose to her feet.

'I'm off now, Darcy, but don't be surprised if you find that me and Jonny have, *you know*, got it together again. Maybe we'll even get it on properly this time, now you're finally out of the picture.'

'You're welcome to him.' Darcy remembered his sneering face and vile words on the phone before. Whoever he was, there was no coming back from this now. 'You're both completely immature. You both put your own needs before anyone else's. The trouble is, of course,' she paused for impact, 'that he doesn't love you and never has.'

Alex headed for the door. 'If what he had with you was love then I think I'll skip it, thanks. Tell Freya I said hi. You never know.' She opened the door and turned to Darcy with a closed-lip smile. 'One day I might be her step-mum.'

26

2017 – Darcy

'She said what?' Erika was appalled as Darcy recounted the events of the previous afternoon. After the unsettling visit from Alex and the way Jon spoke to her on the phone, Darcy cried off meeting up with Erika as planned. She just wanted to stay holed up with Freya; there was no way Darcy was letting her out of her sight while Alex was still in Dubrovnik.

By the next day, Darcy was sure that Alex had really gone, and it felt safe for them to emerge from their cocoon. Knowing that Freya needed to get out and do something fun, Darcy had brought her down to the pool where she was splashing about with some other children she'd befriended while Darcy and Erika looked on from the terrace.

'That's not all. About an hour or so later, she sent me this.'

Darcy turned her phone to face Erika, who gasped in genuine horror. 'They're together?'

'So it seems.'

The photo was a selfie of Alex and Jon at the airport. She wore a coquettish smile and he, with his shadowed eyes and two days of stubble, looked haunted but defiant. The accompanying message read: *Thought you'd want to know that he's OK x*

Erika took another look. 'It does have the vibe of a hostage situation. I bet he didn't want to pose for this.' She tapped the table. 'This is all Alex, trying to wind you up.'

'Well, it's abundantly clear that he can't say no where she's concerned.' Darcy sighed and put the phone down. 'He messaged late last night to say he was back home but he didn't mention her.'

'Did you ask him?'

'I didn't want to know, to be honest. He was horrible on the phone yesterday, Erika, basically saying it was my fault he'd gone with her and I was a cold bitch because I wouldn't let him come back here.'

Darcy heard whooping and laughing from the pool and turned to see Freya bobbing in the water, looking happier and more relaxed than she'd seen her for days.

'I know it's a cliché but kids really are so resilient, aren't they?' Erika followed Darcy's eyeline and smiled at Freya having a good time. 'But those two . . .' Erika gestured in the direction of Darcy's phone. 'I could throttle the pair of them.'

'At least they've gone now.' Darcy traced a shape on the table with her finger. 'I know I'm going to have to deal with Jon eventually but I just can't bear the thought of him right now. And Alex really scared me, you know? Turning up like she did yesterday.'

Erika's brow furrowed as something occurred to her. 'Do you think she really was trying to mess with you before? You know, with the face wipes and that top you bought and stuff? I wasn't sure if – forgive me – you were being a bit paranoid at the time.'

'I don't know.' Darcy met Erika's eyes. 'She definitely enjoyed messing with me but whether she planned for those things to happen or she just took advantage when opportunities arose, I guess I'll never know.'

'Libby tried to talk to her about it at the hospital,' Erika began. Darcy involuntarily tensed; she still wasn't sure how she felt about Libby's part in this mess and she hadn't spoken to her since the night of Tatty's awful acci-dent. All news was relayed through Erika and they had studiously avoided discussing Libby. 'She still stayed at the hospital yesterday, by the way, even when Kyle sent Alex away. She wanted to be helpful, she said.'

'Good old Libby.' Darcy's voice was tinged with sarcasm. 'Shame she didn't feel like being *helpful* for me through any of this.'

'Honestly, she's been asking about you the whole time, but she thinks you hate her.'

'*Hate* her? Me?'

'Yeah, for bringing Alex here and back into our lives. For not being more open about what was happening when we were hapless teenagers. For trusting Alex and thinking that she was her friend.' Erika threw her hands wide. 'She feels awful about it all now.'

Darcy said nothing, and Erika continued. 'That's why she stayed at the hospital. She feels so guilty about Tatty's injuries. She traces everything back to the fact that she allowed Alex to come here and didn't have the nous to rein her in when she started causing trouble.'

'That's silly,' Darcy said, eventually. 'None of us knew what she was capable of. Even I thought I was being paranoid sometimes.'

'Well, she'll be back later. Tatty's being discharged today. Maybe you two can have a chat?'

Darcy shrugged and returned to watching Freya splashing and squealing in the water.

Later, the three of them went for lunch and, as they chatted over burgers and salads, Darcy able to eat properly for the first time in days, she appreciated that a bit of time with her daughter and her friend was exactly what she needed right now. In two days, they would be going home and Darcy would have to face Jon – and possibly Alex – again. But for now, she felt safe and like she might actually be able to relax a little.

Back at the hotel, Darcy was surprised to see Libby waiting for them on the terrace. And she was even more surprised to see her sitting beside the most classically handsome man she'd ever seen outside of a cinema screen. The two of them stood and Darcy and Erika shared a look as Freya asked, 'Who's that man?'

'Hi there, I'm Kyle Kaplan.' He smiled affably at them all and offered his hand to shake, even to Freya who giggled as she accepted it. 'I'm Tatty's father.'

He had the poise and innate self-confidence that Darcy would have expected from such a successful and wealthy man, but she was surprised at how instantly likeable he appeared. He'd seemed a bit of a cardboard cutout on his corporate profile, but the man in front of her was vibrant and charming.

She shared a look with Erika and knew they were both thinking the same thing. How could it be that Alex had been married to a man like this – someone who loved her child as his own – and yet she still hadn't been content with her life?

'Tatty's doing well. She's up in her room, packing her things.'

Darcy was taken aback at that and it must have shown on her face because Kyle rushed to reassure her.

'She's fine, my assistant is with her to do all the fetching and carrying. Tatty just didn't want to sit out here in public,' he lowered his voice, 'you know, with her injuries and all.'

'But she's OK?' Freya looked up at him.

'She's getting there, kiddo.' He smiled at her concerned face. 'In fact, she said she'd love to see you if you want to go up there?' Kyle looked at Darcy for permission. 'And I'd love to have a chat with your mom if she has the time.'

Darcy's instinct was to say no; her stomach turned over at the thought of having to talk to Alex's ex-husband, no matter how nice he seemed, and she was still more than a little apprehensive at the idea of letting Freya out of her sight.

'I'll take her up if you like,' Libby said quietly, not quite meeting Darcy's eye.

'I'll go too, if that's OK? I'd like to see Tatty,' Erika added.

Darcy swallowed. 'OK.'

'Thank you, Darcy.' Kyle indicated the chair that Libby had been sitting in and waited until Darcy sat before sitting down himself. 'This is real awkward, huh?'

Darcy gave a little laugh. 'I'll say. I'm guessing you're not here for small talk.'

Kyle sat back and interlinked his fingers; Darcy felt like she was being interviewed for a job she hadn't even begun to prepare for. Her stomach rolled over again as she waited for Kyle to speak.

'Libby told me what's been going on,' he began.

That's more than she did for me, Darcy thought, but said nothing.

'I know that while Lexie – *Alex* – didn't mean to cause Tatty any harm, it was owing to her aggressive behaviour that she ended up getting hurt.'

Darcy nodded. 'I think that shove was meant for me.'

Kyle inclined his head. 'That's what Libby suggested. That's one of the reasons I told her, Alex, to leave. That, and the way she'd been using Tatty as a pawn in her games with your husband.'

Darcy blinked at him. 'Libby has been really thorough, hasn't she?'

'I'll be honest with you, Darcy. I knew some of this already.'

That surprised her. 'Oh?' She sat forward in her seat. 'You did?'

'Tatty has been in contact with me, probably more than her mom knew, or would have been happy about. She tried to take Tatty away from me when we split up, to, I don't know, punish me or whatever. She knew I had no legal claim on her even though she's my daughter as far as I'm concerned.'

Darcy looked at him with sympathy. 'I'm sorry to hear that, not least because it's obvious that Tatty adores you. Did . . .' She faltered. 'Did you end the marriage or did Alex? I don't think she was ever clear about it.'

Darcy remembered how Alex used to talk about getting together with Kyle like it was a fairytale romance, yet she only ever hinted at the details of their breakup.

Kyle sighed. 'I did; we'd got to the end of the line. She'd cheated on me once too often. I was trying to hold out until Tatty was twenty-one, or eighteen at least, but I couldn't take it anymore. Oh yeah,' Kyle nodded, seeing Darcy's expression, 'she cheated on me constantly. The last time was with a business associate; things got really messy. It was humiliating, professionally and personally.'

'I'm sorry,' said Darcy. 'I thought maybe you were on good terms. She spoke well of you, if her word counts for anything anymore, and I thought she was staying in one of your properties in London?'

'I tried to keep her sweet so that she didn't cut me off completely from Tatty. I mean, she couldn't stop her messaging me, but she could have made it difficult for me to see her.' Kyle gestured at his surroundings. 'When Tatty told me they were coming here, I had a bad feeling. Tatty told me that Lexie had fallen back in with some old friends and alarm bells started ringing. Pretty damn loudly.'

'What do you mean? Did Alex talk about us to you?' Darcy was amazed.

'Not for a long time, but I remembered.' Kyle paused and then laughed. 'I'm not making much sense, am I? Let me go back to the start.'

Kyle told Darcy about how he'd met Alex in Spain. It was the same story that Alex had told them, about him teaching her how to make his classic cocktail. He described her as beautiful but brittle, and he could sense she'd been hurt. He had been enchanted by the idea of bringing out her vulnerable side and took it slowly with her, waiting until she was ready to let her guard down.

'Then she introduced me to Tatty.' Kyle's eyes shone as he recalled the moment. 'I was smitten. I always knew I couldn't have kids of my own.' He waved away the pain of that statement as soon as he'd said it. 'Sports injury in my teens; I'd made my peace with it. But when I met that darling girl, it was perfect. Like we were a ready-made family. I was all in. I loved them both so much.'

Darcy tried to hold back the sneer she wanted to pull. Alex didn't deserve to be so lucky. 'Did she tell you who Tatty's biological father was?'

Kyle rolled his eyes. 'She told me, let's say, a version of the truth. She told me that it was her boyfriend at college, who had cheated on her with someone else.'

Darcy took a sharp intake of breath. Even back then, Alex was pretending that Jon was the father of her child.

'Years later, when we were married and I wanted to adopt Tatty, she refused to even look into it. She said the guy was married now and she didn't want to rock the boat.'

'But you know that Jon isn't really Tatty's father? Alex was lying, or maybe just kidding herself. She said it was . . .' Darcy faltered, unable to articulate the rest.

'I know. I know that now, because Libby told me. And it's horrible. I wish she'd told me the truth.' Kyle sighed, cracked his knuckles. 'But before, I'd believed it was someone connected to her old gang of friends. So when Tatty said you were all coming on this vacation, I had a bad feeling that Alex was up to something. She's been like a coiled spring since we broke up and I have always suspected that she never really got over her first love. Your husband,' he added, apologetically with a wry shrug. 'That's why I arranged to be in Europe this week, in case Tatty needed me.'

Darcy looked at Kyle in surprise and admiration. 'You scheduled your work just to be closer to Tatty?'

Kyle laughed. 'I'm her dad,' he said simply. 'In every way that matters. As far as I'm concerned, I'm Tatty's dad.'

27

2017 – Darcy

Darcy listened as Kyle shared many insights into his relationship with Alex, or Lexie as he called her. She was fascinated to hear that the interior design business was nothing more than a vanity project, which failed to make any money either in New York or London.

'Lexie has a good eye for style and I encouraged her to do something worthwhile with her time. I could see her turning into one of those society wives and I wanted better than that for her.' Kyle became quite animated as he talked. 'I paid for her to take classes and my team helped her with the framework of setting up a business. I didn't want to do it all for her, you know, it was meant to be her project, but I sent a few of my associates her way to get her started with clients.'

'But it didn't work out?' Darcy wondered what it would be like to have a husband who actually supported his wife's career choices rather than trying to squash them.

'Hah!' Kyle's voice grew louder and attracted some glances from people nearby. Darcy noticed a few of the women especially giving him a second and even third look. 'She only played at it. She liked putting pretty pictures on her Instagram, but not the actual hard work of pitching to clients and providing a service. Plus, I arranged for her to give a quote to the CFO of one of my companies and, while she was there, Lexie slept with her husband.'

Darcy clapped her hands across her mouth. What a piece of work that woman was. Although, perversely, to know that this wasn't the first time Alex had seduced someone else's husband, entirely shamelessly, made her feel a tiny bit better – that, and the fact that Alex didn't really have a glittering career as a designer. All this time Darcy had been feeling like her 'little' job wasn't something to be proud of, but at least it was a real job; it was all hers and she was good at it.

'Was that your pet name for her? Lexie?'

'No! I knew her as Alex, and I'm trying to get used to going back to that now. At the start, I called her Ally, like her mom did, but she never liked it.' He gave Darcy a rueful *whatcha gonna do?* smile. 'It was all her idea; she wanted to reinvent herself when she moved to New York.'

Darcy could well believe it. 'Were you happy, in the beginning?'

A shadow passed across Kyle's face. 'For a short while. Then I began to realise that she didn't love me, not really.

I mean, I think she liked me, and she thought I was good husband material. She certainly liked all the benefits of being married to me.' Who wouldn't, Darcy thought, as Kyle continued. 'She had a destructive streak and it stopped her from relaxing and being happy. She was always searching for something better. That's what all the surgery was about; it wasn't for me.'

Darcy thought of young Alex, all knees and elbows, padding her bra and trying to appear sophisticated. Would it have made any difference if she'd been kinder to her back then? Darcy batted that thought away; there was nothing she could do about that now. 'She still seems quite immature and I know her parents used to indulge her. I just thought she was a bit spoiled, you know, an attention-seeker.'

'I fear it's more than that, Darcy. I think she's a narcissist.' Kyle paused to let that sink in. 'I tried to get her to see my shrink, but she said it was me who had the problem. And now I know that she has spent half of her life in love with an idealised version of your husband, it at least partly explains why she's always been so unfulfilled.' He shook his head in a kind of sorrowful despair. 'Everything we had going for us, yet it wasn't enough. And all because she was eaten up with the supposed injustice of her childhood sweetheart picking you instead of her.'

'What a waste, for all of us.' Darcy's heart went out to Kyle; he was rich and handsome, yes, but he truly seemed like a decent man. What he said made so much sense. She knew that Alex had always thought the world revolved around her. Looking at things with fresh eyes, Darcy could see that the way Jon, and that awful barman guy, had treated her, before she was mature enough to handle it, had damaged her, badly. 'But, Kyle, I have to ask. Do you think she's dangerous? She has honestly terrified me these last few days.'

Kyle put his hands out. 'I really don't think so.'

'Really? Even after Tatty?' Darcy remembered the panic she felt when Alex forced her way into their hotel room, with Freya out on the balcony. It seemed silly now, out in public, surrounded by easy-going holidaymakers, but at the time it had felt very real.

'She's reckless and that's why I want her away from Tatty. That, and the fact that Tatty wants some space from her after everything that's happened. But I don't believe she would deliberately cause you, or anyone, physical harm.' He hesitated before adding, 'Although, she may still have her sights on your husband. I don't think she's fully found closure there yet, just to warn you, in case you think a reconciliation might still be on the cards.'

'It's not,' Darcy said immediately. 'Let them make each other miserable for all I care.' As long as she keeps away from Freya, she added in her head.

Kyle extended a hand which Darcy accepted. 'Thank you for meeting with me, Darcy. I still feel somewhat responsible for Alex's behaviour and I wanted to give you my take on the whole situation.'

Darcy smiled. 'And I feel a bit responsible for what happened to Tatty, so thank you too. It's been quite . . . cathartic.'

'Shall we go up and see how things are going with the girls?' Kyle rose to his feet.

Darcy hesitated. 'Do you think Tatty will want to see me, after everything?'

'She doesn't blame you for any of this. Come and see for yourself.'

As Darcy walked with Kyle, she noticed again the heads turning as he passed and wondered what it must have been like when he and Alex had been together. People probably thought they were movie stars. For a moment she basked in the reflected glory, before she noticed a passing woman's eyes slide from him to her. Darcy dropped her head, hoping people weren't wondering why this striking man was accompanied by such an ordinary-looking woman.

'Kyle, I'll meet you up there in a minute.' Darcy avoided his eyes, feeling the pinpricks of teardrops in her own. Before he could protest, she whirled around and headed back towards the terrace, calling behind her, 'Go on ahead, I'll be right there.'

She sped up, trying to outrun the tears, and strode out across the terrace to the edge of the coastal path.

Was this the way it was always going to be from now on? Feeling ugly and worthless, as if everyone was looking down on her? She hugged herself as she cried, looking down at the waves crashing to the shore, desperately wishing there was a way back to a time when she felt secure in who she was and what she had to offer the world.

'I thought I was never going to get you on your own.'

The voice startled Darcy. She whipped around to find Alex standing behind her, eyes glinting in the afternoon sunshine. 'No,' Darcy sobbed, her insides plummeting. 'Not again. I thought you were at the airport! Why can't you just leave me alone?'

'Where am I supposed to go, Darcy?' Alex spread her hands wide as if it were a reasonable question. 'Back to London? New York?' She took a step closer. 'My marriage is over, and my daughter hates me. I've got nothing, and nobody, left.'

Darcy swallowed and backed away. 'I thought you went with Jon.'

Alex made a face. 'I paid for him to get home seeing as he was too broke to buy his own flight.' She stepped closer again. 'But I wanted to come back here and have one more shot at sorting things out for good.'

Alex turned to look out over the water's edge and Darcy took her opportunity to move again. She was within sight of the pool terrace; if she could just get back to the hotel where more people were around then she would feel safer.

'Are you trying to get away from me?' Alex looked amused. 'You weren't in such a rush to get away from my ex-husband, were you? I saw you two sitting together, having a good old chat. I wonder who you were talking about.'

Darcy's face flamed at the thought of Alex watching them. 'This is mad.' She shook her head and continued walking.

'I bet you think you can make him fall in love with you as well, don't you?' Alex spat out as she followed. 'As if he'd want you.'

At the edge of the terrace, with the hotel in sight, Darcy felt strong enough to stop and face her. Recognising something in Alex's expression, Darcy almost laughed. 'You're actually jealous of me talking to Kyle, aren't you?'

Alex said nothing, but Darcy saw the pain in her eyes. This woman was a mass of contradictions, she realised, and there was no point in arguing with her any longer.

'I'm sorry, Alex. Genuinely,' Darcy added, when Alex looked at her in surprise. 'I've been thinking about what you said and you're right about a lot of it. I was unkind to you at school and maybe I should have insisted you come home with me the night of the Leavers' Ball.'

Alex remained silent, so Darcy continued. 'I couldn't help falling in love with Jon, and him with me. But I had no idea he was stringing you along all that time. The truth is,' she took a deep breath, 'I didn't think about you much at all back then, and I'm sorry I wasn't a better friend to you.'

At that moment, Darcy decided to give herself a break. She had a lot going for her, she realised, and she vowed to take this opportunity to get back to being herself, Darcy Starr. Maybe she'd never be the one turning heads ever again, but actually, she was OK with that. She could be a good mum and a good friend and, hell, she could be a good hotel receptionist and organiser of dance school events too.

Most importantly, she was going to stop painting such a rosy picture of her life to the people around her. Why had it been so important to her that everyone thought her marriage was perfect? The pressures of social media played a part, but it was her own ego too, she realised. She needed to be honest with everyone about her relationship with Jon and decide what she wanted from her future, for her and for Freya.

'It's time to start afresh, Alex. For you and me.' Darcy hoped she sounded more confident than she felt. 'And that means keeping your distance. From me, and from—'

'Tatty,' Alex bit out.

'Well, yes, until she's ready to—'

'No.' Alex pointed. 'Tatty.'

Darcy followed the line of Alex's finger and saw a group of people emerging from the hotel entrance. Tatty, bruised and hobbling, flanked by Kyle and Libby. Behind them were Freya and Erika.

'Are you OK?' Erika called out to her.

'It's fine. I'm fine.' Darcy broke into a run towards them, trying not to show any shock or horror as she saw the line of stitches along Tatty's cheek. 'Tatty! What are you doing down here?'

'I saw you and Mom from the balcony.' Tatty grimaced, revealing the stark new gap in her teeth. 'I was worried.'

'I'm absolutely fine.' Darcy was touched; Kyle had clearly set a great example for Tatty – she really took after him. 'Your poor face, though.'

'They said her face took the brunt of it; she must have hit the edge of a step as she tumbled. But there are no broken bones or lasting damage that they can find.' Kyle smiled at her. 'And we can fix your teeth and the scars as soon as you're ready, huh?'

'Tatty.' Alex caught up with them and tried to reach for her daughter but Kyle swiftly blocked her.

Alex gritted her teeth. 'Stop trying to keep me away from her. She's MY daughter. Mine.'

'Please will you just go, Mom?' Tatty's voice was full of contempt. 'Why are you still here?'

'I wanted to see you, to check you're OK.'

Erika made a noise of disbelief. 'If that's the case then why were you out here harassing Darcy?'

As Alex scowled like a petulant teenager, it hit Darcy that she wasn't frightened anymore. And perhaps, she thought, Alex knew that now too, because she kept her eyes averted and said nothing.

'If you don't leave us alone – and that includes Darcy – I'll tell the cops that you pushed me down those stairs,' Tatty said quietly. 'And I have three reliable witnesses, don't I?'

'Hell yeah.' Erika couldn't agree quick enough.

'If that's what you want.' Darcy nodded.

'There you go then,' said Kyle, gently but firmly. 'It's over.'

Alex turned to Libby. 'You too?' Darcy held her breath, waiting to hear what she said.

'You pushed her, Alex.' Libby raised her eyes to meet hers. 'All of this is on you.'

Alex dropped her arms to her side in surrender. '*Now* you grow a backbone.'

'Enough.' Darcy stepped forward. 'I meant what I said about being sorry, but you've behaved appallingly. You've hurt all of us here, some of us more than others.' Darcy shared a grim look with Tatty. 'You need to give people space. *And* you need to sort your own head out.'

Alex finally met Darcy's eyes with a last hint of defiance. 'And what if Jon gets in touch?'

Darcy felt the weight of their daughters watching and listening. She had to rise above the provocation, she needed to be the better person. 'That's no longer my concern,' she said evenly.

Alex shook her head and Darcy could see that she was beaten. Turning to leave, Alex called back over Kyle's shoulder, 'I do love you, Tatty. I'm sorry.'

'Too late, Mom,' said Tatty sadly, as she watched Alex walk away.

28

Darcy – 2017

Darcy watched as Pete twirled Libby for a second and a third time, oohing with everyone else when he effortlessly dipped her back, then clapping as they took hold and moved elegantly as one around the floor.

'Pete's like a new man these days,' she murmured to Erika, who was standing beside her. 'I reckon he must've been quite shaken up by the change in Libby since Dubrovnik.'

After Alex's departure four months before, Kyle offered to arrange new flights for them all if they didn't want to stay there any longer. Libby had accepted, saying she wanted to get home to Pete after everything that had happened, but Darcy suspected the real reason was because Libby was still uncomfortable around her.

Darcy declined Kyle's offer, explaining that she'd given Jon until Saturday to get out of the house and would rather keep out of his way until then. Plus she wanted a little more time to psych herself up before facing their mutual friends and family at home, and telling them what had happened between them. Erika decided to stay too, and along with Freya, they made the best of their final days in the sunshine.

When they returned home, Libby declared that she was postponing the wedding, saying it didn't feel right to continue celebrating. Darcy hadn't known what to say; there was still a huge Alex-shaped hole of unspoken feelings in their friendship and she thought it might be a while before they were truly comfortable with one another again. But when she'd heard from Erika that Pete was devastated and that he and Libby were both miserable, Darcy saw an opportunity to try and make things right.

They'd talked on the phone, both treading on eggshells, trying not to make things worse between them. Darcy had reminded herself not to take Libby for granted. She and Erika often laughed about her being flaky and indecisive, but she had a good heart and cared deeply about the people closest to her. Darcy knew she should show her friend more respect and she urged Libby not to throw away her own happiness for the sake of what had gone before. Nothing could change the past; they could learn its lessons, but they had to look to the future.

Erika turned to Darcy now with a secret smile. 'Don't tell Libby I told you, but they took dance lessons.'

Darcy was agape. 'No! Pete went to a dance class?'

'They agreed he'd take lessons if his brother's band could play the song.' Erika nodded to the stage where

Pete's younger brother and his friends were having an admirable go at playing 'Love Is All Around'. 'Sweet, really,' she added, wincing as they hit a bum note. 'Let's agree that their enthusiasm makes up for the musical quality, shall we?'

Libby and Pete swept along their side of the dance floor, Libby throwing them a huge grin as she chasséd past them. As they waved back, Darcy sighed. 'She's so bloody happy, isn't she?'

'Delirious,' Erika agreed. 'Sickening, isn't it?'

Darcy dug her in the ribs and they laughed. She knew that once Pete started taking more of an interest in the wedding, the plans had become a lot more fun. Libby admitted that she'd been constrained by how she thought a wedding should be, rather than what suited them as a couple. The menu, the music, even her dress – they'd tweaked everything to make it something they were both comfortable with, and the team effort was charming and unique to them.

'Oh, my God!' Erika squealed as Pete lifted Libby up and spun her around in his arms for the routine's grand finale and everyone clapped and cheered. She nudged Darcy and pointed to where Libby's mum Pam was crying her eyes out, propped up by Auntie Karen, who was cheering loudest of all. 'This is TOO MUCH!'

Freya appeared beside Darcy. 'The cake table is open,' she mumbled, through a mouthful of sticky iced doughnut.

'So I can see.' Darcy smiled, taking a tissue from her purse and handing it to her daughter.

'Some wedding, huh?' Kyle arrived with Tatty beside him. Darcy, still grateful for the support he'd given her, gave him a warm embrace as the girls greeted each other. Kyle had insisted that he and Tatty shouldn't encroach on Libby's special day but was clearly delighted to have accepted an evening invitation to join the celebrations.

Tatty's new teeth looked great and her bruises had healed; all that remained was the scar on her cheek. Kyle had invested in specialist, high-coverage makeup and she looked beautiful and confident. Darcy was so pleased to see her smiling again.

Libby appeared beside them, breathless and beaming, her curls in an exuberant cascade around her face. 'What did you think?'

'You were amazing,' Freya enthused, pink icing all around her mouth.

'You both were, really,' said Darcy, with a twinkle at Erika. 'I thought it was Fred and Ginger swooping their way past us just now.'

'Oh, you guys. And Kyle's here!' Libby suddenly noticed him, flying at him with a hug. 'Let me bring Pete to meet you, I've told him so much about you.'

Libby dashed off again, her dress swishing behind her, and Darcy wondered how Alex would feel if she could see how the group had embraced Kyle and Tatty.

Everyone had such genuine affection for the husband and daughter who she'd so mistreated, while she still remained the outcast.

'Erika, thank you again for organising that work placement.' Kyle stepped forward for Erika's trademark air kisses. 'Tatty has had an amazing time in London.'

'No problem at all. She's done really well.' Erika smiled at Tatty. 'We're all going to miss her when you take her home.'

Darcy had initially been dubious when Erika said Tatty was coming back to London to do some work experience at her firm. 'Her dad is literally Kyle Kaplan, he has a hundred businesses she could do her placement at,' she'd said at the time.

But Erika was supportive of the idea. 'I think she wants something that's her own and maybe even wants some closure on what happened last time she saw us all. Besides,' Erika had pulled herself up straighter, 'I can be her mentor. God knows she needs a positive female role model.'

'Here he is!' Libby returned, clutching Pete's arm. He was starry-eyed with a grin that split his face in half; Darcy had to turn away as his naked, unabashed joy was an arrow to her heart. She pushed aside the memory of Jon looking at her like that on their wedding day, the lovelight in his eyes filling her with absolute certainty that she'd found her happy ever after. Moments like this still winded her. She coughed and rummaged in her handbag as Libby made the introductions.

'I'll get us all some drinks. Girls, give me a hand?' Erika took Tatty and Freya to the bar and, as Kyle engaged Pete in a chat about their honeymoon plans, Darcy looked up to find Libby beside her.

'Hey,' said Darcy, awkward now that it was just the two of them. 'It's been a brilliant day, so very beautiful.'

'Thank you. I hope . . .' Libby tailed off and took a deep breath. 'I hope it doesn't seem insensitive. Like we are showing off how happy and in love we are.'

Darcy laughed, a genuine, warm laugh. 'Libby! That's exactly what a wedding is for. Enjoy it. It's your moment.'

Libby took Darcy's hands into her own. 'Look, this is probably not the time or the place but I'm feeling . . . all the feelings today, and I want you to know I never meant to put Alex ahead of you. I know she was my friend back in the day,' she continued, as Darcy opened her mouth to interject, 'but she hadn't been for years. Not like you. You and Erika made room for me when Alex went, and I love our little gang of three; I always have. I wish she'd never come back.'

Darcy's throat was too full to speak so she squeezed Libby's hands and nodded.

'And I want to be clear that I didn't know about her and Jon the whole time, not really. Some of it I thought was made up, other bits I forgot as time passed.' Libby locked her eyes onto Darcy's. 'Once I started to realise what was going on, it was too late. I thought that speaking up might make things worse. You know I'm rubbish with confrontations.'

Darcy did know, and she appreciated how hard it must be for Libby to say all of this to her, in the midst of her wedding celebrations too. 'She made fools of us all. I know you must have felt torn.' Darcy had no appetite to be angry with Libby; it felt like kicking a puppy. 'And I had my guard up from the moment she came back, which made me snippy and suspicious. I wasn't being a great friend to you either, I was too wrapped up in myself.'

'I'm just so sorry about you and Jon, especially when I'm all . . .' Libby let go of Darcy's hands and gestured to her wedding dress.

'Libby, please don't be silly.' Darcy laughed again. 'I don't begrudge you your happiness. Love isn't a zero sum game. And I'm doing fine. Honestly.'

Libby scrutinised Darcy's face, making her feel exposed. But the truth was, she wasn't doing too badly since Dubrovnik. Jon had, reluctantly, moved out as requested and was renting a room near his work until the financial settlement could be sorted. He saw Freya twice a week and he'd asked to come home, several times, but Darcy stood firm.

'There's definitely no going back for you and Jon?' Libby asked.

'After the way he spoke to me on the video call and then posed for that photo with Alex, no way. If he really regretted what he'd done, he wouldn't have gone near her again.' Darcy thought back to all the apologies that she returned home to, when he was contrite, blaming his behaviour on his grief and lack of sleep. 'He's like a completely different person to me now. His cheeky charm doesn't cut it anymore.'

Libby nodded her understanding. 'And you've been going great guns at work, I hear?'

Darcy had been focusing on the promises she'd made herself in Dubrovnik. She'd been working full time since Jon moved out and a promotion was within her sights. Her school mum friends helped with pick-ups and drop-offs so that Darcy could make the extra money she needed and the dance school parents surprised her by helping more with the events so that she didn't need to organise everything.

Darcy had been so touched by the way everyone had been quietly compassionate, just getting on with the daily grind away from the social media circus, and she regretted not being open with them sooner.

'Yeah, work is great actually.' Darcy smiled. It was hard going, but she never doubted that she'd made the right decision to move forward without Jon. She was making a new life for herself and Freya, and since she'd stopped mentally competing with her friends, she found that they were all more supportive and there for each other than ever.

Darcy had to admit she felt pretty good. All the toing and froing of the past few months had taken its toll mentally, but physically she was feeling fitter and more fired up than she had in a long time. Her hair had grown longer, simply because she hadn't the time to get it cut, and it brushed her shoulders in a natural wave. Her dress may have been preloved, but it fit her perfectly, as if it were made for her, the soft navy fabric enhancing her curves, with the silver scarf she'd panic-bought in Waterloo station all those months ago finally having its time to shine, as a twinkly wrap around her shoulders.

Whenever she thought of Alex, Darcy couldn't help making the inevitable comparisons – finding out that your husband has been cheating on you will do that to a woman – but even without Alex's model looks and enviable wealth, she knew she could hold her own. Not least because neither of those things mattered a jot in the end. Darcy was, once again, a woman who knew her worth; she no longer needed to pretend, to herself or anyone else, that life was perfect.

'Thank you.' Darcy grinned as Erika returned holding two bottles of champagne, trailed by the girls with a fistful of glasses each. Erika saw Darcy and Libby smiling at each other and nodded her approval.

'To Libby and Pete!' Erika cried, popping the cork of one bottle and handing the other one to Kyle to open.

'Libby and Pete!' they echoed joyfully.

Tatty and Freya held up the glasses as the bubbles were slopped clumsily between them and they all drank, even Freya, who was permitted a tiny measure.

'Thank you all for being here,' said Libby, entwining herself with Pete who simply beamed and nodded profusely. 'It means so much. To us!' she toasted.

'To us!' they chorused.

The band began a shaky but heartfelt rendition of 'Baby I Love You' and Pete pulled Libby back onto the dance floor.

Erika sighed as she glanced around. 'Where's my happy ever after?'

'I don't think we just get one "happy ever after" you know?' Darcy sipped her champagne. 'I mean, I thought I had mine and look how that turned out!'

'Has anyone heard anything from Alex, do you know?' Erika turned to her as Freya dragged Tatty, Kyle in tow, to sample more cake. 'Last time I broached the subject with Tatty, she said her mom was still in Spain.'

Alex had closed all of her social media accounts after she left them in Dubrovnik, but they'd heard via Tatty and Kyle that she'd fled to be with her elderly parents again.

'I hope she stays there for good, to be honest.' Darcy still woke up in the night, heart racing, after nightmares featuring stone steps, convinced Alex was standing over her. In the cold light of day, Darcy knew that Alex was damaged, not dangerous, but she still felt happier knowing there was the Channel between them. 'But no, I haven't heard anything and I don't think she's been in touch with Jon. Not that he'd say, even if she had.' Darcy watched the couples on the dance floor, a lump in her throat. 'You know what, I think she did me a favour really.'

'Come on.'

'No, really.' Darcy had thought about this a lot. 'If Jon had been the man I thought he was, Alex wouldn't have been able to touch us, whatever she did.' She turned back to Erika with a small smile. 'But as it turned out, it was frighteningly easy to destroy what we had. So, he couldn't have been.'

Erika topped up their glasses. 'Do you miss him?'

'I miss the man I thought he was.' Darcy sighed as she took a sip of bubbles. 'And I'm so sad for Freya, but I've no doubt that I've done the right thing. I wasn't happy even before Alex came back.' Darcy felt good to admit that honestly at last. 'I was unfulfilled and becoming a bore. Her actions just sped up the inevitable.'

'So now you're young, free and single again, just like me.' Erika clinked her glass to Darcy's.

Darcy laughed. 'Well, the single part is true at least.'

'Hey! We're still young! Here's to the next chapter. For all of us.'

'The next chapter!' Darcy raised her glass, laughing as she saw Freya bounding towards them, icing all over her face once again. 'Don't you look a sight?'

Freya grabbed Darcy's free hand. 'Come on, they're playing Taylor Swift.'

'*Are* they?' Erika grimaced, turning her ear towards the band. 'I suppose it could be.' She took Darcy's glass from her and nodded towards the swirling energy of the dance floor. 'Go on, live a little.'

Darcy laughed again as she allowed Freya to pull her into the throng. She vowed to do exactly that.

Acknowledgements

My thanks go to everyone who helped bring this book to life. To my agent Diana Beaumont for seeing potential in the first version of the manuscript, and to all the team at DHH Literary. To my editors, Melissa Cox and Georgia Marshall, for their vision and guidance, and also to so many people in the wider Bonnier team and beyond: Enisha Samra, Eleanor Stammeijer, Florence Philip, Stuart Finglass, Evie Kettlewell, Stacey Hamilton, Chelsea Graham, Alex Kirby, Alex May, Emma Hargrave and Paris Ferguson. All have had a hand in helping to get *A Girl's Girl* onto the shelves and I am truly grateful.

A special shout-out to Writers' HQ, without whom this story would still have been languishing on an unfinished word document. To Sarah Lewis and all of Team WHQ, please know that I will always give full credit to your community, retreats and resources for getting me started on a path to publication. To 'flashy' Kathy Hoyle and all of the Flash Face Off regulars, then and now, your support and encouragement made me take

"

my writing seriously (although not *too* seriously!) and gave me confidence to put my stories out in the world. You are amazing writers; please forgive me for abandoning flash in order to write novels!

To Jo Gatford, now at The Joy of Fixion, for giving her time to help me with applications and for bucking me up after one particularly disappointing rejection by saying, 'But you're still going to do it anyway, right?'. That simple statement, as if it were just a case of pushing on regardless, kept me going when it would have been so easy to give up.

Of all the brilliant people I met through Writers' HQ, special thanks go to Claire Schön, my first beta reader for early chapters of this book. Thank you for the chats and for the coffee in Vienna! I can't wait to see where your writing journey takes you next.

I finished writing my first draft with the help of Curtis Brown Creative's novel writing course led by Suzannah Dunn. Several years later our gang is still meeting online to share ideas, motivate each other and be general cheerleaders for each other's progress. Thanks to Caroline McCartney, Cathy Bridge, Cindy Etherton, Emily Scott, Jay Jacobs, Melissa Jane Knight, Skye Stranger and Susan Swabey, especially those of you who did the full read of my (very long!) first draft and gave such helpful feedback. I feel very lucky to have found such a great group of fellow writers.

To all my family and friends, a huge thank you for always being excited for me, even when I have to keep good news quiet, or things seem to be taking forever to happen! Your support means the world. And, of course, the biggest of thanks to Scott, for his unwavering belief and support. This book is for you.